HAWKFALL

George Mackay Brown (*1921-96*) was one of the twentieth century's most distinguished and original writers. His lifelong inspira-
tion and birthplace, Stromness in Orkney, moulded his view of the
world, though he studied in Edinburgh, and later under Edwin
Muir at Newbattle Abbey College. From 1941 onwards he battled
tuberculosis, and increasingly lived a reclusive life in Stromness,
where a regular stream of publication from 1954 onwards included
Loaves and Fishes (1954), *A Calendar of Love* (1967), collections of
short stories *A Time to Keep* (1969) and *Hawkfall* (1974), a widely-
read novel *Greenvoe* (1972), *Time in a Red Coat* (1976) and a steady
stream of prose and poetry, notably the novel *Beside the Ocean of
Time* (1994) which was shortlisted for the Booker Prize and winner
of the Saltire Book of the Year. His work is permeated by the layers
of history in Scotland's past, by quirks of human nature and
religious belief, and by a fascination with the world beyond the
horizons of the known.

He was honoured by the Open University and by Dundee and
Glasgow Universities. The enduringly successful St Magnus Festival of poetry, prose, music and drama held annually in Orkney
keeps his memory alive, and is his lasting memorial.

GEORGE MACKAY BROWN

Hawkfall and other stories

Polygon

This edition published in Great Britain in 2004 by
Polygon, an imprint of Birlinn Ltd
West Newington House
10 Newington Road
Edinburgh
EH9 1QS

www.birlinn.co.uk

ISBN 1 904598 18 8

First published in 1974 by The Hogarth Press

British Library Cataloguing-in-Publication Data
A catalogue record for this book is available on request from the
British Library

Typeset by Hewer Text Ltd, Edinburgh
Printed and bound by AIT Nørhaven A/S, Denmark

To
PETER and BETTY GRANT

Contents

Acknowledgements

Some of the stories in this book have appeared in *The Scotsman*, *The Glasgow Herald*, *Lines Review*, and in *Neil M. Gunn, The Man and the Writer* (essays for the eightieth birthday of Neil Gunn), *Scottish Short Stories 1973* (Collins/Scottish Arts Council), *The Sixth Ghost Book* and *The Eighth Ghost Book* (Barrie and Jenkins)

Hawkfall

(i)

He was dead. The spirit of The Beloved One had gone on alone into the hall of death. His body was left to them for seven days yet so that they might give it a fitting farewell. Now it was time for it too to be sent after. The priests washed his old frail bluish body with water that had been drawn at sunrise. They arrayed him in his ceremonial vestments: the dyed woollen kirtle, the great gray cloak of wolfskin, the sealskin slippers. Across his breast they laid his whalebone bow, and seven arrows of larch. In his right hand they put the long oaken spear. The old mouth began to smile in its scant silken beard, perhaps because everything was being done well and according to the first writings.

Now it was time. All was ready.

A young man blew a horn on the hillside. The six bearers of the dead lifted the body and set out with it from the Temple of the Sun. They crossed between the two lochs, over a stone causeway. They walked solemnly, keeping step, towards the House of the Dead a mile away. Women walked alongside, wailing and lamenting, but in a ritual fashion, not as they would weep over the cruelty of a lover or the loss of a bronze ring. There were six women: a very old woman, a woman with the blark mark of widowhood on her brow, a woman with the ripe belly and breasts of pregnancy, a woman with a red bride-mark on her cheek, a tall girl with new untapped breasts, and a small child of five or six years. They flung their arms about in anguish, they beat their heads and covered their faces with their hands, their shoulders convulsed in loud wails as they stumbled blindly behind the corpse. (But from time to time one looked shrewdly to see where she was putting her feet; and sometimes one wailed till she had to stop for breath, and then she would turn her head and smile to one or other of the chorus, before falling once more to her prescribed lamentation. The little girl uttered cries like a bird, looking round from time to time at the other women and imitating their gestures.)

The procession arrived at the House of the Dead. Boys were waiting at the lee of the wall with unlit lamps at their feet. The priests laid down their awesome burden. The women wailed louder than ever. The old one knelt on the ground and shrieked; she held her skinny arms out as if all the world's joy and love had been reft from her.

A priest turned and rebuked these distracted ones. Foolish women, he said sternly, to weep so, when you should know that a great chief is going now into his nuptial joys, so that the light may be reborn, with primrose and tern, seal and cornstalk, and that you yourselves may be possessed with all abundance.

Meantime the boys kneeling at the lee of the House of the Dead had been putting flint sparks to their lamps, and guarding the small flames anxiously from the wind. And sometimes, so bright the spring sun shone, it seemed their precious flames were lost. But no: as they stooped in under the low lintel of the House of the Dead, all five of them, one after the other, the lamps glowed like opal in the gloom of the long corridor. So they passed in to the central chamber, uttering an elegy in their high or newly-broken voices.

> He is gone from us, The Brave Hunter
> He is gone from us, The Opener of Wells
> He is gone from us, Fosterer of the
>   Children of the Sun (the kindly
>   kindled fires, the lamp flames in
>   winter)
> He is gone from us, our Shield
> He is gone from us, The Wise Counsellor
> He is gone from us, The Corn Man . . .

After them came the dead chief with one bearer in front and one behind, for it was impossible for more than one person to enter at a time. Very low they had to stoop, these grown men, at the entrance to the House of the Dead. Almost on their knees they had to proceed along the stone corridor; for death should make men lowly and humble, and so they groped their way forward like moles into the flaming heart of the howe.

The central chamber filled silently up with the priests of the sun. The boys stood against the dripping walls, holding their lamps high. The bearers of the dead reassembled. They lifted their king-priest in his litter. A huge square stone block had been levered out of the wall and lay on the floor. Inside the tomb they could see, shadowy and flickering, the bones of former rulers, a knuckle bone, ribs, a skull. Now they prepared this latest traveller for his journey. They laid on him brooches of silver and horn, agates, polished cairngorms, a bronze sword; beside his head a silver cup to refresh him if perhaps he should falter in the arms of his dark bride.

The loaded body passed into the aperture. The stone was lifted and set in the wall once more. One by one the priests of the sun knelt and kissed the stone, and passed out, stooping low for a score of paces, into the spring wind and the sun.

The boys followed with their lamps. Outside they extinguished them; but the sun was so bright that the flames were only small invisible quivers. The boys puffed their cheeks over them. A little smoke rose.

And there on the inside slope of the great fosse that circled the House of the Dead sat the six women, laughing at some lewd story that the old crone was telling. The big-bellied woman seemed to shake the earth with her thunderous mirth. Even the widow smiled. The child was on the far side of the fosse, stooping and rising, daisies spilling out through her fingers.

A priest rebuked them. 'Foolish women,' he said, 'do you still not know that your king and your high priest is dead?' . . . The women turned away and drew their shawls over their faces, but the shoulders of the child-bearer continued to shake for a long time.

A thin cry shivered across the still waters of the loch. Many voices responded with a shout. In the Temple of the Sun a new priest-king had been chosen. At the very moment of entombment the power had fallen upon a chosen one.

The priests, the women, the boys walked slowly and silently, in procession as they had come, to the Temple beyond the two lochs. Soon they would know who the new father of the people was to be.

He stood in the heather, his upper body naked, alone in the still centre of the circle of huge monoliths: a young man, scarcely more than a boy, a virgin: on him the choice had fallen, his name the voice of the gods had uttered. 'This is the man,' proclaimed the caucus of ancient priests who alone could interpret the unutterable will of the gods. And, the choice having now been made, these old ones fussed around here and there, issuing orders to priests and acolytes and people, anxious that everything should be done in accordance with the ancient writings.

The young man with his bright body stands in the centre of the Temple.

He will never again kiss a country girl in the dark of the moon. He must bear now all his days the burden of perpetual virginity so that all else might be fruitful in field, in loch, in the great sea, in the marriage beds. In him the sorrows and triumphs of the tribe will be enacted ritually, and through his mouth the ancient wisdom interpreted; until at last, after very many years, the sun becomes a burden to him and he fares gladly to the House of the Dead and to the dark bride.

A priest kneels before him, puts into his hand a flint knife.

The ceremonies of initiation and consecration will last for a whole week. These rites are solemn, ancient, intricate, and of an almost impossible delicacy (for let a word be spoken wrong, or a gesture obscure the sun, or a foot step withershin, and much misfortune may stem from the flaw).

A young boar is dragged squealing across the heather to the Father of the People. Four priests manhandle the gnashing squealing slithering outraged beast. They up-end it in front of the Father of the People. Gravely, nervously, compassionately he bends over and pushes the flint knife into the boar's gullet. Blood spurts over his arms and shoulders. The boar twists about, staggers to its feet, looks about it very bewildered, runs a few steps this way and that way, stops, stumbles, slowly keels over on its side, hind legs faintly kicking. The priest-king holds cupped hands under the terrible throat wound. The people crowd about as he stands and scatters the sacrificial blood among them.

Now an ox is sacrificed. It is a quiet patient beast. It thrashes and goes limp under the knife. Blood is showered to the four quarters of the sun, and falls among the people. Happy the man who has a single red spot on his coat.

The arms and shoulders and breast of the Beloved of the Sun are smeared and daubed as if a tattered scarlet shirt had been thrown over him.

A hooded falcon is carried through the heather on a priest's fist; and is unhooded; and glares once, fiercely, at the celebrant; and flares out and flutters under the knife and is still. And again a small scattering of the life-giving essence.

For the animals bless us with their blood: whom the sun and moon and stars love, and who love those brightnesses in return, but who cannot articulate blessing, the innocent ones; they bless the wintry hearts of men with passionless perpetual streams of sacrifice.

That same day, near a village on the west coast of the island, the men prepared for the first fishing of the year. Two by two the fishermen stood beside their boats among the sheltering rocks. Then with a cry and a heave they swung the inverted boat up over their heads, and turned, an immense purposeful four-footed insect, across the broad sand to the edge of the water; and with a cry and a heave were again two fishermen and a floating curragh.

Next they brought down to the sea their stack of crab-pots. With concentration, a dark intentness, they stowed them on board. The stone brine-prisons in the Skara Brae houses were almost empty of limpets and dulse and whelks and mussels, but today they were after more succulent fish, the crab and the haddock. Creel by creel was handed from shore to boat.

In one of the Skara Brae houses an old mouth, so very dry and whiskered and shrunken that the young ones forgot sometimes whether it belonged to a man or a woman, began to mutter over the ashes. 'The Beautiful One is dead.' It soughed out the same words, over and over again. Once it said, 'His mouth was a delight to my mouth.' Then, over and over again, like the creaking of ash when a fire is dying, 'The Beautiful One, the Beautiful One, he is dead.'

A young woman came to the sea-bank and called to the busy fishermen, 'The chief has died between the two lochs. Old Mara, she has seen it.'

The fishermen paid no attention to her. It was a good day for fishing: a pewter sea and a gray sky. The crabs had put on their new hard coats. They would have issued from their crannies and ledges to see what polyps and algae they could prey upon. And they would certainly not despise the bait that men offered them.

The fishermen worked on.

Three women came and stood on the low sea-bank that protected the village. A fierce elderly woman cried to the fishermen, 'Does a man work the day his father dies? The Father of the People is dead. He who feeds us is dead, the Provider. Do you want a darkness to fall on us?'

Two of the curraghs were afloat. The men in them hesitated and were half turning back to the sand. A young man with a curiously flattened nose spoke across the water. 'Pay no attention to the women. What if some old man or other is dead? We have been making creels all winter for this day.' He handed the oars to his companion in the boat and leapt aboard. Half-a-dozen groups were still stowing creels aboard. The first three curraghs drifted slowly into the west.

(ii)

A boat scraped on the stones of the steep green island. Two young men leapt from the bow and dragged the boat clear of the water. A man with a hawk on his fist stepped from the slippery stones to the sand. He was a tall dark ugly man, with a hook nose and a sharp gray eye. The falconer followed him on to the island. The dark man flung the hawk from him. It would not go; it fluttered and flared and swung on his hand, rooted there, a fierce flaring of wings. The falconer stooped to it, whispered, offered it his hand, sang. The bird hopped gently from one fist to the other. Then the dark man walked up the beach, leapt over the low sea-bank, and ran across a field to a carved stone doorway. He entered the Hall boisterously.

In the church a stone-throw away the clergy and the boys were trying out their voices at a new setting of a penitential psalm:

> *Miserere mei, Deus, secundum*
> *magnam misericordiam tuam*
> *Et secundum multitudinem*
> *miserationum tuarum dele iniquitatem meam*

A cantor was trying to make a proper contrast of voices, a better interweaving of treble with bass and tenor. 'Try once again,' said the offended clerical voice. 'Once more now.'

> *Miserere mei, Deus, . . .*

The dark man's feet thudded over the wooden floor of the Hall. The fire in the central hearth was almost out, charred logs with one yellow flame gulping among them. The man stopped and clapped his hands. A boy came running from the women's quarters beyond. 'Blow up the fire,' said the man. 'It's February, not June. Bring in more logs. Start a flame with some broken peats.'

'Yes, lord,' said the boy, and lifted a large straw basket from the hearth.

He was a rather ugly boy; he seemed to have no proper nose-bridge, so that his nostrils flared out over his cheeks; also his face was a constellation of freckles; but in spite of these defects everyone in the Hall found him attractive, and the women especially were inclined to spoil him.

'Lord,' he said now, pleadingly, 'please give me leave to go to the burn after dinner. There is an otter in the burn. I have sharpened a long stick.'

'Tomorrow,' said the man. 'Today there are more important things to do.'

The boy pouted a little. He turned and carried the basket in front of him to the fuel-hoard outside.

At the far end of the long Hall a woman sat at a loom. She was still beautiful though her hair was streaked with gray and there were wrinkles about her eyes and mouth. Around her sat three girls. One was on a low stool. The two on the floor had their feet tucked demurely under their skirts. The three girls were sewing. They drew coloured woollen threads through one long undulation of linen. Truncated pictures appeared on the linen – the wing of a raven, the leg of a soldier, the stern of a ship.

The men who had hauled the boat ashore entered, carrying dead birds and hares, and passed through into the kitchen, a hound flowing and lolloping among their legs.

The dark man approached the women round the loom. He strode across the tapestry. One of the girls cried 'O' and put her hands to her mouth as the deerskin shoes, soiled with sand and mud and seaweed, brushed against the linen. The man bent over the woman at the loom. She tilted her face towards him. 'Ingibiorg,' he said. He kissed her once on the mouth (still red and beautiful, though with wrinkles and unwanted hairs about the corners now). He touched her coiled bronze braided hair gently. Then he passed out of the chamber into the dark corridor beyond.

The boy came staggering back into the Hall with logs and peat in the basket. He dumped it down beside the hearth. The girls called out to him to take care.

The dark man took off his hunting jacket in his room. He took off his hat with the swan's feather in it. He took off his red woollen shirt. He kicked off his shoes. He went to the door and clapped his hands. He loosed the thong at his waist and slid his skin trousers off and threw them on the heap of clothes on the bed. He turned. A silent figure stood in the door with a garment over his arm. The naked man went down on his knees and stretched out his arms for the penitential sackcloth to be put on him.

'*Mis-er-er-e*,' said the ill-natured voice from the choir of the church. 'You are not exactly at a feast when you sing that. You are not in a dance-hall or a tavern. Not exactly. You are souls in torment. You are standing in holy fire. Pray that it may be the cleansing fire of Purgatory and not that other unquenchable brimstone. Now once again – and remember your sins and be sorry for them while you sing it – *Mis-er-er-e.*'

The bass voices made utterance, dark with sorrow.

The man in sackcloth followed the summoner across the field to the church. The walls still had skirtings of snow, under the blue cold sweep of sky. Revay Hill had a white worn cap. Bare feet followed bare feet across the grass and into the gloom of the church. The penitent knelt beside a pillar and, shaking with cold, tried to remember his sins. The killing of his nephew Rognvald in the seaweed in Papa Stronsay. The burning of Rognvald's men earlier that same night. The holocaust of the King of Norway's men the next morning, a heap of reeking corpses on the shore of Kirkwall. He tried to imagine these things, the sword in the guts – a lingering bitter death that; the fire climbing from belly to chest to beard, bones crackling and marrow bubbling and the man still not dead, unless he had mercifully choked on a lump of smoke; the axe in the skull between one word and another. He tried to imagine the sins he had committed, and to be sorry for them, but he could think of nothing except the spasms of cold that were going through his body.

Meantime the Mass had begun. 'Introibo ad altare Dei,' sang the Bishop in his fine Latin that he had learned to pronounce in the colleges of Paris.

'Ad Deum qui laetificat juventutem meam,' responded the choristers in the coarser Latin of the north.

Kyrie eleison. Christe eleison. Kyrie eleison. Backwards and forward the voices shuttled, weaving the unseen garment of penitence, weaving the sackcloth.

There was silence. The penitent looked up. An acolyte was bringing to the Bishop the bason of ashes. The boy knelt before the altar, delivered the ashes, knelt again, retired. The penitent swung his head round the church slowly. Ingibiorg his wife was kneeling behind him, but in the clothes that she had worn at the loom; only her hair was covered with a gray cloth. Three gray-kerchiefed girls knelt beside her. The falconer and the young men were there in their hunting clothes, their feathered caps on the stone floor beside their knees. Erlend his second son knelt over by the statue of Saint Olaf. The cook was there, carrying his ladle as though it would take a blessing from being in church and pour out better broth and stew. He did not see the boy who looked after the fires in the Hall. The stewart was there. The men from the fishing boat had brought their nets. The ploughmen and the cattlemen and the shepherds and the keeper of the pigsty were there, and their women. All those cheeks were gaunt in the taper light, as if sorrow had indeed hollowed out their faces. He alone wore the sackcloth for them all.

De profundis clamavi, Domine. A bass voice rose up, imploring, out of woeful pits of shame. *Domine, exaudi orationem meam,* sang the tenors. The phrases were a little brighter, as if hope were a possibility – it was there, somewhere, surely – it was not entirely extinguished. At least sorrow was something – the people of Orkney had this day put off the many-coloured coat of vanity.

But had they? Thorfinn Sigurdson, Earl of Orkney, Shetland, Caithness, Sutherland, Ross, the Hebrides, Man, Lord of the Western Sea, could not concentrate on anything because of the great qualms that shook his body. Springs of coldness rose from his knees where they touched the stone floor and passed up through his loins and his belly and his chest and his face. His clasped hands shook. He tried to concentrate on his sins. Unfaithfulness to the Lady Ingibiorg on three occasions this past winter, with one of the handmaidens (the innocent-looking one) and with Sven the ploughman's eldest daughter and with the Gaelic girl in Caithness – O God, he could not even think of the girl's name or her appearance because of the cold gules that were chilling the sinuses of his forehead and obliterating his ears and fingers.

Sacerdores tui induantur iustitiam: et sancti tui exultent, sang the farm boys, their pure high blessed notes rising to the roof.

And I did not go to Mass at Christmas midnight, because I had drunk too much honeyed ale. And I accuse myself of the constant sin of pride. And while many of my people eat limpets and roots I never fail to stuff my belly out with roasts of pork and trout from the grill and Irish wines. And I . . . But he existed within the heart of an iceberg.

Benigne fac, Domine, in bona voluntate tua Sion: ut aedificentur muri Jerusalem, sang the redeemed voices, bass and treble and tenor part of a single whole, interwoven, reconciled, a fitting Lenten garment to offer to the Lord.

In the following silence the worshippers heard, borne into the church on the uncertain east wind, very faintly, the cry of a transfixed otter.

The Bishop descended from the altar, carrying the bason. He paused before the Earl. The Bishop dipped his thumb in the ashes. He marked a gray cross on the forehead of the Earl. *Memento, homo, quia pulvis es, et in pulverem reverteris . . .*

All the people bowed their heads, waiting for the ashes of humiliation to be written on their brows.

(iii)

The principal clerk at the Palace of Birsay, Jonathan Fraser, a Scotsman, sat at a table in the library on the morning of June the tenth and wrote, as every morning, the diary of Patrick Stewart his master as far as he had observed the Earl's business, pastimes, conversation, bodily health, etcetera, on the previous day, the ninth of June. The clerk wrote with a quill upon parchment, dipping the point frequently in a stone bowl of ink, elaborating the capital letters with fine intricate flourishes, and cursing sometimes under his breath when the ink failed in the middle of a well-conceived phrase, or if the quill required the penknife.

The 9th day of June in the year of the Lord 1593

His lordship rose too late for divine service. *I am concerned, yet not concerned, touching the state into which religion has fallen,* he saith to me breaking his fast with white bread and a capon limb and a small beaker of goats' milk. *They are up and down like a seesaw, Presbyter and Bishop, sermon and sacrament, black gown and white gown. The cursing that they put one on another! (Yet all holds: I observe not one blasted with perdition.) I think, Master Fraser, these preaching men are not necessary unto us. What are their prayings but puffs of air? Yet kirk serveth to hold the people in awe. Therefore I say I*

*am concerned and not concerned. Make an apology to Canon Fulzie
that I did not attend his Matins this morning.*

His lordship received at noon Master Simon Buttquoy his factor
and they sat an hour and more over the estate books, going as it
were with a comb through every farm and cot and the rental each
paid. And, *By God,* said his lordship, *this is a mouse's yield that they
make. How can they be well governed and protected, yea, and
cherished, when this is all that the estate receives from these Orkney-
men? It is not before time that we are come hither into the north.
There will be here a new ordering of things, Master Buttquoy.*

At half past two in the afternoon, his lordship having sat down
to a light repast of hare-broth and crab and barley bread with a
bowl of Spanish wine, and last a gobbet of white cheese, ordered
the horses saddled and the hounds leashed. There was much
merriment round the table. Master Abercrombie described how
he had gotten lost in deep snow in the parish of Orphir in the
previous winter, going about some business of the estate, so that he
saw small prospect of reaching either Birsay or Kirkwall before
nightfall. He called therefore at a cottage on the side of a hill. The
man of the house gave him buttermilk and oatmeal for refreshment. Alack, said the crofter, there are two beds, I and my old
Margit Ann sleep in one, and the bairn in the other. Would you
pass the night with our lass, sir? . . . But Master Abercrombie, not
choosing (as he said) to have his night broken with a child's
bawlings and shittings, assured the man he would be comfortable
enough in the deep straw chair before the hearth, with a blanket
about his knees. And so the night passed, somewhat sleepless. Then
morning came, and the family assembled to break their fast. First
came to the table the man of the house, and then Margit Ann his
spouse (an ugly enough old beldame) and then 'the bairn', who
was a lass of sixteen years, with new-formed breasts and hair like a
torrent of sunshine, and all the meal-time she looked slyly and
shyly and yearningly at Master Abercrombie, the red and the white
roses coming and going upon her cheeks . . .

His lordship had great mirth from that tale.

When the table was a scatter of crusts and cheese parings and
empty goblets, they rose and went out to the stable yard where the

Wylie, and myself. I think none spoke except this small-faced architect. And his lordship, who would have broken such impudence and arrogance with some salutary obscene barbed witticism on other occasions, listened as meek as a dove to the creature, the only begetter of his future palace in Kirkwall.

Simon Buttquoy begged to be excused; he had to preside over an interrogation in the cellar.

Nor did M. Bouchet care for the lobster and cheese sauce.

He cupped his hand over the buttock of the girl that carried in the cheese.

Over by the fire, when viol and lute began to play, M. Bouchet covered his ears.

Carrying my writing materials, I followed Master Buttquoy down to the cellar.

In the cellar the interrogation of Adam Thorfinnson, farmer in Garth in the parish of Saint Michael, commenced. Two years since, Earl Patrick Stewart was put in possession of ancient deeds and titles in which it was plainly set out that the Earl's predecessors had had sole ownership of the lands of Garth in Saint Michael parish. He had therefore required, in all civility, the said Adam to make due acknowledgement of his (Adam's) ancestors' usurpation of the said lands. This usurpation had occurred in that difficult time when there was no clear distinction between Norse and Scottish in the islands and two diverse laws, languages, codes, contended one with another in inextricable confusion; which ravelment was intensified by the Norse use of the patronymic; according to which, for instance, Adam's father was called Thorfinn Paulson, his grandfather Paul Swanson, his great-grandfather Sweyn Janson, and so on back to an original called William Otter, or Flatnose, who, vehemently claimed the said Adam, was gifted these lands of Garth in perpetuity by his master, a Norwegian earl called Thorfinn Sigurdson. This claim had no written documentation but was, claimed Earl Patrick, rooted in fable; and it is likely, said his lordship, that this Earl Thorfinn, if he existed at all, fought against dragons and had his helmet hammered by mountain trolls and took an ice maiden to wife.

Now that the dove of peace was fallen and furled in the north, the Earl required Adam to quit the said lands of Garth at the season of Martinmas. Of his charity the Earl would not press for past payment of rent, an onerous sum indeed if a century's unpaid rent were to be computed, together with the interest on the same. And the Earl further offered the said Adam the tenancy of the farm of Lang Klett in the same parish, which farm to some degree had reverted to bog and heather with long unoccupancy, but a young man of Adam Thorfinnson's vigour (argued the factor) could speedily restore these acres to their former yoke and yield.

The Earl had required Adam Thorfinnson, eighteen months since, to put his mark to a document drawn up by Master Lorimer the sheriff and myself, acknowledging the undoubted rights of the Earl in this matter, but Adam Thorfinnson had up to the present steadfastly refused.

The said Adam had therefore been removed under duress from the farm and lands he occupied unlawfully to the Palace of the said Earl Patrick Stewart in Birsay, in order that one only question be put to him, namely, did he propose to yield Garth to its rightful owner Patrick Stewart; the interrogator to be Master Simon Buttquoy, factor to the said Patrick Stewart.

Adam Thorfinnson answered, *No.*

Thereupon Adam Thorfinnson was shown the iron boot, the wedges, the hammer; the Earl's men made a great clattering on the stones with these instruments.

Adam again answered, *No* – he had the lands from his father and his father's father before him.

The iron boot was thereupon put on the right leg of Adam of Garth, and it reached to his knee. A wooden wedge was inserted between bone and metal. A naked-shouldered man stood by with a raised mallet.

Answer, said Simon Buttquoy.

No, said Adam Thorfinnson.

Strike, said Simon Buttquoy.

The wedge took the full weight of the hammer. Adam Thorfinnson's face was silvered with a sweat.

Answer, said Simon Buttquoy.

I call upon God to witness, said Adam Thorfinnson, *that I have worked these acres well and enriched them yearly with manure and seaweed. I have opened two wells about the place, and a quarry. With my own hands last summer I built a barn. I have greatly enriched the place.*

Strike, said Simon Buttquoy.

The hammer fell and the iron rang and a bone cracked.

I have a son that is to come after me, said Adam Thorfinnson. *I would not have him inherit the wildnerness and wetness of Lang Klett.*

His head was fallen on his breast.

I had not seen this Adam Thorfinnson previously. He had the usual appearance of the peasantry, thick shoulders and red cheeks, and in addition his nose was squashed somewhat as if he had been kicked by a horse or perhaps had it broken in a tavern brawl – this gave to his face a hard obdurate cast.

Now two guardsmen held him by the shoulders.

You are young, said Simon Buttquoy. *You are strong. It is well known that you are a good and a provident farmer. In six years the Lang Klett will be as rich a place as any to be seen in the west part of Orkney. There is a burn. You could quarry big stones. All that district stands in sore need of a mill.*

No, said Adam Thorfinnson.

Strike, said Simon Buttquoy. The hammer fell. The iron rang. Adam Thorfinnson swooned in his chair. A guardsman wound his hands through Adam Thorfinnson's hair and jerked his head back. Another dashed water into Adam Thorfinnson's face. Adam Thorfinnson looked around as if he had but newly arrived among us. He half smiled. Then his whole body was deluged with pain and he groaned for the first time. Simon Buttquoy went over to the chair where he was held. Simon Buttquoy looked close at him with much seriousness and a shaking of his head. *Adam, Adam*, he said, *what possesses you? What in the name of God ails you? A cripple man will not be able to plough the Lang Klett. A man with one leg shorter by six inches than the other will make poor twisted cuttings with his scythe. The parish children run after men like that and mock them. In the name of God, all Earl Patrick asks of you is to put your mark to that parchment with the seal upon it, over there on the table.*

There was silence for a full minute. Adam Thorfinnson looked at the man who stood guard over the door. He put his tongue to his dry lips. He looked at the sergeant with the mallet. His throat swole with another groan. Then he leaned towards Simon Buttquoy as to a trusted friend, and whispered a word.

I cannot hear you, said Simon Buttquoy. He gestured to me to bring over the parchment and quill to the chair where the farmer was held.

Adam Thorfinnson said in a loud firm voice, *No.*

Simon Buttquoy straightened himself.

Sergeant, said he, sadly, *put in another wedge.*

(iv)

The young laird and the graying minister sat at either side of a blazing fire. Through the library window of the Hall the laird could see the drifting snowflakes. He lifted a decanter from the table and poured a little liquor into the minister's glass. The minister raised his free hand in futile remonstrance. 'Come,' said the laird, 'it's a cold afternoon and you have a three mile ride in front of you. The brandy is good, admit that.'

'It is a very good brandy,' said the minister. 'A delicious spirit indeed.'

The laird replaced the glass stopper in the decanter.

'And so you see, Mr Liddle,' he said, 'what an invidious situation has been forced on me. Provide a dozen men, say their lordships in the letter, for His Majesty's ships before New Year's Day, out of the parish, the bounty to be two guineas a man . . . This is what will happen now. I will ask this man and that to volunteer. O yes, some will say, and others will look at their boots and mumble, and the proud ones will walk away from me and turn and glare from the end of the road. But a dozen, say, agree. O yes, anything to please the laird in the Hall. They shuffle and touch their bonnets. After Christmas I send the officers round the parish to summon them. Not a skin. Not a rumour. They have vanished from the face of the earth. One has gone to the Hudson's Bay. One is in Rousay buying a mare. One is in Birsay looking for a wife. One never came back from the fishing . . . Of course I know where they are. They are hiding in the caves until the officers of the Press Gang have left the islands. They are fed and comforted by night, in secret, by their women. Not one man from this parish reaches Portsmouth or The Nore. And my reputation with the lords of the Admiralty will have sunk to zero.'

He jerked a satin cord at the wall. There was a distant tinkling.

'It is truly a disgrace,' said the minister.

'It is not,' said the laird. 'I sympathize with these lads. Have you seen the three that were sent home to Hamnavoe after Trafalgar? Learmonth my factor saw them. One with his right leg shot away. One like a wraith with consumption. One furrowed from nape to buttocks with the lash, a broken man. I would winter in a cave myself to stay out of these hell-ships.'

A man stood in the library door.

'Andrew,' said the laird, 'have you lit the fire in the spare bedroom?'

'I have that,' said Andrew.

'A good fire, Andrew,' said the laird. 'It will be a cold night. Is my wife still sewing in the parlour?'

'The mistress retired to her room an hour ago and more,' said Andrew. 'Poor body, she has a sore head.'

'Andrew,' said the laird, 'the decanter is empty. See to it.'

'No more for me,' said the minister.

'And bring in more peat,' said the laird, 'a full basket.'

'Andrew withdrew, closing the door softly behind him.

There were about a hundred wedding guests in the barn of Eldquoy. The men looked very uncomfortable in their dark suits and white stiff collars. The guests stood about in small murmuring groups, the women at one end, the men at the other. All at once there was a silence. The man of the house, the bride's father, stood in the door with a keg of ale in his hands. Behind him stood his wife and two of his daughters. The goodwife carried a tray of white crumbly cheese, the girls had boards of oatcakes and bere ban-nocks. The man of the house advanced and looked round the company till he spied the oldest of his guests. Gravely he approached him and held out the ale-vessel. The old man drank, and passed the keg to his neighbour, then dipped his fingers among the slices of cheese and bannock. He said something; everyone laughed. The ale and bread went from mouth to mouth in a slow sunwise circle. Everyone ate and drank.

Meantime, in the best room of the farmhouse, two women were lacing the bride into her white gown. They sat her down on a wooden stool. They pulled white stockings over her legs that were fresh from yesterday's ritual washing. They unpinned her coils and braids and shook out her long black hair and sent the combs rippling through it. A girl came in and put white shoes on the bride's feet.

'So what kind of a living can anyone drag out of such primitive agriculture?' said the laird. 'A strip here and a strip there, oats one year, barley the next. Drive the beasts out beyond the township wall once the seed is in – the pigs, the geese, the cows, the garrons – let them root and roam about the hill all summer. Pray in the kirk for the rain to fall and the sun to shine. But one year the crop is high and burnished and another year the worm is in it. Kill the beasts and salt them down for the winter, for there's nothing to feed them till the grass begins to grow again. And steep the malt and get drunk. And when the last of the salt meat is eaten bait the lines, push out the boat, try a haul out west. It won't do.'

'*In the sweat of thy brow shalt thou labour*,' said the minister. 'They know no better. This is how it has always been. They are content.'

'It won't do,' said the laird. 'In the first place I cannot maintain this house and my other house in the Canongate of Edinburgh, and educate my son and daughter forby, on the rents I wring out of this parish at present. The earth is rich, she could yield a hundredfold more.'

'It is simply to upset them unnecessarily,' said the minister, 'to instruct them in a new mode of agriculture. It's more than that. It is to fill their heads with dangerous ideas. No. I am sorry to disagree with you, but I must repel what you say. I think of France and I shudder.'

'Your glass is empty,' said the laird.

'No more,' said the minister, and got to his feet. 'The wedding is at four o'clock. They will be starting to walk over the hill in the snow.' . . . He set his empty glass down on the table.

'It isn't three o'clock yet,' said the laird, and poured another dram into first the minister's and then his own glass. 'You'll ride there in a half-hour.'

He pulled the satin cord beside the fireplace. A remote tinkle seemed to echo the fall of the brandy into the glasses.

'Enclosures,' said the laird. 'Root crops. Grasses. The tilth squared into proper fields and rented for cash to the eager energetic ones. This is the agriculture of the future. Other benefits will fall from the good hands of Ceres – clean bright cottages – a physician in every parish – a school and a schoolmaster in every parish.'

Andrew appeared in the doorway.

'Saddle Mr Liddle's mare, Andrew,' said the laird. 'And see that the fire in the spare room is well banked.'

Andrew nodded and withdrew.

'So Knox thought,' said the minister. 'I cannot see it myself. What will become of hierarchy? Nobody will know where he stands. It will be all a chaos. I wish fervently not to be alive on that day.'

The minister was still on his feet. He drank with some vehemence. His upper lip was wet to the nostrils when he set down his glass on the table.

'You are a Tory,' said the laird good-humouredly, 'in an age of enlightenment. There is nothing to be done with the likes of you but put your head on a block.'

'Exactly,' cried the minister. 'That's what they did in France. Exactly so.' He was as red in the face as a turkey-cock.

Andrew stood in the door. 'The mare is ready,' he said.

'Have one for the road,' said the laird.

Outside the barn there was a sudden tumult of boys' voices. They were calling for the bridegroom, over and over again, their voices high and shivering in the winter air. A few of the bolder ones beat with their fists on the door. Again the bridegroom's name was called, cajolingly at first. 'Tom Langclett! Tom, Tom! It's cold out here. We're starving, Thomas.'

The barn door remained shut.

Their voices modulated into mockery and insult. They shouted over and over again the nickname of the bridegroom – 'Flatnose! Flatnose! Tammag Flatnose!'

The bridegroom came at last and stood in the door with his hands full of copper coins. He threw his heaped hands skywards. Pennies and halfpennies and farthings showered among the shouts and clutching fingers and fell softly on the snow. Then the separate boys became one wild distracted beast, tearing and rooting and howling and grovelling for the bridegroom's bounty. They churned the snow into a swift gray chaos. The bridegroom retired. The barn door was shut. When the bride and her attendants came out of the house for the wedding procession there was only one boy left, standing in the lee of the barn with bleeding fingers. The boy wept softly under the softly falling snow.

A fiddler stood beside the peat-tack. He put his fiddle to his throat and drew the bow across the strings. He stepped forward, flashed a wintry magic from his breast over the barnyard. The wedding guests issued out of the barn as if in obedience to his summons – first bride and groomsman, then bridegroom and bridesmaid, then two by two the entire bridal company. They followed the fiddler out of the farm on to the road, and turned right, and set off, laughing and chattering and poking fun at this one and that, two by two, a long serpentine progress towards the manse that lay just over the shoulder of the hill two miles away. *Woo'd and married an' a'*, shrieked the fiddle. Only the bride kept silent all the way, as the white snow fell softly and incessantly on her whiteness.

The minister's horse champed the snow in the courtyard. The minister stood in the open door in his coat and cravat. He gestured excitedly with his hat. He had plainly drunk more than was good for him. The laird had him by the elbow and was trying good-naturedly to urge him towards his horse. Holding a lit candle in one hand, Andrew passed up the stairs behind them with two thick soft white blankets clasped to his breast.

'It has started already,' cried the minister. 'Secession in the kirk. There is this meeting-house for seceders that has been opened in Kirkwall. They speak of having another in Hamnavoe. And another in Birsay, if you please . . . Why do they no longer attend Sabbath worship from the farm of Howegarth, John Rendall and his wife and six bairns? Why is Harald the shepherd's seat empty? I wager you haven't seen Angus Gow the blacksmith in his pew this two month past. No. And why not? Because they have joined this damned Secession.'

'The wedding,' said the laird gently.

'The heresy is spreading,' said the minister, flourishing his hat in the laird's face. 'You would not think the wolf would plunder in such a distant sheepfold as Orkney. Harry Germiston from Gray-stones, I didn't see him in his pew last Sabbath.'

'The wedding,' said the laird. The hoof of the mare drew a long groove in the snow.

'It is this liberalism,' said the minister . . . 'I am coming, Molly,' he called to the mare, 'have a little patience.' . . . He turned back to the laird, stifled a belch with his hat and said, 'I fear I have abused your hospitality.'

'No, no,' said the laird, 'but you will need all your time if you are to be at the manse to meet the wedding party.'

'Their weddings,' said the minister. 'I swear I sometimes have to laugh. There she stands in front of me, all in white, a virgin, a vestal, and with a big belly on her simply bursting with fruitfulness. Six or seven months gone. When the Blotchnie wedding was over I went back to my study and I poured out a dram for myself and I laid my head on the desk and I shook with laughter. And no wonder. For Bella-Jean of Blotchnie had to be carried straight from her wedding to her lying-in.'

'Tell me,' said the laird, 'this girl who is being married today, how is it with her? Is she far gone?'

'Mary of Eldquoy is a good girl,' said the minister. 'No-one has ever pointed the finger at her. She will wear her white blamelessly. Of that much I am sure.'

'They will be waiting at the locked door of the manse,' said the laird patiently. 'In the snow.'

'I never join in their receptions,' said the minister. 'This family and that invite me, but I do not go. I know well enough what goes on at these wedding bacchanalias, after midnight, once the whisky takes a hold of them. It is a great time for the next generation to be sown all over the parish, a country wedding. Not only in the nuptial bed.' He winked at the laird. 'Fornication rampant under the stars . . . Molly, I am coming now.'

An upper window flushed with the rousing of a fire in the hearth.

The minister mounted his mare, throwing his leg with a certain formal abandonment. He waved his hat twice towards the door of the Hall, where the laird stood with a hand raised. The mare, urged on, plodded forward through the soft snow.

The laird went in and closed the door. He returned thoughtfully to the flickering library. He put the glass stopper in the decanter. He stirred the fire with the brass poker. He wandered over to the book-clad wall. He fingered a volume here and there, pursing his lips, dropping on one knee occasionally to examine a title near the floor. He withdrew a tall calf volume and opened it at random.

Thou hast seen the falcon adrift between two clouds, how it seemeth on a sudden to check and to hang motionless in the pure upper stream, and keepeth a high lonely speculation there awhile; anon it seemeth to stumble on a steep blue step of sky, and falleth free; no, rather it hurleth itself downward, earthtrue, and maketh a brief check again above the tranced prey; then its claw reacheth down to make an immaculate consummation; and the earth is hallowed again with red lustral drops.

A gray cat cried thinly at his knee; he rubbed the furry throat with his knuckles till the cat was all one breathing purr. The window darkened. Snowflakes fell on the panes like gray silent moths, and clung there for a moment, and became black quick beads. The laird rose to his feet and closed the heavy curtains.

He returned to the bookshelves. He drew out a volume of poems and opened it idly.

> My banks they are furnished with bees
>> Whose murmur invites one to sleep;
> My grottos are shaded with trees,
>> And my hills are white-over with sheep.
> I seldom have met with a loss,
>> Such health do my fountains bestow;
> My fountains all border'd with moss,
>> Where the harebells and violets grow.

His lips moved occasionally, relishing the words. He brought the book over to his chair beside the fire. He arranged the candelabrum on the table so that the brightest waverings of light moved over his chair. He sat down and lifted the book and turned a page. The cat crouched in the hearth, its hind leg stuck straight out, and burrowed violently in its belly for a flea. Then it sat up and blinked and leapt on to the laird's knee and sought for first the hard calf edge of the book and then a dreaming knuckle. It purred occasionally. It padded the velvet lap with its velvet feet and found a place at last and curled up and closed its eyes. The long sensitive fingers turned a page.

> But where does my Phyllida stray?
>> And where are her grots and her bowers?
> Are the groves and the valleys as gay
>> And the shepherds as gentle as ours?
> The groves may perhaps be as fair,
>> And the face of the valleys as fine;
> The swains may in manners compare,
>> But their love is not equal to mine.

The fiddler was almost exhausted. Apart from the long bridal procession to the manse and back he had kept the dance going for five hours and more in the barn of Eldquoy. Around ten o'clock the music began to falter. The groomsman brought him a glass of whisky and the ale-keg. The dance stopped. Then the music resumed, with all its old energy but with a mistake here and there – rents in that coarse-spun sark of song.

It was all too energetic for the older guests. They had retired to the benches along the wall.

The night was cold for kissing under the stars, but there was a constant coming and going of the younger guests through the barn door. A girl would come in with snowflakes clinging to her hair. 'Where has thu been?' some old man would ask her, then turn and wink at the other old men. Then her cheeks would flush more than ever, and the old men would wheeze and clap their knees with their hands and wipe tears from the corners of their eyes. And a minute later the girl's partner would come in from the chaste kisses of the snow and turn from her as if she was nothing to him; and seek the circling whisky jug.

Another young man would seize a girl by the wrist in the middle of a reel and pull her towards the door. The girl would look anxiously to see if her father was noticing. He was not – he was seated over by the wall, smoking his clay pipe and gossiping behind a whirl and a shriek of dancers – but her sister who carried round a tray of sliced mutton had turned round and was eyeing every move. She plucked her hand from the hand of her partner, very offended, and joined some elderly women at the north end of the barn whose days of dancing and love were over.

The fiddler raised his bow high in the air. He needed more refreshment.

The bride and bridegroom sat in a corner of the barn in some kind of secret painful consultation. The girl was upset. Her mouth trembled. Her new husband bent forward and murmured consolingly to her. She waved away the chicken and the bannock; no, she couldn't eat. She pressed the lace handkerchief to her hot cheeks. The dance had such fury and impetus in it now that only the bridesmaid, who came to tell her she must mix the most important drink of the evening, the Bride Cog, noticed her distress. The bridesmaid hastened to tell the host, who was arranging the whisky, the honey, the ale, the Jamaican sugar, the rum, about the varnished well-turned wooden vessel. Sombrely the bride's father eased his way through the dancers till he reached the bride. He bent down and spoke earnestly to the girl, occasionally turning for confirmation to the bridegroom. It was no use; the bride would not be comforted; her eyes were brilliant with new tears. The mother and the youngest sister came, easing their way past the knees of the seated whispering nodding old ones. The mother took the bride's hand and sat down beside her. This made things worse than ever; the bride bent her head into her hands and her fingers were wet with tears; a few drops shone over her knuckles on to the floor.

Nothing of this little drama could be heard for the noise of the dance. Once more the fiddler had faltered, and the whisky bottle had been passed to him. The music resumed, a jig, but hardly recognizable on account of the waywardness of the performance. 'My God, what's he trying to do, strangle a cat?' said the beadle to the blacksmith. The young ones, men and girls, threw up their arms and circled each other.

The mute mime in the corner of the barn had been observed by a very old woman seated near the door, alone. She was so old and so incapacitated with rheumatism that she had to be excused every task, such as carrying round portions of chicken and keeping the mouths of the men wet. Everyone paid her deference as they passed, half in awe and half in raillery. An old man, hurrying past her after the circling ale vessel, would stop and say a few laughing words to her. She would smile and shake her head and say nothing. Now she noticed the sorrow of the bride, and the cajolery and threatening and pleading all about her. She rose. She balanced her twisted body on a long stick. She shuffled and hobbled along the wall. Half-drunk dancers dragged their partners out of the way of this painful progress. The bridegroom made way for her beside the bride; taking the old one's elbow gently and easing her down on to the bench. At once she sent them all away: bridegroom, host, hostess, sisters, aunt. They were ravelling up a very simple situation – leave the girl to her. They went without question; they mingled with the wedding guests. The bride and the old woman sat alone in the corner.

Because of the stamping of feet and the laughter and the rant of the fiddle nobody knew what words passed between the old woman and the girl. But the girl listened with growing absorption to what she heard now; as if she tasted, sip by quickening sip, the mellowness that many winters bestow on the chalice that must be drunk by all women born. The withered hand touched, in turn, the young mouth and the breast and the thigh. Presently the bride smiled. She turned and kissed the gray sagging cheek. The old woman put her hand, last, to the bride's belly, and nodded decisively. Thus indeed it must be.

The music had stopped once more, finally this time it seemed, for the fiddle had fallen on the floor with one wild despairing shriek and the fiddler was making his way unsteadily among the stone jars of ale. It was midnight. He had saturated the entire parish with music. He could give them nothing more. He had emptied himself utterly. The groomsman set him down against the wall and put a mug of ale between his hands.

A couple came out of the night, shyly, lightly clung about with snowflakes.

The bride stood at the main table, smiling, and mixed the Bride Cog. She emptied the whisky bottle and the rum bottle into the vessel, then a reluctant golden flood of honey, then a jar of Jamaican sugar like old soft snow. From the farm kitchen two men carried in a pot of scalding hot ale.

The host tasted the liquor, and nodded.

Bridegroom and bride carried the vessel first to the sibyl in the corner. She frowned into the rich rising fumes.

Then mouth after mouth tasted the blessing as it went round sunwise, until everyone had drunk; they even touched the liquor to the mouth of a child who lay half asleep in his mother's arms.

Three young men urged Walter Flett the weaver into the fiddler's chair. They sat him down and put the fiddle into his hands. A girl urged him with a kiss on the cheek. Walter raised the bow. He could dispense only a thin sour music. But by now they were past caring for excellence. The strings shrieked and keened. The feet beat on the floor once more. A wild cry rose to the roof beams.

In the middle of this dance there came two slow loud knocks at the door. The host crossed over and lifted the sneck. Andrew the servant from the Hall stood there. He had a lantern in his fist. He squeezed the snow out of his beard. 'It's time,' he said. 'The master's waiting.'

No, he wouldn't come in. No, he wouldn't take a dram. The master was ready now. They must hurry.

A new cloak was put over the bride's shoulders. Her hair was pushed under a new finely-knitted lace shawl. The two sisters fussed round her. The mother murmured encouragement and consolation into her ear. Nobody moved in the barn; it was as if the appearance of Andrew had turned them all to stone. The bride's eyes sought out the bridegroom, but he had passed from the barn into the house as soon as the summons came. The old woman nodded: a slow resigned sorrowful fall of the head: this must be. The father, muffled hurriedly in a gray cloak and a gray bonnet, touched the bride on the elbow. Andrew and the host and the bride passed out into the snow. The groomsman shut the door. The barn broke out again with its babble of a hundred tongues. Walter Flett put the fiddle under his chin. The true fiddler slept against the wall. The barn swooned and lamented and, slowly but with gathering impetus, began to turn.

The bridegroom stood alone at the cold kitchen window of Eldquoy. He saw the three small dark figures moving up the ridge towards the Hall. They dwindled in the snow. At last all that he could see was the frail flicker of the lantern.

But his mind, as he stands with his face against the pane, is possessed with another image. He sees himself on the moor one day next summer. He has his gun over his shoulder. He is after grouse and hares. A horseman breaks the skyline, urging his horse through the heather, going in the direction of the village. It is the young laird. They are alone, those two, in the world. Horse and horseman come nearer. The hunter waits. The handsome laird is now within the radius of death. The tenant with the flat ugly nose, Thomas Langclett, turns to face him. He raises his gun to his shoulder . . .

It would never happen that way. If he did find himself in such a situation, alone with the ravisher of his bride, he knew he would never shoot. Instead he would take off his cap and mutter a polite greeting; perhaps, if the laird lingered to speak (for he was otherwise an agreeable gentleman) he would thank him humbly for allowing him to shoot over his lands again that year.

The mind of the bridegroom throbbed with a bitter impotent rage.

No, but what he would truly like to do would be to shoot the minister in his own kirkyard.

An upper window of the Hall flushed with the firelight and the candles inside.

(v)

Mr Humphrey Langclett murmured and smiled farewell in the town square to Mr John F. Norton the draper, Mr Thord Swann the ironmonger, and Captain Aram. It was a beautiful morning in June. The sun poured up the steep seaward closes of Hamnavoe and barred the main street with alternate brilliance and shadow. Draper and ironmonger and retired skipper smiled and raised their sticks in farewell to Mr Langclett, and moved on northwards along the street.

Those four walked, every morning whatever the weather, winter and summer, as far as the boatyard and back, discussing national politics and the affairs of the town and sometimes, with smiles and tolerant headshakings, some intriguing titbit of local gossip.

Mrs Andrina Holm was standing at the window of the jeweller's shop, gray head under gray shawl humbled to the town fathers going past.

Mr Langclett, before he inserted the key into the main shop door, saw that the parlour curtains upstairs were drawn against the sun. The breakfast dishes were washed now, obviously, and the cat and the canary fed.

Today, at dinner-time, Harriet would have to be told. He had promised. It would not be an easy announcement to make by any means.

The shop had a glass-panelled inner door. When Mr Langclett depressed the latch and pushed, the little bell gave out a bright *ping*. There was a dark fragrant delicious smell inside the shop, compounded of apples, cloves, liquorice, coffee, treacle, tobacco, and the other items of merchandise that Mr Langclett sold. Mr Langclett tugged at the blind-cord in the window. The sun came dazzling in. A bluebottle throbbed and bounced in the large pane; another lay inert between the bowl of oranges and the jar of brandy-balls.

The eye of a stuffed hawk glittered from the counter.

Mr Langclett removed his jacket and hung it on a hook. It was quite warm in the shop. Upstairs now there was a rumble, a small shrieking of castors, a thud, muted measured flutters. Harriet was making the beds. His daughter's domestic routine never varied from day to day.

The shop door pinged.

Mr Langclett, bent over the open account book on the desk, was aware of a hovering doleful presence. He turned with a sigh; it was of course Mrs Brewton. She stood at the counter with her shopping bag. He noticed that she had no purse in her hand. Mrs Brewton said, sadly, that it was a beautiful morning but that she expected they would pay for it with some bad weather later on. Two pounds of sugar, please. A jar of raspberry jam. A tin of salmon (what on earth was a fisherman's family wanting with tinned salmon?). Twenty woodbines. A packet of cream crackers . . . She thought that was all. O no, a bar of milk chocolate for Linda. Linda had a bit of a cough. She had kept Linda from school till tomorrow at least. Linda was kind of delicate, the poor bairn.

And she would pay before closing time. Sando would be back from the lobsters by then.

'There's five pounds odd against you in the book, you know,' said Mr Langclett after a pause, glancing towards the ledger on the desk.

'I know, I know,' said Mrs Brewton. She took a woodbine out of its packet. 'I told Sando about it.' She had matches in her apron; she rattled the box. 'Sando says he'll settle as soon as ever he's in from the sea.' She scratched the match into flame.

'Well, I hope so,' said Mr Langclett in a tone of mild reproach.

Mrs Brewton's cheeks hollowed and her bosom heaved. Her mouth emitted a hank of blue-gray smoke. She began to cough.

The smoke shredded out. She put her free fist to her mouth. Coughing, Mrs Brewton sought the door, and coughing still crossed the street towards the steep sunlit close where, in squalor and contentment, the Brewtons lived.

Mr Langclett had heard more than once about this week-end settling-up, which sometimes took place and sometimes not; it depended on whether and to what extent Brewton was on the booze.

There was a sound of subdued voices upstairs. Harriet was having a morning visitor. That was unusual. Very few visitors came to the Langcletts'; it was a discreet withdrawn household. The muted exchange of voices went on – the quiet murmurs of Harriet mingling with elegiac plaints and queries. Mr Langclett realized with a start that no other voice in Hamnavoe resembled that voice – the visitor could only be Andrina Holm. What on earth did Harriet and Andrina Holm have to say to one another? Andrina Holm had not been near his premises for a year – in fact since the day he had rebuked her for slandering Captain Aram. She had said in his shop before other customers that Captain Aram took his rum bottle into the kirkyard and sat on the kerb of his young wife's grave and got drunk there – so-and-so and so-and-so and so-and-so had seen the performance – who ever heard the like? – what a disgrace . . . Mr Langclett knew these talebearers to the bone. They hawked slander and gossip about the doors under the pretext of being the old wise kindly ones, and that Andrina Holm was the wickedest gossip of all.

Upstairs the dialogue went on.

The thought of what he himself must say to Harriet at dinner-time brought a dew of sweat to his upper lip. He had promised to do it. This was the day. When he and Martha met at the cemetery gate for their Thursday afternoon walk along the sea-banks, he would tell her that he had kept his promise: he had broken the news to Harriet, everything was now settled. *Ping.* He paused. He smiled. His breath fluttered with pleasure when he thought of Martha and himself walking between the cornfields and the sea, under the great blue sweep of sky.

A tall stranger, buoyantly and happily smiling, was offering him a bill across the counter. If he would be so kind as to put this notice in his window. A beautiful Irish brogue. Mr Langclett took his reading spectacles out of his waistcoat pocket, shook out the horn legs, and poised, glintlingly, the frame over his ramshackle nose. The stranger held his head a little to one side, quizzically.

EVANGELICAL MEETING / *There will be an Evangelical Meeting in the Temperance Hall every night next week, from Sabbath on, beginning (D.V.) at 8 p.m. / Speaker, Mr Albert Murphy, the noted Ulster evangelist. / All are welcome.*

'I'm sorry, I never put bills in my window,' said Mr Langclett, handing the sheet back to Mr Albert Murphy. The evangelist's face lost its dimples, though it remained serene. He tilted his head even more, as if estimating Mr Langclett's worth in the scale of spirituality.

'Not even for the Lord's sake?' he asked.

Mr Langclett shook his head. 'I've told you,' he said.

'I see,' said the evangelist. He was smiling again, all forgiveness. 'God bless you.'

Mr Langclett watched the tall dark figure, smiling and touching his dark hat to Mrs Thomasina Smith and Wilma Freyd who were slowly circling about each other on the pavement, clasping their shopping bags, gossiping – one face shocked, the other dimpled with pleasure – and saw him stooping under the lintel of Webster the tailor's shop, smiling, and tightly clasping the notice that Mr Langclett had rejected, going out of the light into a cave of cloth and shadows.

Don't hold with that sort of thing, extremes, all that sickly smiling too, like a tin of syrup lying with the lid loose, as if they and they alone basked in the divine favour. Such arrogance. 'For the Lord's sake.' The Lord was well enough served in this town, three kirks – no, four, counting the Piskies – forby the Pentecostals and the Brethren and the Salvation Army.

Upstairs in the parlour the dialogue was still going on, with Harriet's contributions punctuating only briefly the mournful sing-song of Andrina Holm. Mr Langclett tilted his head. He listened. He could not distinguish one word; he had an uncanny feeling, as if he was a ghost just out of hearing of the chorus of the living. *Ping.* Poor Emily entered the shop, bearing a copy of *The Orcadian*. Harriet would have nothing to complain of. He would see to that. She would have a roof over her head. She would of course never get married now – with men she was either shrill or silent – she was thirty-two – the first fadings and moth-marks of spinsterhood were on her. Emily – pink face and almond-shaped eyes – proffered, wordlessly, the newspaper.

'Well, Emily,' said Mr Langclett, 'Thursday again, is it? Is this my *Orcadian*? That's a good girl, Emily. And how is mother, fine, eh?'

Emily, in a light hollow voice, said yes, that her mama was fine, and Silver had had four kittens in the coal-shed last night, and the water-closet was chocked and there was a stink but a man was coming to see to it.

Mr Langclett laid a penny and a halfpenny on the counter, in payment of *The Orcadian*. (Emily brought him his copy every Thursday morning from the newsagent's.) He took down a sweet jar from the middle shelf, unscrewed the lid, groped inside with his forefinger to slacken the coagulated mass, and laid three 'jelly babies' on the counter.

Emily put a long yellow gum into her mouth, mindlessly. She was the girl from next door. Mrs McCorbey had been very hurt when the medical officer, last month, had described Emily as a mongol. But a mongol she undoubtedly is, thought Mr Langclett, noting again the almond eyes, pink and white skin, bulbous jowls, broad nose, tongue lolling in the mouth.

'Thank you, Emily,' he said kindly.

Emily picked up the remaining two sweets in her chunky fingers and left the shop. She stood outside in the street for a moment, slatting her eyes against the sun, and bent to stroke Spot, the ironmonger's collie pup, dancing and barking happily round her. Mr Langclett, once more unfolding his spectacles, saw that Andrina Holm had left the house and was stationed at the mouth of the close opposite, looking left and right along the street.

Mr Langclett's eye glided over the solid block of advertisements on the front page of *The Orcadian*, then he opened the paper and spread it flat out on the counter. HARBOUR BOARD FINANCES.

DISASTROUS FARM FIRE IN NORDAY. HAMNAVOE COUN-
CILLOR RESIGNS. He reserved the serious reports for his after-
dinner cup of tea. One column in the centre page he always read
first: *Births, Marriages, Deaths, In Memoriam*. His eye leapt down
the rung of names – Adamson, Buchan, Dennis, Eason, Farquhar,
Isbister, Learmonth, Langclett. What Langclett would that be? He
read.

> In loving memory of Cecilia Langclett (née Graham), wife of
> Humphrey Langclett, general grocer, Hamnavoe, and dear
> mother of Harriet, who passed to her rest 9th June, 1920
> > A year has passed since the sad day
> > When that dear one was called away.
> > Here we can only sit and sigh,
> > Hoping some day to meet her again on high.

Mr Langclett stood behind the counter as though he had been
struck on the face. Cissie's death. This was terrible. He had clean
forgotten that today – yes, the ninth – was the first anniversary.
After a long illness borne with Christian patience. He saw again the
waxen face on the pillow. He saw the first strewment of clay on the
coffin. Harriet had never once mentioned the anniversary to him.
Harriet had inserted the announcement without consulting him.
Ping. The newspaper creaked in his hand.

'Well, Humphrey, there must be something very interesting in
the paper today.'

He had not even heard William Corston come in. His mouth
was cold with shock. When he spoke the words came bleak and
wintry.

'Nothing much,' he said. 'Deaths. I see that Tim Isbister has died
in New Zealand. You won't mind him. He was in my brother
James's class at school. In Wellington, New Zealand.'

'Before my time,' said William Corston. There was a pause.
'Humphrey, it's more than my tobacco I've come for.' He cleared
his throat and consulted, briefly, his silver watch. William Corston
had a proposal of some delicacy to put to Mr Langclett – that much
was obvious. 'I suppose you might just have an idea what I mean.'

Mr Langclett began to shake his head slowly. 'Humphrey, this town will be none the worse of your services.'

William Corston's right hand, shyly seeking Mr Langclett's on the counter, depressed with the thumb the knuckle of the forefinger. Mr Langclett's cold mouth relaxed in a small swift private smile. William Corston was a far more earnest freemason than himself: all these signs were a mysterious potent language to him; without that communication, as far as William Corston was concerned, the pillars of the world would collapse – all would revert to superstition and popery and the beasts of the night.

'You're wasting your time,' said Mr Langclett.

'Think about it, man,' said William Corston gravely. 'You would be a welcome face at the table.'

'I'm sorry,' said Mr Langclett.

'You more than anybody,' said William Corston. 'I said to the Provost after Monday night's meeting, "Well (said I) there's Coubister resigned, and the only man in Hamnavoe to fill his place is Humphrey Langclett. But (I said) I doubt he'll refuse, as usual" . . . "We can but try," said the Provost . . . So that, in short, is why I'm here, Humphrey.'

'No,' said Mr Langclett.

'A long family tradition of municipal service,' said William Corston. 'Archibald Langclett, your grandfather, provost of the town. Your father a bailie. Wasn't there a Langclett in the first Council of all, in 1817?'

'Thomas Langclett,' said Mr Langclett. 'He was the eldest son of the miller of Lang Klett. He came to Hamnavoe and founded this business in 1809.'

They stood silent for a moment, reverencing the dust of the generations.

'I'm sorry to disoblige you, William,' said Mr Langclett at last. 'But I don't like that sort of thing. All that wrangling, bitterness. And folk knocking at your door at all hours, wanting you to do this and that for them. I just have no talent for it.' More solemnly he said, 'It's not good for business either, I can tell you that.'

William Corston considered these arguments, then shook his head at Mr Langclett in friendly displeasure.

'You know this, Humphrey,' he said, 'we're going to hound you. Every election time, every time there's a vacancy, we're going to be after you. You're going to get no peace at all.'

'I have plenty on my plate as it is,' said Mr Langclett. *Ping.* 'Museum Committee, Lifeboat Committee, Liberal Party. The Lodge. The Bowling Club.'

A thick-set man shambled into the shop, bearing between his fingers a dark disc. He came and stood right between Mr Langclett and William Corston; he put a barley breath all over the shop. 'I found this when I was digging the garden,' he muttered. 'The boys in the pub, they told me to bring it here. Sando Brewton said, *Humprey Langclett is the man to show it to.*'

(Mr Langclett was one of the leading antiquarians and naturalists in the town. People brought to him the flint arrowheads, the fossils, the foreign coins that are hidden in every nook and corner of Orkney.)

'Now then,' said William Corston sharply, 'Mr Langclett and I happen to be discussing important business.'

Mr Langclett accepted the coin. He breathed on it. He pulled a handkerchief from his pocket and rubbed the metal vigorously. He opened the counter drawer and brought out a magnifying glass. He squinnied through the glittering convex, turning the coin over and over, this way and that.

'You mustn't come bothering Mr Langclett with every bit of rubbish you dig up,' said William Corston to Robert Jansen.

Robert Jansen shuffled his feet and hung his head.

'A James the Sixth shilling,' said Mr Langclett at last. 'That's what it is. *Rex Scotorum.* And the lion on the other side.' He offered the lens and the coin to William Corston. 'Have a look, William.'

William Corston glanced into the curve; a gravured lion was startlingly enlarged.

A reverence for history, for the dead magnificent dust that had lorded it over the humbler dust of their fathers, held them in a deeper silence. The coin passed between them like a sacred object.

'Now Robert,' said Mr Langclett, 'that was an interesting thing you found. It isn't *very* valuable. I mean it wouldn't fetch much on the market, maybe a pound or thirty shillings. Now what I'm thinking is this. If you go back to the pub some of them will try to get it off you for a pint. Or you might easily lose it. The best thing, Robert, would be for you to present it to the town museum. The Museum Committee would be very pleased. They would send you a letter of thanks. I'm sure we don't have a James the Sixth shilling in our coin case. Now what about that, eh?'

Robert Jansen's blunt fingers received back the small heraldic round. He muttered that he would have to think about it. Obviously the men in the pub had told the poor simple creature that this find had made him the wealthiest man in Hamnavoe.

'Mr Langclett will see that it is placed in the town museum for you,' said William Corston. 'Just leave it with him, man.'

But Robert Jansen, still muttering, passed out into the sunlight. He turned this way and that on the cobbles, uncertain now whether to go back to *The Arctic Whaler*, or bear his treasure to the safety of his house, or perhaps indeed after all return it into the wise keeping of Mr Langclett.

Andrina Holm had crossed the street and was standing now at the very threshold of the shop, shielding her brow against the steady torrent of noon light. Once she turned and squinnied in through the glass panel of the door: old-ivory face, soft shadowy whiskered mouth, blue eyes-tones in warped leather purses.

'What way can Jansen afford to drink?' said William Corston. 'He's on poor relief. I can't think why the health people don't do something about him. They say his room's in a filthy state.'

'That was interesting,' said Mr Langclett. 'The house Robert lives in, it's one of the oldest houses in the town, you know. A coat-of-arms over the door, a worn inscription on a sandstone shield. You can just make out a date, 1596, I think.'

'An ounce of the usual mixture anyhow,' said William Corston. 'Then I must be getting back.'

'Think of it,' said Mr Langclett. 'A Stewart walking in his Hamnavoe garden on a summer evening after his dinner. Some illegitimate son of that Earl Patrick Stewart in Birsay, Black Pat. He would have been a near cousin too, of course, of the King of Scotland. Well, then, there he walks, with one of his fancy-women. He takes out his lace handkerchief to wipe the claret and the ox-fat from his mouth. A coin falls out. A small tinkle among the stones – he never hears it. Three hundred and thirty years later his house is a slum. The rose garden is a tattie patch. Robert Jansen turns up the coin with his spade.'

'Humphrey,' said William Corston, 'you should have been a writer of romances.'

Mr Langclett smiled. He loved the relies of history: those small objects that have fallen intact between the great millstones of necessity and chance.

William Corston laid his tobacco pouch on the counter. 'They'll be wondering in the office where on earth I've got to,' he said.

Mr Langclett, opening the tobacco jar, glanced through the window. His heart gave two erratic thumps – a lift – a swoon – a lingering delicious flutter. Was it? Yes, it was her. Alone, primly, a woman was descending the steep close opposite. She carried her shopping bag in front of her. She had lifted, becomingly, her skirt above her ankles, the better to negotiate one of the short flights of steps that led down from her house to the street and the shops. Miss Martha Swift was going as always on a Thursday to get her messages before closing time. Mr Langclett flushed with pleasure. Where would she go first? She reached the street and turned left. Sorenson the butcher's. Old Sorenson – poor blind soul that he was – would serve her in the light of common day. *Obliged, Miss Swift. Your change now. Thank you so much.* That such a one should care for Humphrey Langclett. The woman smiled at some person coming towards her along the street. *Ping.* She lingered, her lips moved. She passed, elegant and perfect, out of the window frame.

Mr Langclett's hands held, enchanted, the stone tobacco jar.

'And a box of matches,' said William Corston. He laid a considered row of coins on the counter.

That such a dear person should ever conceivably care for an ageing ugly graceless man like himself. It was as if fragrance and dew should enter into a stone kirkyard rose, and that the wind should shake it, and that it should bleed with overspill of petals.

A faded voice broke the spell: 'A quarter pound of tea, if you please.' A fumble, a sigh, a shuffle. It was Andrina Holm. 'I saw a certain person on the street this minute. I had to laugh. Tip-tipping along. Too grand to speak to the likes of me, of course. The grand-niece of Governor Swift of Hudson's Bay, if you please. That same madame, she had a fine carry-on with the marines in the war-time. Officers only, though. Nothing under a lieutenant ever crossed her threshold. They usually stayed to their breakfast.'

'I am serving Bailie Corston at the moment,' said Mr Langclett.

The soft ancient mouth went on. 'I've just been speaking to your Harriet, Mr Langclett. She's a gem of a girl, that. I never saw such a shining well-kept house. You're a lucky man to have a daughter like Harriet. Ceylon tea. One thing Harriet can't abide, in any shape or form, and that's loose behaviour, especially in folk that are of an age to know better.'

'I do not stock Ceylon tea,' said Mr Langclett.

'A loyal girl she is too,' said Andrina Holm. 'Loyal as the day, to her home and her family and to them that are no longer here.' Utterance of dark evil wisdom. Crepitation of the dust of grave-stones.

'You are not welcome in this shop,' said Mr Langclett. 'I told you that some time ago.'

'Harriet will be a lamp to your age,' said Andrina Holm, turning away. 'When your time comes she will close your eyes. I can buy my tea somewhere else.'

The glass panes clashed and rattled upon her departure.

'I swear to God,' said William Corston, 'I can't abide that old creature. She puts the grues on me.'

Mr Langclett's hand trembled as he emptied rather more than an ounce of Virginia mixture out of the aluminium scoop into William Corston's tobacco pouch.

William Corston drew the silver watch from his waistcoat pocket and looked at it. 'Five to one,' he said. He laid his hand on Mr Langclett's and said very earnestly, 'Humphrey, do what your best instincts tell you to do.'

From above came a rattle of plates, and the smaller music of knives and forks and spoons being laid on the table.

William Corston passed out into the street. There he raised a hand to Thomas Webster the tailor who was putting the wooden shutters on his shop window.

The street was total brightness now. The noontide sun poured northwards through the street, a full silent golden flood. In the afternoon the shadows of tall houses would begin slowly to encroach again from the west, and by evening this heart of Hamnavoe would be a deep cool ravine.

High on the side of the hill the school bell rang.

Mr Langclett's eye fell bleakly on the *In Memoriam* column in the newspaper. All Hamnavoe would have read that awful piece of piety before nightfall. He could imagine the mockery at the foot of this close, at the head of that pier, in house-doors all along the street: *What an old hypocrite, Humphrey Langclett!* Of course all the town knew, and had known for a long time. Harriet, Andrina Holm, John F. Norton, Thord Swann, Captain Aram, William Corston, Robert Jansen, Mrs Brewton, even poor Emily: they all knew about him and Martha. It must be all of three months since the first farmer's wife had seen the two of them walking westward above the shore and next morning had told the story at the van door. A strange thing – you always act as if it is a honeyed secret between the two of you. How foolish he had been, to think otherwise.

A desolating image came into his mind: Martha sitting in her kitchen at Holm View, within the next half hour, waiting for the potatoes to boil. She opens *The Orcadian*. She reads the *In Memoriam* column, the death warrant of their love.

Harriet had contrived things with admirable skill. To make doubly sure, she had enlisted the services of Andrina Holm.

His community had condemned him through the mouth of that old hag.

It *was* shameful, the more he thought about it. Drinking rum in the kirkyard, kissing in the kirkyard. Death is swallowed up in lust. He understood the impiety of the living and the rebuke of the silent dead. *Dear Cissie, I am truly sorry. The dream will pass. Not a word will I say to my daughter today. I will be what I was meant to be, a sober respectful widowed business-man, a lonely walker in the sun and the snow for a year or two. Then I will come and lie down beside you at last in the faithful dust.*

There came two loud thumps on the ceiling. It was the signal that dinner was ready. On Thursday it was always Irish stew, followed by custard and prunes, and finally a cup of tea.

Yelling chattering cooing bands of school children appeared and disappeared across the open door, eddying homeward. One small face drifted and hung in the glass of the shop window, above the apples and the brandy-balls, in a wide-eyed impossible dream of sweetness, then drifted away again.

Shop girls began to flow in both directions along the street. It was early closing day in Hamnavoe. This fine afternoon the beaches and the golf course would be well attended, and every plot of ground would have its elderly gardener. He himself, at a quarter past two, was due to put on his tweed jacket and his dark blue tie, and take his silver-handled walking-stick out of the rack in the lobby, for another meeting among the tombs.

Not today. He could not do it. Perhaps never again. The stones, love and death, that whirl upon one another at the centre of every man's life, were slowing down for Mr Langclett. Soon they would stop. He knew now that there would be no grains of his to nourish the future. No innocent beautiful mouth would eat at the table between Martha and himself. His generation must perish from the land.

Between father and daughter a lasting silence would be kept.

Mr Langclett stood at the shop door with his key in his hand. The burning flagstones were possessed, extravagantly, by a solitary figure. Sando Brewton had emerged from *The Arctic Whaler*. A bottle was stuck awry in his jacket pocket. He stood for half-a-minute swaying on the cobbles. Then, blind and blundering, he set a course for home.

Mr Langclett returned into the shop. He drew the blind down the droning window; the shop was all gloom and fragrance once more. The stuffed hawk was lost in the shadows.

The heart is bruised in that thunder and contention of stones. They would stop soon. Then he would have peace.

The door between the house and the shop opened. Harriet,

dressed all in black, stood in the glimmering rectangle. She said nothing. She stood and looked at him. She had come to summon him, wordlessly, to his stew and prunes.

Stone upon fruitless stone laid.

'Harriet,' said Mr Langclett, 'I have something to say to you.'

The Fires of Christmas

The Earl of Orkney in the winter of the year 1046 was Rognvald Brusison: a young courteous popular man. A few weeks previously he had made sure of his earldom by surrounding his uncle's hall in Orphir and setting fire to it. Everyone had perished in the flames except women and servants, who had been allowed to leave. The body of Earl Thorfinn, Rognvald's uncle, was presumably among the charred corpses that were found in the hall next morning. (But, in fact, among all that roaring dapple of red and black Earl Thorfinn had taken his wife Ingibiorg in his arms and leapt with her through a gap at the end of the house. That same night he rowed twenty miles with scorched arms across the Pentland Firth to Caithness.)

The time drew on to Christmas. Earl Rognvald was now sole lord of the islands. He had nothing to fear. Apart from secure possession of his earldom he was high in favour with his overlord, King Magnus of Norway. Earl Rognvald meant it to be a Christmas of high rejoicing in Orkney. That meant huge quantities of ale.

The Earl left Kirkwall for the island of Papa Stronsay with a company of men to get malt for the brewing. His little pet dog sat on his knee in the stern of the boat. Behind him in Kirkwall he left the tough loyal guardsmen that had been lent to him by the Norwegian king. There would be no need for such magnificent warriors in the small island of Papa Stronsay.

The Earl was welcomed by the farmer who made the famous malt. After supper that first night the Earl and his men were sitting round the hospitable hearth. It was a cold evening. Rognvald told a man to go out and fetch more peats from the stack. The small dog lay stretched out at his feet. Then, either because he was drowsy on account of the sea journey and the warmth, or because he had tilted too many ale-horns, the Earl made a slip of the tongue. He said, 'We'll be old enough by the time this fire is out.' In those doom-ridden days a slip of the tongue was a portent. What does it signify, if you mean to say one thing and you actually say something quite different? It means that your own intentions are being overset by the master-workings of fate; the fallible tongue has become an oracular instrument. Earl Rognvald, drowsy and content at the hearth, had meant to say, 'We'll be warm enough by the time this fire is out.' He had actually said, 'We'll be old enough by the time this fire is out' – a bleak sinister thing for one young man to say to other young men; as if time was about to telescope suddenly for them, and all the stages of their manhood, maturity, wisdom, and age were to be packed into one last night.

There was silence in the farmhouse after fate had spoken through the mouth of the Earl. They knew there was no appeal against it. 'It's likely,' said Rognvald at last, 'that my uncle Thorfinn is alive.'

Scarcely had he said this when fire broke out everywhere, from roof and doors and gables. The little comfortable fire in the centre of the house was drowned in tumults of flame, like a rockpool by the ocean. Earl Thorfinn was alive, there was no doubt about it.

As always, the courtesies of a burning were observed. Women, servants, unarmed men were allowed out. None was to die but the warriors. The fire was now at its height, red cloven skyward-pouring torrents; it made the stars gray cinders. A priest appeared at the door from inside, in a white linen gown. 'Give the priest a hand,' said Earl Thorfinn. (Priests too were sacrosanct.) But this particular priest put one hand on the half-door and vaulted clean over the heads of the besiegers, and was lost in the darkness beyond.

'That,' said Earl Thorfinn, 'is Rognvald. Nobody could do a thing like that but Rognvald. Follow him.'

Thorfinn's men split into groups and searched the shore in the darkness. It seemed likely he would try to do the same as Earl Thorfinn had done at the time of the Orphir burning – that is, get hold of a fishing boat and row to the safety of another island. There was a burst of barking beside a rock – Rognvald's pet dog, trying to

defend him, had betrayed him. They put their daggers here and
there into the usurper. The priest gown was patched red.

There remained the Norwegians in Kirkwall, Magnus's royal
bodyguard, a formidable troop of men.

Next morning Earl Thorfinn's men loaded the malt for the Yule
brewing on board the dead earl's ship and rowed towards Kirkwall.
The Norwegians came down to the beach, unarmed, to greet the
homecomers and the festive cargo. Earl Thorfinn had thirty of
these easterlings killed on the spot. The shore was strewn with
corpses. Only one survived; he was given a passage to Norway in
order to break the news to King Magnus.

In the small island in the north the dove-shaped hands of monks
lifted a body from the shore, red with blood and seaweed, and
ferried it over to the island of Papay where there was a small
monastery and where Saint Tredwell worked her miracles of
healing. But Rognvald Brusison's wounds were beyond healing.
There, in that holy ground, they buried him.

Eighty-nine winters passed in the islands. At Christmas in the year
1135 Earl Thorfinn's great-grandson Paul Hakonson was Earl of
Orkney: a mild peaceable man, trying to hold his precarious
earldom between enemies to the north and enemies to the south.
His chief captain was a man called Sweyn Breastrope, a creature of
sombre strength who (it was said) communed with the devil in the
moon-dark nights of winter. The earl leaned on that monolith for
the safety of his person and his state. In return Sweyn Breastrope
served Earl Paul with brutish devotion.

Earl Paul decided to spend the Christmas of 1135 at his hall in
Orphir. Next door to the hall was a church, built probably by his
father Earl Hakon after his penitential voyage to Rome and
Jerusalem.

In the hall on Christmas eve fires were lit and the long tables laid
with meat and fish and bread. The earl's men sat or sprawled at the
benches, and stewards went round all afternoon filling their horns
with ale. Now and then, through the babble and hornclash and
laughter, the earl's poet would stand up and recite a few verses.
Hounds slept beside the fire. The darkness came down early, and

torches were lit. At the centre of the high table sat Earl Paul, and
Sweyn Breastrope sat at his right side.

In the church next door the services for the eve of the Nativity
were beginning. Fragments of psalms filtered into the drinking-
hall, and reminded the retainers of the true nature of their
celebrations. Christ was about to be born; Mary and Joseph were
already in the stable under the inn, with the ox and the ass and the
bright scatter of straw . . . But in the hall many of the earl's men
were already drunk.

A stranger, a young man from Caithness on the Scottish shore of
the Pentland Firth, was let into the hall from the bitter night
outside and taken right up to Earl Paul. The young man, whose
name was Sweyn Asleifson, had terrible news: his father and all his
family except one brother had been burnt to death in their house in
Caithness by Earl Paul's enemies, because the family had always
been loyal to the earl.

Earl Paul made the young man sit at the table beside him, a high
honour. On his other side Sweyn Breastrope propped his head in
his hands. He was already more than half drunk.

The night wore on. Ale-horns foamed and swiltered; trays of
bread and beef were carried round by the stewards. Sometimes a
few of the earl's men would rise up from the benches and go next
door into the church. Office followed office, Nones after Sext, then
Evensong. It was getting on for midnight, when the Mass of the
Nativity would be celebrated.

In the hall the feast got louder and more confused. Suddenly the
main door opened and a fisherman stood there. He brought bad
news. Sweyn Asleifson's brother had been drowned that afternoon
in the Stronsay Firth.

Sweyn Asleifson from Caithness, now doubly bereaved, sat at the
earl's table in a stupor of grief. Earl Paul did his best to comfort
him. 'No-one,' he announced to the company, 'is to do or say
anything to upset Sweyn Asleifson.' Then he put a kiss of peace on
the stranger's cheek.

At that the man on the other side of Earl Paul growled like a
beast into his tankard. Sweyn Breastrope was jealous.

There is a state of desolation when a man cannot get drunk, no matter how much he drinks; so that, whereas Sweyn Breastrope was getting drunker and drunker as midnight approached, Sweyn Asleifson emptied his ale-horn regularly and sat there like a cold statue.

This was a further matter of grievance. Eyvind the chief cupbearer heard Sweyn Breastrope muttering into his ale-horn, 'Sweyn will be the death of Sweyn.' . . . 'Sweyn must be killed by Sweyn.' . . .

In the church they began to sing Evensong. Earl Paul invited Sweyn Asleifson to accompany him to the service. He would be safer among the priests; he would get more consolation from the psalms than from the drinking songs. The young man rose and followed the earl to the door. At the door Eyvind took him aside and told him what old Sweyn had said. 'You must kill him,' said Eyvind, 'or he will certainly kill you.'

Earl Paul went into Evensong alone. Sweyn Asleifson hid behind some barrels at the door. He took his axe from his belt and drew the blade over his forearm. A few brief blond hairs fell silently on the flagstone.

Sweyn Breastrope noticed Earl Paul and Sweyn Asleifson leaving the hall together. He took out his sword, shouted for his squire – a man called John – lurched to his feet, and went staggering after them. In the darkness outside, between hall and church, he would do what had to be done.

As he reached the threshold Sweyn Asleifson rose up from behind the ale barrels and struck him flush on the forehead. Most men would have fallen dead from that axe-stroke. Sweyn Breast-rope only staggered. He shook blood from him like a shower of heavy red coins. With his fading senses he struck out at the first shape he saw and killed his man John – 'he hewed him down to the shoulder', we are told in the Saga.

Sweyn Breastrope, Earl Paul's great and trusted captain, died of his wound during the night.

In the church the Mass of the Nativity began.

The choir sang the Sanctus. *Pleni sunt coeli et terra gloria tua. Benedictus qui venit in nomine Domini. Hosanna in excelsis* . . . God came, a poor child, into the world of violence, hunger, treachery. Earl Paul knelt there before the high altar and was glad of it.

Sweyn Asleifson was on horseback, between Orphir and the shore of Firth, going helter-skelter under the stars, a wild gallop. He slept that night in a farmhouse in the small island of Damsay. Next day he sailed across the bay to Egilsay, where Bishop William of Orkney was celebrating Christmas in the island of Saint Magnus's martyrdom. There he received the bishop's pardon and blessing.

Later this young killer, Sweyn, was called the greatest of all the vikings, and his name was known and feared from Shetland to the Scilly Isles. He died in a broken Dublin street, an old man, with the sword in his hand and a prayer in his mouth.

Earl Paul came back to his festive hall after Mass. There all was drunkenness, disorder, blood, and the two Sweyns gone from him, each into a different darkness.

It was Christmas morning.

Soon, in the church, they began to sing Matins.

These two Yuletide happenings, as recorded in the Saga of the Orkney Earls, are separated by almost a century. The second event is as violent and bloody as the first. Men's lives still issue from the inexorable hands of fate. But in the meantime the blood of Saint Magnus had been shed. The second drama is not so dark and hopeless as the first. Fate had given way, to some extent at least, to grace.

Tithonus

FRAGMENTS FROM THE DIARY OF A LAIRD

They are all, especially the women, excited in Torsay today. There is a new child in the village, a little girl. The birth has happened in a house where – so Traill the postman assured me – no one for the past ten years has expected it. The door of Maurice Garth the fisherman and his wife Armingert had seemed to be marked with the sign of barrenness. They were married twenty-one years ago, when Maurice was thirty and Armingert nineteen. One might have expected a large family, five or six at least, from such a healthy devoted pair. (They had both come from tumul-tuous households to the cold empty cottage at the end of the village.) But the years passed and no young voice broke the quiet dialogue of Maurice and Armingert. To all the islanders it seemed a pity: nothing but beautiful children could have come from their loins.

I was hauling my dinghy up the loch shore this afternoon – it was too bright a day, the trout saw through every gesture and feint – when I saw the woman on the road above. It seemed to me then that she had been waiting to speak to me for some time. I knew who she must be as soon as she opened her mouth. The butterings of her tongue, and the sudden knife flashes, had been described to me often enough. She was Maggie Swintoun. I had been well warned about her by the factor and the minister and the postman. Her idle and wayward tongue, they told me, had done harm to the reputation of more than one person in Torsay; so I'm sure that when I turned my loch-dazzled face to her it did not wear a welcoming expression.

'O sir, you'll never guess,' she said, in the rapt secret voice of all news bearers. 'A bairn was born in the village this morning, and at the Garth cottage of all places – a girl. I think it's right that you should know. Dr Wayne from Hamnavoe took it into the world. I was there helping. I could hardly believe it when they sent for me.'

The face was withdrawn from the loch side. A rare morning was in front of her, telling the news in shop, smithy, manse and at the doors of all the crofts round about.

I mounted my horse that, patient beast, had been cropping the thin loch-side grass all morning and cantered back to The Hall over the stony dusty road.

Now I knew why a light had been burning at two o'clock in the cottage at the end of the village. I had got up at that time to let Tobias the cat in.

This is the first child to be born in the island since I came to be laird here. I feel that in some way she belongs to me. I stood at the high window of The Hall looking down at the Garth cottage till the light began to fade.

The generations have been renewed. The island is greatly enriched since yesterday.

I suppose that emotionally I am a kind of neutral person, in the sense that I attract neither very much love nor very much dislike. It is eight years since I arrived from London to live in the island that my grand-uncle, the laird of Torsay, a man I had never seen in my life, left to me. On the slope behind the village with its pier and shop and church is The Hall – the laird's residence – that was built in the late seventeenth century, a large elegant house with eighteen rooms, and a garden, and a stable. I am on speaking terms with everyone in the village and with most of the farmers and crofters in the hinterland. Certain people – William Copinsay the shopkeeper, Maggie Swintoun, Grossiter from the farm of Wear – I pass with as curt a nod as I can manage. If I do have a friend, I suppose he must be James MacIntosh who came to be the schoolmaster in the village two summers ago. We play chess in the school-house every Friday night, summer and winter. Occasionally, when he is out walking with his dog, he calls at my place and we drink whatever is in the whisky decanter. (But I insist that his dog, a furtive collie called Joe who occasionally bares his teeth at passers-by, is not let further than the kitchen – Tobias must not be annoyed.) Mac-Intosh comes from Perth. He is a pleasant enough man. I think his chief interest is politics, but I do nothing to encourage him when he starts about the Irish question, or the Liberal schism, or the suffragettes, or what the Japanese can be expected to do in such and such an eventuality. I am sure, if I let him go on, that some fine evening he will declare himself to be a socialist. I set the decanter squarely between us whenever I hear the first opinionated murmurings; in those malty depths, and there alone, will any argument be.

I think MacIntosh is quite happy living in this island. He is too lazy and too good-natured to be hustled about in a big city school. It is almost certain that he has no real vocation for his job. He has gone to the university, and taken an arts degree, and then enrolled in teaching for want of anything better. But perhaps I do him wrong; perhaps he is dedicated after all to make 'clever de'ils' of the Torsay children. At any rate, the parents and the minister – our education committee representative – seem to have no objection to him. My reason for thinking that he is without taste or talent for the classroom is that he never mentions his work to me; but there again it could simply be, as with politics, that he receives no encouragement.

There is a curious shifting relationship between us, sometimes cordial, sometimes veiled and hostile. He becomes aware from time to time of the social gulf between us, and it is on these occasions that he says and does things to humble me – I must learn that we are living now in the age of equality. But under it all he is such a good-natured chap; after ten minutes or so of unbated tongues we are at peace again over chess-board or decanter.

Last night MacIntosh said, between two bouts of chess in the school-house, 'It's a very strange thing, I did not think I could ever be so intrigued by a child. Most of them are formed of the common clay after all. O, you know what I mean – from time to time a beautiful child, or a clever child, comes to the school, and you teach him or her for a year or two, then away they go to the big school in the town, or back to work on the farm, and you never think more about them. But this pupil is just that wee bit different.'

'What on earth are you talking about?' I said.

'The Garth girl who lives at the end of the village – Thora – you know, her father has the fishing boat *Rain Goose*.'

'Is that her name, Thora?' I said. (For I had seen the quiet face among a drift of school-children in the playground, at four o'clock, going home then alone to Maurice and Armingert's door. I had seen bright hair at the end of the small stone pier, waiting for a boat to come in from the west. I had seen the solemn clasped hands, bearing the small bible, outside the kirk door on a Sunday morning. But beyond that the girl and I had never exchanged a single word. As I say, I did not even know her name till last night.)

'She is a very strange girl, that one,' said MacIntosh. 'There is a *something* about her. Would you please not drop your ash on the mat? (There's an ash tray.) I'm not like some folk. I can't afford to buy a new mat every month. Mrs Baillie asked me to mention it to you.'

My pipe and his dog cancel each other out. Mrs Baillie is his housekeeper.

'To me she looks an ordinary enough child,' I said. 'In what way is she different?'

MacIntosh could not say how this girl was different. She was made of the common clay – 'like all of us, like all of us,' he hastened to assure me, thereby putting all the islanders, including the laird and Halcro the beachcomber, on the same footing. Still, there was something special about the girl, he insisted, goodness knows what . . .

MacIntosh won the third hard-fought game. He exulted. Victory always makes him reckless and generous. 'Smoke, man, smoke in here any time you like. To hell with Mrs Baillie. Get your pipe out. I'll sweep any ash up myself.'

I met Thora Garth on the brae outside the kirk as I was going home from the school-house. She put on me a brief pellucid unsmiling look as we passed. She was carrying a pail of milk from the farm of Gardyke.

Fifteen years ago, in my grand-uncle's day, the island women stopped and curtsied whenever the laird went past. A century ago a single glance from the great man of The Hall turned them to stone in their fields.

All that is changed.

Traill the postman had put a letter through my window while I was at the school-house. The familiar official writing was on the envelope. I lit the lamp. I was secure in my island for another six months. The usual hundred pounds was enclosed, in a mixture of tens and fives and singles. There was no message; there was usually no need for the Edinburgh lawyer to have anything special to say. He had simply to disburse in two instalments the two hundred pounds a year that my grand-uncle left me, so that I can live out my life as a gentleman in the great Hall of Torsay.

Thora Garth returned this morning from the senior school in Hamnavoe, at the end of her first session there. I happened to be down at the pier when the weekly mail steamer drew alongside. Several islanders were there, as always on that important occasion. The rope came snaking ashore. A seaman shouted banter to the fishermen and Robbie Tenston the farmer of Dale (who had just come out of the hotel bar). The minister turned away, pretending not to have heard the swear-words. I found Maurice Garth standing beside me. 'What's wrong with the creels today?' I said to him . . . 'I'm expecting Thora,' Maurice said in that mild shy murmur that many of the islanders have. 'She should be on the boat. It's the summer holidays – she'll be home for seven weeks.'

Sure enough, there was the tilted serious freckled face above the rail. She acknowledged her father with a slight sideways movement of her hand. At that moment I was distracted by an argument that had broken out on the pier. Robbie Tenston of Dale was claiming possession of a large square plywood box that had just been swung ashore from the *Pomona*.

'Nonsense,' cried William Copinsay the general merchant. 'Don't be foolish. It's loaves. It's the bread I always get from the baker in the town on a Friday.'

chief man in the island, I should be doing something about it, but I am morbidly afraid of making a fool of myself in front of these people.) Robbie could have taken the merchant in his great earth-red hands and broken him. He could have picked him up and flung him into the sea. He tried first of all to shake himself free from the hysterical clutchings of William Copinsay. He struck Copinsay an awkward blow on the shoulder. They whirled each other round like mad dancers between the horse-box and the gangway. Then – still grappling – they achieved some kind of a stillness; through it they glared at each other.

God knows what might have happened then.

It was Thora Garth who restored peace to the island. It was extraordinary, the way the focus shifted from the two buffoons to the girl. But suddenly everyone on the pier, including the skipper and the fighters and myself, was looking at her alone. She had left the steamer and was standing on the pier beside the disputed box. She had one hand on it, laid flat. With the other she pointed to William Copinsay.

'The box belongs to him,' she said quietly. 'Robbie, the box belongs to Mr Copinsay.'

That was the end of the fracas. Robbie Tenston seemed to accept her verdict at once. He pushed Mr Copinsay away. He muttered a grudging 'Well, don't let him or anybody ever call me a fool again.' He walked up the pier, his face encrimsoned, past Maggie Swintoun and the other women who were flocking to the scene, too late, with their false chorus of commiseration and accusation. 'That Robbie Tenston should be reported to the police,' said Maggie Swintoun flatly. 'It's that pub to blame. It should be closed down. Drink is the cause of all the trouble in Torsay. Them in authority should be doing something about it.' . . . She kept looking at me out of the corner of her eye.

Mr Copinsay sat on his box of bread and began to weep silently.

I could not bear any more of it.

The seamen had returned to their work, swinging ashore mailbags, crates of beer, saddlery, a bicycle, newspapers. Steve Mack the skipper was lighting his pipe and looking inland to the island hills as if nothing untoward had happened.

And indeed – though I hated to agree with Copinsay – ther
no doubt that the box contained bread; the incense of new ba
drifted across the pier.

'Don't you call me a fool,' said Robbie Tenston in his
dangerous drinking voice. 'This is a box of plants, if you wan
know. It's for my wife's greenhouse. The market gardener wrot
say that it was coming on the boat today. That's why I'm he
man. Let go of it now.'

Copinsay and Robbie Tenston had each laid hands on the ro
that was round the box. A circle of onlookers gathered ragged
about them.

The trouble was, the label had somehow got scraped off i
transit. (But Robbie must have been stupid to have missed tha
delicious smell of new rolls and loaves. Besides, roots and greenery
would never have weighed so much.)

They wrestled for the box, both of them red in the face. It had all
the makings of a disgraceful scene. Four of the crew had stopped
working. They watched from the derrick, delighted. The skipper
leaned out of his cabin, grinning eagerly. They could have told who
owned the box by rights, but they wanted the entertainment to go
on for some time yet.

Mr Evelyn the minister attempted to settle the affair. 'Now
now,' he said, 'now now – it is simply a matter of undoing the
rope – please, Mr Copinsay – Robert, I beg you – and looking
inside.'

They paid no attention to him. The farmer dragged the box
from the weaker hands of the merchant. Copinsay's face was
twisted with rage and spite. 'You old miserly bastard!' shouted
Robbie.

The skipper leaned further out of his cabin. He put his pipe
carefully on the ledge and clapped his hands. Maggie Swintoun and
a few other women came down the pier from their houses,
attracted by the hullabaloo.

At that point Copinsay flung himself on Robbie Tenston and
began to scratch at his face like a woman. He screamed a few
falsetto incoherences.

The dispute had reached a dangerous stage. (I felt that, as the

I left the women cluck-clucking with sympathy around Copinsay Agonistes. I took my box of books that was sent each month from the library in the town – there was never likely to be any fighting about that piece of cargo – and walked up the pier.

From the gate of The Hall I looked back at the village. Thora Garth was greeting her mother in the open door of their cottage. Maurice carried his daughter's case. The woman and the girl – the one was as tall as the other now – leaned towards each other and kissed briefly. The dog barked and danced around them.

On the top of the island, where the road cuts into the shoulder of the hill, a small dark figure throbbed for a minute against the sky. It was Robbie Tenston bearing his resentment and shame home to Dale.

This evening I called in at the hotel bar for a glass of beer – a thing I rarely do; but it has been, for Orkney, a warm day, and also I must confess I am missing James MacIntosh already – he went home to Perth for the summer vacation two days ago. Seven weeks without chess and argument is a long time.

Maurice Garth was sitting in the window seat drinking stout. I took my glass of beer across to his table.

'Well,' I said, 'and how is Thora liking the big school in Hamnavoe?'

'She isn't clever,' he said, smiling. 'I doubt she won't go very far as a scholar. But what is there for a lass to do in Torsay nowadays? Everybody's leaving the island. I suppose in the end she might get some kind of a job in the town.'

'It was remarkable,' I said, 'the way Thora put a stop to that fight on the pier this morning.'

'Oh, I don't know,' said Maurice. 'That pair of idiots! Any fool could have seen that it was a bread box. I hope we'll hear no more about it. I hope there isn't going to be any trouble about it with the police.'

'They might have done each other an injury,' I said. 'It was your Thora who brought them to their senses. I never saw anything quite so astonishing.'

'No, no,' said Maurice, raising his hand. 'Don't say that. Thora's just an ordinary lass. There's nothing so very strange about it. Thora just pointed out what was what to that pair of fools. Say no more about it.'

Maurice Garth is a placid man. Such vehemence is strange, coming from him. But perhaps it was that he had drunk too many glasses of stout.

There has been a fine morsel of scandal in the village this morning. The Swintoun woman has been going about the doors at all hours, her cheeks aflame with excitement. It seems that the younger son of Wear, the main farm in the island, has been jilted. Everything has been set fair for a wedding for three months past. Consignments of new furniture, carpets, curtains, crockery have been arriving in the steamer from Hamnavoe; to be fetched later the same afternoon by a farm servant in a cart. They do things in style at Wear. The first friends have gone with their gifts, even. I myself wandered about the empty caverns of this house all one morning last week, considering whether this oil painting or that antique vase might be acceptable. The truth is, I can hardly afford any more to give them a present of money. In the end I thought they might be happy with an old silk sampler framed in mahogany that one of my grand-aunts made in the middle of Queen Victoria's reign. It is a beautiful piece of work. At Wear they would expect something new and glittery from the laird. I hoped, however, that the bride might be pleased with my present.

The Rev. Mr Evelyn was going to have made the first proclamation from the pulpit next Sunday morning. (I never attend the church services here myself, being nominally an Episcopalian, like most of the other Orkney lairds.)

Well, the island won't have to worry any more about this particular ceremony, for – so Traill the postman told me over the garden wall this morning – the prospective bride has gone to live in a wooden shack at the other end of the island – a hut left over from the Kaiser's war – with Shaun Midhouse, a deck hand on the *Pomona*, a man of no particular comeliness or gifts – in fact, a rather unprepossessing character – certainly not what the women of Torsay would call 'a good catch', by any means.

I am sorry for Jack Grossiter of Wear. He seems a decent enough young chap, not at all like some others in the household. His father of all men I dislike in Torsay. He is arrogant and overbearing towards those whom he considers his inferiors; but you never saw such cap-raisings and foot-scrapings as when he chances to meet the minister or the schoolmaster or myself on the road. He is also the wealthiest man in the island, yet the good tilth that he works belongs to me, and I am forbidden by law to charge more than a derisory rent for it. I try not to let this curious situation influence me, but of course it does nothing to sweeten my regard for the man. In addition to everything else he is an upstart and an ignoramus. How delighted he was when his only daughter Sophie married that custom house officer two years ago – that was a feather in his cap, for according to the curious snobbery of folk like Grossiter a man who has a pen-and-paper job is a superior animal altogether to a crofter who labours all his life among earth and blood and dung. The eldest son Andrew will follow him in Wear, no doubt, for since that piece of socialism was enacted in parliament in 1882 even death does not break the secure chain of a family's tenure . . . For Andrew, in his turn, a good match was likewise negotiated, no less than Mr Copinsay the merchant's daughter. Wear will be none the poorer for that alliance. Only Jack Grossiter remained unmarried. Whom he took to wife was of comparatively small importance – a hill croft would be found for him when the time came. I could imagine well enough the brutish reasonings of the man of Wear, once his second son began to be shaken with the ruddiness and restlessness of virility. There was now, for instance, that bonny respectable well-handed lass in the village – Thora Garth – what objection could there be to her? She would make a good wife to any man, though of course her father was only a fisherman and not overburdened with wealth. One afternoon – I can picture it all – the man of Wear would have said a few words to Maurice Garth in the pub, and bought him a dram. One evening soon after that Jack Grossiter and Thora would have been left alone together in the sea-bright room above the shore; a first few cold words passed between them. It gradually became known in the village that they were engaged. I have seen them, once or twice this summer, walking along the shore together in the sunset.

Now, suddenly, this has shaken the island.

The first unusual thing to happen was that Thora went missing, one morning last week. She simply walked out of the house with never a word to her parents. There had been no quarrel, so Armingert assured the neighbours. For the first hour or two she didn't worry about Thora; she might have walked up to Wear, or called on Minnie Farquharson who was working on the bridal dress. But she did not come home for her dinner, and that was unusual, that was a bit worrying. Armingert called at this door and that in the afternoon. No-one had seen Thora since morning. Eventually it was Benny Smith the ferryman who let out the truth, casually, to Maurice Garth, at the end of the pier, when he got back from Hamnavoe in the early evening. He had taken Thora across in his boat the *Lintie* about ten o'clock that morning. She hadn't said a word to him all the way across. It wasn't any concern of his, and anyway she wasn't the kind of young woman who likes her affairs to be known.

Well, that was a bit of a relief to Maurice and Armingert. They reasoned that Thora must suddenly have thought of some necessary wedding purchase; she would be staying overnight with one of her Hamnavoe friends (one of the girls she had been to school with); she would be back on the *Pomona* the next morning.

And in fact she did come back on Friday on board the *Pomona*. She walked at once from the boat to her parents' door. Who was trailing two paces behind her but Shaun Midhouse, one of the crew of the *Pomona*. Thora opened the cottage door and went inside (Shaun lingered at the gate). She told her mother – Maurice was at the lobsters – that she could not marry Jack Grossiter of Wear after all, because she had discovered that she liked somebody else much better. There was a long silence in the kitchen. Then her mother asked who this other man was. Thora pointed through the window. The deck-hand was shuffling about on the road outside with that hangdog look that he has when he isn't working or drinking. 'That's my man,' Thora said – 'I'm going to live with him.' Armingert said that she would give much pain and grief to those near to her if she did what she said she was going to do. Thora said she realized that. 'I'm sorry,' she said. Then she left the cottage and walked up the brae to the farm of Wear. Shaun went a few paces with her through the village, but left her outside the hotel and went back on board the *Pomona*; the boat was due to sail again in ten minutes.

Thora wouldn't go into the farmhouse. She said what she had to say standing in the door, and it only lasted a minute. Then she turned and walked slowly across the yard to the road. The old man went a few steps after her, shouting and shaking his fists. His elder son Andrew called him back, coldly – his father mustn't make a fool of himself before the whole district. Let the slut go. His father must remember that he was the most important farmer in Torsay.

Jack had already taken his white face from the door – it hasn't been seen anywhere in the island since. I am deeply sorry for him.

I ought to go along and see these people. God knows what I can say to them. I am hopeless in such situations. I was not created to be a bringer of salves and oils.

I saw the minister coming out of the farmhouse two days ago . . .

The eastern part of the island is very desolate, scarred with peat-bogs and Pictish burial places. During the war the army built an artillery battery on the links there. (They commandeered the site – my subsequent granting of permission was an empty token.) All that is left of the camp now, among the concrete foundations, is a single wooden hut that had been the officers' mess. No-one has lived there since 1919 – inside it must be all dampness and mildew. Tom Christianson the shepherd saw, two days after the breaking of the engagement, smoke coming from the chimney of the hut. He kept an eye on the place; later that afternoon a van drove up; Shaun Midhouse carried from van to hut a mattress, a sack of coal, a box of groceries. He reported the facts to me. That night, late, I walked between the hills and saw a single lamp burning in the window.

Thora Garth and Shaun Midhouse have been living there for a full week now – as Mr Copinsay the merchant says, 'in sin'; managing to look, as he says it, both pained and pleased.

Two nights ago Armingert and Maurice came to see me.

'Shaun Midhouse is such a poor weed of a creature,' said Armingert in my cold library. 'What ever could any girl see in the likes of *that*?'

Maurice shook his head. They are, both these dear folk, very troubled.

'Jack Grossiter is ill,' said Armingert. 'I never saw a boy so upset. I am very very sorry for him.'

'I will go and see him tomorrow,' I said.

'What trouble she has caused,' said Armingert. 'I did not think such a thing was possible. If she had suddenly attacked us with a knife it would have been easier to bear. She is a bad cruel deceptive girl.'

'She is our daughter,' said Maurice gently.

'We have no business to inflict our troubles on you,' said Armingert. 'What we have come about is this, all the same. We understand that you own that war-time site. They are sitting unbidden in your property, Thora and that creature. That is what it amounts to. You could evict them.'

I shook my head.

'You could have the law on them,' she insisted. 'You could force them out. She would have to come home then, if you did that. That would bring her to her senses.'

'I'm sorry,' I said. 'There is something at work here that none of us understands, some kind of an elemental force. It is terrible and it is delicate at the same time. It must work itself out in Thora and Shaun Midhouse. I am not wise enough to interfere.'

There was silence in the library for a long time after that.

Armingert looked hurt and lost. No doubt but she is offended with me.

'He is right,' said Maurice at last. 'She is our daughter. We must just try to be patient.'

Then they both got to their feet. They looked tired and sad. They who had been childless for so long in their youth are now childless again; and they are growing old; and an area of their life where there was nothingness twenty years ago is now all vivid pain.

I knew it would happen some day: that old school-house dog has savaged one of the islanders, and a child at that. I was in the garden, filling a bowl with gooseberries, when I heard the terrible outcry from the village, a mingling of snarls and screams. 'Joe, you brute!' came James MacIntosh's voice (it was a still summer evening; every sound carried for miles) – 'Bad dog! Get into the house this minute!' . . . And then in a soothing voice, 'Let's see your leg then. It's only a graze, Mansie. You got a fright, that's all . . . That bad Joe . . . Shush now, no need to kick up such a row. You'll deafen the whole village.' . . . This Mansie, whoever he was, refused to be comforted. The lamentation came nearer. I heard the school-house door being banged shut (my garden wall is too high to see the village): James MacIntosh had gone indoors, possibly to chastise his cur. Presently a boy, sobbing and snivelling in spasms, appeared on the road. He leaned against a pillar to get his breath. 'Hello,' I said, 'would you like some gooseberries?'

Greed and self-pity contended in Mansie's face. He unlatched the gate and came in, limping. There was a livid crescent mark below his knee. He picked a fat gooseberry from my bowl. He looked at it wonderingly. His lips were still shivering with shock.

'That damn fool of a dog,' I said. 'Did he seize you then? You'd better come into the kitchen. I'll put some disinfectant on it. I have bandages.'

The cupped palm of his hand brimmed with gooseberries. He bit into several, one after the other, with a half-reluctant lingering relish. Then he crammed six or seven into his mouth till his cheek bulged. His brown eyes dissolved in rapture; he closed them; there was a runnel of juice from one corner of his mouth to his chin.

The day was ending in a riot of colour westward. Crimson and saffron and jet the sea blazed, like stained glass.

'The disinfectant,' I said. 'It's in the kitchen.'

He balanced the last of the gooseberries on the tip of his tongue, rolled it round inside his mouth, and bit on it. 'It's nothing,' he said. 'I was in the village visiting my grand-da. It was me to blame really. I kicked Joe's bone at the school gate. I must be getting home now. Thora'll be wondering about me.' . . .

So, he was one of the Midhouse boys. He looked like neither of his parents. He had the shy swift gentle eyes of Maurice his grandfather. He relished gooseberries the way that old Maurice sipped his stout in the hotel bar.

'And anyway,' he said, 'I wouldn't come into your house to save my life.'

'What's wrong with my house?' I said.

'It's the laird's house,' he said. 'It's The Hall. I'm against all that kind of thing. I'm a communist.' (He was maybe ten years old.)

'There isn't anything very grand about this great ruckle of stones,' I said. 'It's falling to pieces. You should see the inside of it. Just look at this wilderness of a garden. I'll tell you the truth, Mansie – I'm nearly as poor as Ezra the tinker. So come in till I fix your leg.'

He shook his head. 'It's the principle of it,' said Mansie. 'You oppressed my ancestors. You taxed them to death. You drove them to Canada and New Zealand. You made them work in your fields for nothing. They built this house for you, yes, and their hands were red carrying up stones from the shore. I wouldn't go through your door for a pension. What does one man want with a big house like this anyway? Thora and me and my brothers live in two small rooms up at Solsetter.'

'I'm sorry, Mansie,' I said. 'I promise I won't ever be wicked like that again. But I am worried about that bite on your leg.'

'It's the same with the kirk,' said Mansie. 'Do you think I could have just one more gooseberry? I would never enter that kirk door. All that talk about sin and hell and angels. Do you know what I think about the bible? It's one long fairy-tale from beginning to end. I'm an atheist, too. You can tell the minister what I said if you like. I don't care. I don't care for any of you.'

The rich evening light smote the west gable of The Hall. The great house took, briefly, a splendour. The wall flushed and darkened. Then with all its withered stonework and ramshackle rooms it began to enter the night.

The gooseberry bush twanged. The young anarchist was plucking another fruit.

'I don't believe in anything,' he said. 'Nothing at all. You are born. You live for a while. Then you die. My grandma died last year. Do you know what she is now? Dust in the kirkyard. They could have put her in a ditch, it would have been all the same. When you're dead you're dead.'

'You'd better be getting home then, comrade, before it's dark,' I said.

'Do you know this,' he said, 'I have no father. At least, I do have a father but he doesn't live with us any more. He went away one day, suddenly. Oh, a while ago now, last winter. Jock Ritch saw him once in Falmouth. He was on a trawler. We don't know where he is. I'm glad he's gone. I didn't like him. And I'll tell you another thing.'

'Tomorrow,' I said. 'You must go home now. You must get that bite seen to. If you don't, some day there'll be an old man hobbling round this village with a wooden leg. And it'll be you, if you don't show that wound to your mother right away.'

'Rob and Willie and me,' he said, 'we're bastards. I bet I've shocked you. I bet you think I said a bad word. You see, Thora was never married. Thora, she's my mother. I suppose you would say "illegitimate" but it's just the same thing. The gooseberries were good. They're not your gooseberries though. They belong to the whole island by rights. I was only taking my share.'

The darkness had come down so suddenly that I could not say when the boy left my door. I was aware only that one smell had been subtracted from the enchanting cluster of smells that gather about an island on a late summer evening. A shadow was gone from the garden. I turned and went inside, carrying the bowl of gooseberries. (There would be one pot of jam less next winter.) I

traversed, going to the kitchen, a corridor with an ancient iner-
adicable sweetness of rot in it.

I have been ill, it seems. I still feel like a ghost in a prison of bone. I
have been very ill, James MacIntosh says. 'I thought you were for
the kirkyard,' he told me last night. 'That's the truth. I thought an
ancient proud island family was guttering out at last.' . . . He said
after a time. 'There's something tough about you, man. I think
you'll see the boots off us all.' He put the kettle on my fire to make
a pot of tea. 'I don't suppose now,' he said, 'that you'll be up to a
game of chess just yet. Quite so.' He is a sweet considerate man. 'I'll
fill your hot-water bottle before I go,' he said, 'it's very cold up in
that bedroom.'

The whole house is like a winter labyrinth in the heart of this
summer-time island. It is all this dampness and rot, I'm sure, that
made me so ill last month. The Hall is withering slowly about me. I
cannot afford now to reslate the roof. There is warping and
woodworm and patches of damp everywhere. The three long
corridors empty their overplus of draught into every mildewed
bedroom. Even last October, when the men from the fishing boat
broke the billiard-room window, going between the hotel and the
barn dance at Dale, I had to go without tobacco for a fortnight or
so until the joiner was paid. Not much can be done these days on
two hundred pounds a year.

'James,' I said, 'I'm going to shift out of that bedroom. Another
winter there and I'd be a gonner. I wonder if I could get a small bed
fitted into some corner of the kitchen – over there, for example,
out of the draught. I don't mind eating and sleeping in the same
room.'

This morning (Saturday) MacIntosh came up from the school-
house with a small iron folding bed. 'It's been in the outhouse since
I came to Torsay,' he said. 'The last teacher must have had it for
one of his kids. It's a bit rusty, man, but it's sound, perfectly sound.
Look for yourself. If you'll just shift that heap of books out of the
corner I'll get it fixed up in no time.' . . .

We drank some tea while blankets and pillows were airing at the
kitchen fire. I tried to smoke my pipe but the thing tasted foul – the

room plunged; there was a blackness before my eyes; I began to sweat. 'You're not entirely well yet by any means,' said the schoolmaster. 'Put that pipe away. It'll be a week or two before you can get over the door, far less down to the hotel for a pint. I'm telling you, you've been very ill. You don't seem to realize how desperate it was with you. But for one thing only you'd be in the family vault.'

People who have been in the darkness for a while long to know how it was with them when they were no longer there to observe and evaluate. They resent their absence from the dear ecstatic flesh; they suspect too that they may have been caught out by their attendants in some weakness or shame that they themselves make light of, or even indulge, in the ordinary round. At the same time there is a kind of vanity in sickness. It sets a person apart from the folk who only eat and sleep and sorrow and work. Those dullards become the servants of the hero who has ventured into the shadowy border-land next to the kingdom of death – the sickness bestows a special quality on him, a seal of gentility almost. There are people who wear their scars and pock-marks like decorations. The biography of such a one is a pattern of small sicknesses, until at last the kingdom he has fought against and been fascinated with for so long besets him with irresistible steel and fire. There is one last trumpet call under a dark tower . . .

This afternoon, by means of subtle insistent questions, I got from James MacIntosh the story of my trouble. He would much rather have been sitting with me in amiable silence over a chess-board. I knew of course the beginning of the story; how I had had to drag myself about the house for some days at the end of May with a gray quake on me. To get potatoes from the garden – a simple job like that – was a burdensome penance. The road to the village and the tobacco jar on Mr Copinsay's shelf was a wearisome 'via crucis', but at last I could not even get that far. My pipe lay cold on the window-still for two days. Sometime during the third day the sun became a blackness.

'Pneumonia,' said James MacIntosh. 'That's what it was. Dr Wayne stood in the school-house door and barked at me. *The laird up yonder, your friend, he has double pneumonia. By rights he should*

*be in the hospital in Kirkwall. That's out of the question, he's too ill.
He'll have to bide where he is . . . Now then* (says he) *there's not a hell
of a lot I can do for him. That's the truth. It's a dicey thing,
pneumonia. It comes to a crisis. The sick man reaches a crossroads,
if you understand what I mean. He lingers there for an hour or two.
Then he simply goes one way or the other. There's no telling. What is
essential though* (says the old quack) *is good nursing. There must be
somebody with him night and day – two, if possible, one to relieve the
other. Now then, you must know some woman or other in the island
who has experience of this kind of thing. Get her . . .* And out of the
house he stumps with his black bag, down the road, back to the
ferry-boat at the pier.

'So there you lay, in that great carved mahogany bed upstairs,
sweating and raving. Old Wayne had laid the responsibility fairly
and squarely on me. I had to get a nurse. But what nurse? And
where? The only person who does any kind of nursing in the
island is that Maggie Swintoun – at least, she brings most of the
island bairns into the world, and it's her they generally send for
when anybody dies. But nursing – I never actually heard of her
attending sick folk. And besides, I knew you disliked the woman.
If you were to open your eyes and see that face at the foot of the
bed it would most likely, I thought, be the end of you. But that
didn't prevent Mistress Swintoun from offering her services that
same day. There she stood, keening and whispering at the foot of
the stair – she had had the impudence to come in without
knocking. *I hear the laird isn't well, the poor man* (says she). *Well
now, if there's anything I can do. I don't mind sitting up all night
. . .* And the eyes of her going here and there over the portraits in
the staircase and over all the silver plate in the hall-stand. *Thank
you all the same,* said I, *but other arrangements have been made . . .*
Off she went then, like a cat leaving a fish on a doorstep. I was
worried all the same, I can tell you. I went down to the village to
have a consultation with Minnie Farquharson the seamstress. She
knows everybody in Torsay, what they can do and what they can't
do. She demurred. In the old days there would have been no
difficulty: the island was teeming with kindly capable women who
would have been ideal for the job. But things are different now,

Minnie pointed out. Torsay is half empty. Most of the houses are in ruin. The young women are away in the towns, working in shops and offices. All that's left in the way of women-folk are school bairns and "puir auld bodies". She honestly couldn't think of a single suitable person. "*Now* (says she) *I doubt you'll have to put an advertisement in The Orcadian.*"'

'I knew, as I walked back up the brae, that by the time the advertisement – "Wanted, experienced private nurse to attend gentleman" – had appeared, and been answered, and the nurse interviewed and approved and brought over to Torsay, there would have been no patient for her to attend to. The marble jaws would have swallowed you up . . .

'When I turned in at the gate of The Hall, I saw washed sheets and pillow-cases hanging in the garden, between the potato patch and the gooseberry bushes, where no washing has ever flapped in the wind for ten years and more. (You hang your shirts and socks, I know, in front of the stove.) I went into the house. The fire was lit in the kitchen. The windows along the corridor were open, and there was a clean sweet air everywhere instead of those gray draughts. I'm not a superstitious man, but I swear my hand was shaking when I opened the door to your bedroom. And there she was, bent over you and putting cold linen to the beaded agony on your face.'

'Who?' I said.

'And there she stayed for ten days, feeding you, washing you, comforting you, keeping the glim of life in you night and day. Nobody relieved her. God knows when she slept. She was never, as far as I could make out, a minute away from your room. But of course she must have been, to cook, wash, prepare the medicines, things like that. She had even set jars of flowers in odd niches and corners. The house began to smell fragrant.'

I said, 'Yes, but who?'

'She told me, standing there in your bedroom that first day, that I didn't need to worry any longer. She thought she could manage. What could I do anyway, she said, with the school bairns to teach from ten in the morning till four in the afternoon? And she smiled at me, as though there was some kind of conspiracy between us.

And she nodded, half in dismissal and half in affirmation. I went down that road to the school-house with a burden lifted from me, I can tell you. *Well, if he doesn't get better*, I thought, *it won't be for want of a good nurse.*'

'You haven't told me her name,' I said.

'On the Thursday old Wayne came out of The Hall shaking his head. I saw him from the school window. He was still shaking his head when he stepped on board the *Lintie* at the pier. That was the day of the crisis. I ran up to your house as soon as the school was let out at half past three (for I couldn't bear to wait till four o'clock). The flame was gulping in the lamp all right. Your pulse had no cohesion or rhythm. There were great gaps in your breathing. I stood there, expecting darkness and silence pretty soon. What is it above all that a woman gives to a man? God knows. Some strong pure dark essence of the earth that seems not to be a part of the sun-loving clay of men at all. The woman was never away from your bedside that night. I slept, on and off, between two chairs in the kitchen. At sunrise next morning you spoke for the first time for, I think, twelve days. You asked for – of all things – a cup of tea. But the nurse, she was no longer there.'

'For God's sake,' I said, 'tell me who she is.'

'You'll have to be doing with my crude services,' said James MacIntosh, 'till you're able to do for yourself. You should be out and about in a week, if this good weather holds. I thought I told you who she was.'

'You didn't,' I said.

'Well now,' he said, 'I thought I did. It was Thora Garth, of course.'

This morning I had a visit from a young man I have never seen before. It turns out that he is a missionary, a kind of lay Presbyterian preacher. There has been no minister in Torsay since the Rev. Mr Evelyn retired three years ago; the spiritual needs of the few people remaining have been attended to, now and then, by ministers from other islands.

This missionary is an earnest young bachelor. He has a sense of vocation but no humour. Someone in the village must have told him about me. 'Mister, you'd better call on the old man up at The Hall. You'll likely be able to understand the posh way he speaks. He only manages down to the village once a week nowadays for his tobacco and his margarine and his loaf. He has nothing to live on but an annuity – nowadays, with the price of things, it would hardly keep a cat. The likes of him is too grand of course to apply for Social Security. God knows what way he manages to live at all. He's never been a church man, but I'm sure he'd be pleased to see an educated person like you.' . . . I can just imagine Andrew Grossiter, or one of the other elders, saying that to the newcomer some Sunday morning after the service, pointing up the brae to the big house with the fallen slates and the broken sundial.

So, here he was, this young preacher, come to visit me out of Christian duty. He put on me a bright kind smile from time to time.

'I like it here, in Torsay,' he said. 'Indeed I do. It's a great change from the city. I expect it'll take me a wee while to get used to country ways. I come from Glasgow myself. For example, I'm as certain as can be that someone has died in the village this morning. I saw a man carrying trestles into one of the houses. There was a coffin in the back of his van. By rights I should have been told about it at once. It's my duty to visit the bereaved relatives. I'll be wanted of course for the funeral. Ah well, I'll make enquiries this afternoon sometime.'

He eyed with a kind of innocent distaste the sole habitable room left in my house, the kitchen. If I had known he was coming I might have tidied the place up a bit. But for the sake of truth it's best when visitors come unexpectedly on the loaf and cracked mug on the table, the unmade bed, the webbed windows, and all the mingled smells of aged bachelordom.

'Death is a common thing in Torsay nowadays,' I said. 'Nearly everybody left in the village is old. There's hardly a young person in the whole island except yourself.'

'I hope you don't mind my visiting you,' said the missionary. 'I understand you're an episcopalian. These days we must try to be as ecumenical as we can. Now sir, please don't be offended at what

I'm going to say. It could be that, what with old age and the fact that you're not so able as you used to be, you find yourself with less money than you could be doing with – for example, to buy a bag of coal or a bit of butcher-meat.'

'I manage quite well,' I said. 'I have an annuity from my grand-uncle. I own this house. I don't eat a great deal.'

'Quite so,' he said. 'But the cost of everything keeps going up. Your income hardly covers the little luxuries that make life a bit more bearable. Now, I've been looking through the local church accounts and I've discovered that there are one or two small bequests that I have the disposal of. I don't see why you shouldn't be a beneficiary. They're for every poor person in the island, whatever church he belongs to, or indeed if he belongs to no church at all.'

'I don't need a thing,' I said.

'Well,' he said, 'if ever you feel like speaking to me about it. The money is there. It's for everybody in Torsay who needs it.'

'Torsay will soon require nothing,' I said.

'I must go down to the village and see about this death,' he said. 'I noticed three young men in dark suits coming off the *Pomona* this morning. They must be relatives of some kind . . . I'll find my own way out. Don't bother. This is a fascinating old house right enough. These stones, if only they could speak. God bless you, now.'

He left me then, that earnest innocent young man. I was glad in a way to see the back of him – though I liked him well enough – for I was longing for a pipeful of tobacco, and I'm as certain as can be that he is one of those evangelicals who disapprove of smoking and drinking.

So, there is another death in the island. Month by month Torsay is re-entering the eternal loneliness and silence. The old ones die. The young ones go away to farm in other places, or to car factories in Coventry or Bathgate. The fertile end of the island is littered with roofless windowless crofts. Sometimes, on a fine afternoon, I take my stick and walk for an hour about my domain. Last week I passed Dale, which Robbie Tenston used to farm. (He has been in Australia for fifteen years.) I pushed open the warped door of the dwelling-house. A great gray ewe lurched past me out of the darkness and nearly knocked me over. Birds whirred up through the bare rafters. There were bits of furniture here and there – a table, a couple of chairs, a wooden shut-bed. A framed photograph of the Channel Fleet still hung at the damp wall. There were empty bottles and jam jars all over the floor among sheep-turds, and bird-splashes . . . Most of the farm houses in Torsay are like that now.

It is an island dedicated to extinction. I can never imagine young people coming back to these uncultivated fields and eyeless ruins. Soon now, I know, the place will be finally abandoned to gulls and crows and rabbits. When first I came to Torsay fifty years ago, summoned from London by my grand-uncle's executor, I could still read the heraldry and the Latin motto over the great Hall door. There is a vague shape on the sandstone lintel now; otherwise it is indecipherable. All that style and history and romance have melted back into the stone.

Life in a flourishing island is a kind of fruitful interweaving music of birth and marriage and death: a trio. The old pass mildly into the darkness to make way for their bright grandchildren. There is only one dancer in the island now and he carries the hour-glass and the spade and the scythe.

How many have died in the past few years? I cannot remember all the names. The severest loss, as far as I am concerned, is James MacIntosh. The school above the village closed ten years ago, when the dominie retired. There were not enough pupils to justify a new teacher. He did not want to leave Torsay – his whole life was entirely rooted here. He loved the trout fishing, and our chess and few drams twice a week; he liked to follow the careers of his former pupils in every part of the world – he had given so much of his life to them. What did he know of his few remaining relatives in Perthshire? 'Here I am and here I'll bide,' he said to me the day the school closed. I offered him a croft a mile away – Unibreck – that had just been vacated: the young crofter had got a job in an Edinburgh brewery. James MacIntosh lived there for two winters, reading his 'Forward' and working out chess moves from the manual he kept beside his bed . . . One morning Maggie Swintoun put her head in at the kitchen door when I was setting the fire. 'O sir,' she wailed, 'a terrible thing has happened!' Every broken window, every winter cough, every sparrow-fall was stuff of tragedy to Maggie Swintoun. I didn't bother even to look round at the woman – I went on laying a careful stratum of sticks on the crumpled paper. 'Up at Unibreck,' she cried, 'your friend, poor Mr MacIntosh the teacher. I expected it. He hasn't been looking well this past month and more.' . . . She must have been put out by the coal-blackened face I turned on her, for she went away without rounding off her knell. I gathered later that the postman, going with a couple of letters to the cottage, had found James MacIntosh cold and silent in his armchair . . . I know he would have liked to be buried in Torsay. Those same relatives that he had had no communication with for a quarter of a century ordered his body to be taken down to Dundee. There he was burned in a crematorium and his dust thrown among alien winds.

Maggie Swintoun herself is a silence about the doors of the village. Her ghost is there, a shivering silence, between the sea and the hill. In no long time now that frail remembered keen will be lost in the greater silence of Torsay.

The shutters have been up for two years in the general store. William Copinsay was summoned by a stroke one winter evening from his money bags. They left him in the kirkyard, with pennies for eyes, to grope his way towards that unbearable treasure that is laid up (some say) for all who have performed decent acts of charity in their lives; the acts themselves, subtleties and shadows and gleams in time being (they say again) but fore-reflections of that hoarded perdurable reality. (I do not believe this myself. I believe in the 'twelve winds' of Housman that assemble the stuff of life for a year or two and then disperse it again.) Anyway, William Copinsay is dead.

Grossiter died at the auction mart in Hamnavoe, among the beasts and the whisky-smelling farmers, one Wednesday afternoon last spring.

Of course I know who has died in Torsay today. I knew hours before that young missionary opened his mouth. I had seen the lamp burning in a window at the end of the village at two o'clock in the morning.

It is not the old man who has died, either. His death could not give me this unutterable grief that I felt then, and still feel. The heart of the island has stopped beating. I am the laird of a place that has no substance or meaning any more.

I will go down to the cottage sometime today. I will knock at the door. I will ask for permission to look into that still face.

The only child I have had has been taken from me; the only woman I could ever have loved; the only dust that I wished my own dust to be mingled with.

But in the fifty years that Thora Garth and I have lived in this island together we have never exchanged one word.

The Fight at Greenay

Harraymen would go sometimes to the shore through the parish of Birsay. They had to go, for seaweed to manure their fields in spring; occasionally in a hard winter for limpets and dulse to eat. (Harray is the only parish in Orkney that has no seaboard.)

There was fighting often between the Harraymen and the Birsaymen; or between Harraymen and Stennessmen if they chanced to go through Stenness to the shore, coming down between the two lochs to the desolation of Waithe; or between Harraymen and Eviemen if they took the dark road through the hills to the shining beach at Aikerness. In those days the men from the different parishes had no great liking for each other. Only laird and tinker and bird moved freely from district to district.

That year it was seaweed for the furrows the Harraymen were after, strong stuff that had been nourished in mid-Atlantic. The last storm of winter had laid it in heaped red drifts on the shore of Marwick and further north towards Garson and the Palace and the Brough. Their ploughing was done.

Four Harraymen were chosen, for their strength in case it should come to fighting, for their gentleness so that all offence to the Birsaymen should be avoided. They were Peter-with-One-Eye, Malty, the Witch's Boy, and Randy Eric.

They crossed the border into Birsay, going easy and cautious as cats between Beaquoy and the small gray loch of Sabiston. For three miles along the road nothing happened. The world was at peace all round them – larks up beside the sun, first daisies in the ditches. A few Birsaymen were following their oxen and ploughs along the lower slopes of the hill.

They came to the alehouse at Greenay.

'I think,' said Malty, 'we should rest here for a while and draw a quiet breath.'

'No,' said Peter-with-One-Eye. 'There's always trouble in ale-houses.'

Malty's feet began to drag.

'Work first,' said Peter-with-One-Eye. 'We'll stop at the ale-house on our way home. We'll be glad of a drink then.'

Malty turned in at the alehouse door. One by one they followed him. Peter-with-One-Eye went in last, shaking his head.

They drank the ale Malty paid for. Then Peter-with-One-Eye paid for a round; he was the leader, he had his pride to consider.

That spring the Greenay ale was very good and very strong. Nobody objected when the Witch's Boy bought four more mugs.

Their beards were still frothy from the pewter when seven Birsay ploughmen came in, thirsty from their day's work. They sat at a table in the opposite corner from the Harraymen. Maggie, the daughter of Abel of Greenay, brought in another tray of tankards. She was a plain thick-set girl. Nobody in Birsay wanted to marry her. Her temper was uncertain, even though she laughed a good deal, showing her strong teeth.

A Birsayman said, 'I wonder what it's like to have only one eye? One thing sure, it makes a man very ugly to look at.'

Peter-with-One-Eye said to his companions, but loud enough for the whole alehouse to hear, 'I take no offence.'

The men went on with their drinking, the Harraymen at one table and the Birsaymen at the other. Maggie carried in the ale.

Another Birsayman said, 'It must be a hard thing to have a witch for a mother. A hundred years ago a woman like that would have been burned at Gallowsha in Kirkwall.'

The Witch's Boy rose to his feet. Peter-with-One-Eye took hold of his jacket and pulled him back on to his chair. 'We take no offence,' he said. 'We are peaceable folk.'

Maggie was going back and fore all the time between the barrel and the tables. Abel stood in the shadow of the inner door, rubbing his hands between greed and apprehension. There was always a lot of money spent at the season of the plough, but there was inclined to be more rowdiness then also.

A Birsayman with a black beard said, 'There's a drunkard in the parish of Harray who they say is drunk every night of the week. In last winter's snow the prints of his feet went straight to begin with, then there was a wandering, then a circling, and in the centre of the circle the searchers found this drunken beast of a Harryman next morning. There was an empty rum flagon in the snow beside his head. I'm telling you the story as I heard it.'

'This is me they're speaking about,' whispered Malty.

'There is offence now,' said Peter-with-One-Eye loud enough for all to hear, 'but the seed has fallen in a stony furrow.'

Randy Eric ordered a round of drinks.

'It seems to me,' said another Birsayman who was smoking a pipe, 'that the lasses of this parish wouldn't feel themselves safe if they knew that a certain lecher was trekking through our hills after seaweed that belongs by right to us. I think all the same his power with women is exaggerated. No proper Birsaywoman would cast a second look at such a thing.'

Randy Eric began to sweat. His fists were trembling so much that he spilt ale over his moleskin trousers.

Maggie stood before him and laughed.

'Now it is going beyond offence,' said Peter-with-One-Eye. 'Still we will be as quiet as pigeons.'

The Birsayman who had spoken last fell on the stone floor. Randy Eric's tankard had hit him full between the eyes. The burning tobacco died in floods of beer.

They say the fight that followed was the best that ever was fought between Harraymen and Birsaymen. The story is that it went on all night in the alehouse (as if that were possible). The truth is that at the end of twenty minutes Abel of Greenay was able to estimate his broken furnishings.

The Witch's Boy got home next morning. He had three broken ribs and he was spitting blood. His mother put him to bed. She took a dead spider and a lupin root; she roasted them and crushed them and powdered them and mixed them in water from the Magnus well. She said certain words over the cup. The boy's face blanched and shivered on the pillow. By harvest time he was able to swing a scythe as well as any other harvester.

Malty avoided the worst of the fighting by hiding behind the ale barrel. He stayed there all night and got home to Corston in the morning, drunk.

Peter-with-One-Eye lost his other eye in the fight. Till the day of his death a boy had to lead him to kirk and market. 'No offence,' he would say gently if he stumbled on a stone. 'No offence in the world.'

Randy Eric was found next morning in Maggie's bed. This was considered to be a great feat on his part, in the circumstances. The following harvest he married Maggie. Now that old Abel is dead Eric keeps the alehouse in Greenay. Maggie rocks a new baby every winter.

Eric welcomes all Harraymen who are going through Birsay for seaweed and limpets, or to the horse-fair at The Barony, or on any business whatsoever. Nowadays you will sometimes see a Birsay-man and a Harrayman drinking at the same table at Greenay. (I wish all the warring people of the world could be as well reconciled – perhaps if white married black, and Jew and Arab fell in love, and the lady in the Hall were to take a fancy to Ikey the tinker.)

On a winter night the ale drinkers at Greenay hear through the partition the croonings of Maggie over her latest cradle-load.

The Cinquefoil

UNPOPULAR FISHERMAN

There are a few men in the island I don't speak to, one especially: Fred Houton that I used to fish with in our boat the *Thistle* until the day two or three years ago when he struck a savage unexpected blow at my pride.

If he had taken a five-pound note out of my wallet I would have forgiven him, or whisky from my cupboard; or even if he had not turned up for the fishing one morning. For Fred Houton and I understood each other, there was a grudging muted friendship.

He lived with his mother in a croft in the hills, a poor place called Ingarth.

I was pleased enough to see him most evenings. He would throw open the door of my hut without knocking and say, 'Come on, then, boy, we're going for a pint.' Or, if we had no money, we would sit silent and play draughts and smoke till after midnight.

After I got to know Rosie, all that changed. It's true, I had known Rosie all my life – all the islanders are acquainted with one another. And a plain little thing I thought her. She stood all day at the counter of her father's shop above the pier and served the island with groceries, bread, knit-wear, confectionery, tobacco. She was just one among the hundred faces, old and young and ageing, that drifted about the island.

She came to the hut one day with a copy of the *Fishing News* that I hadn't collected for a week. She came dripping with rain; my window was a gray throbbing blur. I asked her in while I rummaged in the cupboard for coppers. She said, 'Your floor could do with a wash.' She said, trembling – the four pennies in her fist – 'That's a poor fire you have.' . . . She stayed for a bite of supper. She was pretty enough with the rain-washed apples in her cheeks. She promised, at the end of the house under the stars, to come back the next night.

Soon it was a strange night that didn't bring Rosie to my hut, with a few fresh-baked scones, or a pot of jam, or a book.

I never really got to like her. I never thought her long freckled face beautiful. She brought a disturbance into my days. I enjoyed fishing more, and breathing, and drinking, because of Rosie.

'If you think I'm going to marry you,' I said, 'you're mistaken. I don't believe in that nonsense. I won't go to the kirk with you on Sunday mornings either.' (I knew she sang in the church choir.)

She said that that was all right as far as she was concerned. But maybe I would change my mind after a time.

There was a certain amount of difficulty with Fred Houton. He would come crashing through the door – as he always did – upon our silence. 'Are you here again?' he would say to Rosie. And to me: 'Come on, come on. They're wanting us to play darts in the pub.'

I told him in the boat one morning when we were setting creels that I would appreciate it if he didn't come so much about my place in future. I let him know – surely the man must have guessed – that there was an understanding between Rosie and me. Then seeing the hurt look on his face, I said, 'Well, say one night a week. Friday – that's always a good night in the pub. We'll have a drink every Friday. Rosie can bide home on Friday and do her knitting. But mind you knock at the door in future.'

One day that winter Fred Houton said to me, 'Look, Gurness, I won't be able to fish with you after Christmas. We'd better come to some arrangement about the boat.'

It turned out that his mother had had a bad twelve-month of it with rheumatism, and the work of the croft, though it was small, was too much for her now. So, Fred had to give up the fishing and resume the work of barn and byre and peat-hill.

I was vexed at the prospect of losing him. He was a good worker (and a luckier fisherman than me, I admit that). But we do not show our feelings in the island. I said, 'That's all right.'

At the new year, I gave him a hundred pounds for his share in the *Thistle*.

That seemed to be the final severance; after that he never stood noisily in my door, even on a Friday evening when my throat was dry. I drank alone on Friday in the window-seat of the pub. I am not good company – I have never had any friends in the island, and I haven't needed them.

I was not even friendly with Rosie. We quarrelled often, that winter, about such things as whether I should get a new suit, for example, or a wireless to hear the weather forecast for inshore fishermen. She would say straight out that I was mean. She would say, ruffling my hair, that really I must try to be more pleasant to people. Some of the answers I gave her made her mouth tremble.

I had a young boy in the boat with me that winter, Jerome Scabra of Anscarth. He learned, slowly, the craft of fishing. I paid him three pounds a week, and he got a few fish home with him at the weekend (if there were any fish).

One Monday evening in March Rosie did not come to the hut. Nor did she come on Tuesday, Wednesday, Thursday.

I ought to have called at the shop. But I know that James Wasdale her father doesn't like me. That wouldn't keep me back, of course – it's all one to me whether they like me or dislike me or have no feelings about me at all. But I don't like the idea that any woman should think me put out on her account. It occurred to me that she might be ill. There was flu in the island, I had heard.

On Friday afternoon I sent Jerome Scabra along to the shop for a tin of tobacco and cigarette papers.

He was back in ten minutes, cutting the air with his shrill mouth.

'Well,' I said, 'are they busy in the shop? Stop that whistling. Old Wasdale fleeces the islanders right and left on a Friday.'

Jerome said there was no customer in the shop when he went in but old Jake Sandside scrounging for this and that.

'This is not the kind of tobacco I use,' I said. 'Who served you? Was it the old man?'

'No,' said Jerome. 'It was Rosie.'

I told the boy to be at the shore at seven o'clock prompt next morning.

Rosie never came back to my hut, except once.

That summer, before harvest, she married Fred Houton in the kirk. I read about it in the local newspaper. I think it is better for a woman to be thirled to a man who makes his living from the land. It is a surer steadier happier life for a girl. The sea is too dangerous.

I hear they have a bairn now. It'll be no beauty. Neither the father nor the mother have much to commend them in the way of looks.

I wish them no harm, all three of them up there at Ingarth.

But I never speak to them. I go past them in the village as if they didn't exist.

Last night a knock came to my door. It was the woman of Ingarth.

'Gurness,' she said, 'Fred and I, we would like . . . please . . . we would like it very much if you would . . . you know, Gurness, we both like you . . . come to dinner with us on –'

I threw the door shut. The door-frame rattled. My hands trembled the way they do when there is a halibut on the hook.

Something makes me happy this winter, out west. The *Thistle* is catching a lot of fish. Young Scabra is – I know it now – a lucky fisherman.

THE MINISTER AND THE GIRL

'For love we were born indeed, and so that we might understand truly what love is we exist for a few years on the earth, and then after our death our dust – if we have understood a little the meaning of love – lies richer in the earth than the dust of those who have devoted themselves entirely to 'late and soon, getting and spending' . . .

'When we are enjoined to love our neighbours, it is surely a difficult thing to do sometimes. For some of the people we meet in the course of our lives are not attractive to us in any way. How can we love this person whose every word on every subject under the sun offends us; even the way he speaks may set our teeth on edge. You, and I, and everybody, has met such a person. We generally avoid his company. Yet the divine injunction is plain – "Love your neighbour" – we are bound as Christians. What does it mean? It does not mean, I think, that we should go about the world with holy long-suffering smiles on our faces for this one and that, high and low, good and bad. By no means; one of the qualities of love is honesty, sincerity. I think it may mean this – we are bound to enter upon any relationship, however fleeting, with a deep respect for the other person. You may say, "Instinctively I do not like this person!" and closer acquaintance may not by any means sweeten your opinion of him. Yet we must think of ourselves as limited people – even the saints are limited – and we simply do not understand. The distasteful person was created by God, he is one of God's children, when we are introduced to him we are in the presence of a marvellous mystery. Before that mystery we must school ourselves to be patient, long-suffering, modest, under-standing. This may not be "love" as St Paul meant it in his great meditation on love in the Epistle to the Corinthians, but it is to stand perhaps on the threshold of love, hoping – if we stay there long enough – that the door may be opened to us.

'Thus it is possible to feel dislike for a person, and yet to be in a state of charity towards him . . .'

The minister of Selskay was interrupted at this point in the writing of his sermon. There was a knock at the door. He put down his pen and called, 'Come in.' No-one answered. Finally he went to the door and opened it. Tilly Scabra stood there. She muttered something that John Gillespie could not quite catch, but he did hear the words 'trouble' and 'help'.

The Scabras were a family that lived at the other end of the island. Even among the crofters and fishermen, who are never snobs, they were poorly regarded. Arthur Scabra, the minister had heard, was not really a bad man, and in fact he had liked him the once or twice they had met and chatted on the road. But this Arthur had come home from doing his National Service taking with him a trollop of a girl from Leith or Granton, and whether they were married or not nobody knew, but anyway they took up residence with Arthur's old mother. Old Mrs Scabra did not live to see her granchildren, but she can't have ended her days in tranquillity; for Angela, Arthur's woman, was not long in showing her mettle. Debts and drink and quarrelling – among such squalid unknown things the old woman took ill, and turned her face to the wall, and breathed her last. Arthur and Angela, after the funeral, found the 'kist' under the bed with the mother's savings in it: a bundle of notes, a few sovereigns, a gold brooch. Then for a month or so Anscarth was the gayest house in the island, with parties two or three nights a week (to which all the young men went, of course); and Angela had new flashy clothes, and new ornaments of appalling ugliness littered the mantelpiece and sideboard. Of course the money gave out, and then the parties stopped, except for the weekend half-bottle and the home-brew; and at Anscarth it was back to the old cycle of debts, drink and quarrelling.

The good folk of Selskay held up their hands at the stories of the on-goings at Anscarth, which up to then had been an austere respectable place. Between one lurid story and another, Angela gave birth to her first-born, a boy.

The sad thing was, she had dragged Arthur down with her. Before going away to his calling-up, Arthur Scabra had been a quiet hardworking boy. He came back after three years utterly changed, and this Jezebel from the street-corners with him. From that day on Arthur had never put a hand to plough or oar. The creature wasn't ill, that was obvious – he could forage all day among the seaweed for whelks or driftwood, in rain or sun – it was just that he had lost the taste for work. 'Arthur Scabra doesn't incline work,' said an old crofter to the minister, and spat, and laughed.

They managed to live, all the same. Hardly a winter passed without another little Scabra filling the cradle in the corner of the house. The dreariness, the drink, the fighting went on monotonously, among periods of tranquillity. If things got too oppressive indoors, Arthur would wander along the shore for an hour or two, probing in this pool and that swathe of seaweed. Then after a time one of the little ones would appear on the banks above and shout across the sand, 'Dad, come on, your dinner's ready.' . . .

Then Arthur would come slowly back, and gather the bairn into his arms, and kiss it. And together they would stoop under the chattering wailing laughing soup-smelling lintel of Anscarth.

One winter little Tilly appeared on earth, and opened her eyes, and wailed. It was the minister's predecessor who had, out of charity, gone to the croft and baptized her; for the Scabras never went to the kirk.

Now here she stood, some sixteen years later, on the doorstep of the manse, muttering something about 'fighting' and 'blood'.

'You'd better come in,' said Rev. John Gillespie.

Extracts from the Diary of a Minister

I knew it would come, sooner or later. They are trying to marry me off. It is the youngest daughter of Fiord who has been chosen. At least, her old madam of a mother has chosen her to be the lady of the manse. Three times this month a note has come from Fiord – through the post, if you please: 'We would be very happy,' said the first note, 'if you could find time to come to tea on Friday afternoon. There will be no other guests. Bet has been baking a cake with cherries in it. We know you like that' . . . I couldn't go – I had this presbytery meeting in the town. The second invitation, a week later, I accepted. A drearier afternoon I have rarely put in. There we sat round the table in the parlour, eating the cherry-cake and sipping tea: Mrs Dale the hostess, and Mrs Hunda the doctor's wife, and Bet. Pressed, I said the cake was very good (so it was). The conversation was mostly about the wickedness of strikers, the scandalous things that were shown on TV, Arthur Scabra's laziness . . . Almost before I knew it the ladies had withdrawn and I found myself alone with Bet Dale. The poor girl had been instructed to put on an impressive show – it was all chatter, giggles, blushes, long silences. I couldn't stand much of that. 'My respects to your mother,' I said. 'The cake was marvellous. Thank you.' . . . She gave me a last hurt look. Then I went.

What she told old madam I do not know. All was not yet lost. Another billet-doux a few days later through the letter-box: 'We *did* enjoy your company that afternoon last week, especially Bet.

She hasn't stopped talking about it since. Bet, I know, is intelligent, and she is starved of serious conversation in this island. So *please* come to tea on Friday afternoon, 4 p.m.' . . . Starved of conversation! Bet's destiny, I'm sure, lies in a farmhouse, with children and cheese-making and the growing of roses. She would be deadly miserable in a house like this. I wrote this morning: 'Dear Mrs Dale, Thank you for your invitation. Unfortunately I am not able to accept. I find that afternoon tea is bad for my digestion.' . . .

I think I have made at least two more enemies in Selskay; and one of them quite powerful.

Now it is Mr James Wasdale the merchant having a go, on behalf of his daughter Rosemary who sings in the choir.

Rosie is a more interesting girl than Bet Dale, though much plainer. I sense depths in her. She might suddenly do something unexpected – goodness knows what. She has a high true sweet soprano.

What did I find on my doorstep a few weeks ago but a bottle of Beaujolais, well wrapped against the eyes of passers-by. No note to say who the donor was. The mystery was explained that same evening when I went to the shop for my tobacco: 'O, Mr Gillespie, and did you get the wine all right? . . . Well, I thought you might like it. Rosie called with it, but you were out. No, no, of course not, you mustn't pay – it's a gift. A pleasure, Mr Gillespie.' . . . A few days more, and the second cannon in the campaign was fired – Rosie at the door with a parcel: beautiful crisp brown paper, virgin string. She held it out to me. 'For you, Mr Gillespie,' she said . . . 'But what is it? Who is it from?' . . . 'It's a fair-isle jersey. I knitted it. I'm a good knitter. I didn't knit it for you. My father said I was to take it here, to you, as a present. So here it is.' . . . I said I had plenty of jerseys. I thanked her. But really, if it was for giving away, somebody else who needed it should have it – Jake Sandside, for example, or Arthur Scabra. 'I think so too,' she said. 'But please, you take it, and give it to one of them. Then I can tell my father I handed it over at the manse door.' She is a strange honest girl. I like her, and I think she respects me, but her affections are elsewhere

. . . I gave the jersey to Jake Sandside who has no shirt under his jacket.

The last dying shot in the campaign was fired today. Mr Wasdale the merchant comes to me, very troubled, after closing-time. 'It's about Rosie, you see, Mr Gillespie. I'm worried about her. Perhaps if you spoke to her. I'll tell you what the position is, as far as I can make it out.' . . . Rosie, it seems, has fallen for somebody quite unsatisfactory – none other than that great growling bear of a fisherman called Gurness who lives alone in a hut on the point. Sometimes, it seems, she isn't home all night. Mr Wasdale is very very worried – Gurness is a mean violent man. It is terrible, terrible. He never thought his Rosie, etc.

I promised to speak to Rosie about it. But what right have I to put my blundering hands upon that most delicate and subtle web, the heart's affections?

This is the saddest of all – old sweet balmy Miss Fidge, the seacaptain's daughter, who lives in the big granite house on the side of the hill, has taken a fancy to me! That it should come to this! I noticed the first onset of affection about a month ago, as she was leaving the church after the morning service. (She has been a devoted church-woman all her life.) Instead of the slight formal bow to me, as she passed, she lingered, she was all smiles and crinkles, she got in the way of other worshippers who were following her. 'A dear beautiful sermon,' she said. 'O how it touched my heart!' And I trying to nod and smile goodbye to this one and that one and the other one. 'You are a gifted young preacher – greatly gifted – the hearts of everyone were so touched – I could tell – O yes, indeed.' In fact it had been a rather poor sermon, not in my usual earthy-subtle style at all; a disappointment to me at the time of writing and at the time of delivery; not one for my book of collected sermons, to be published when I am ninety years old and past caring what anybody thinks. 'A little spiritual gem!' . . . 'Well, thank you, Miss Fidge, God bless you' (eager to get back into the church and have a word with the beadle about the faulty heating). 'You are a dear good young man. I bless the day you came to Selskay. I feel that in some way you are a son to me, a spiritual offspring.' . . . It was time to bolt after that. Old Flaws the beadle must have noticed my blushes . . . And so it has gone on even unto this present: that gray austere old lady dotes on me. What she has left of tenderness is spent on me. She monopolizes me after the morning services every Sunday now – the other parishioners never get a chance at all with her. It is touching – sometimes when she beams at me a vanished ghost of beauty – that must have been fifty years ago – flits across her tired face. It suddenly occurred to me yesterday that, in her present frame of mind, she might easily leave me everything in her will. That would be terrible! – she has poor cousins, I hear, in Gateshead and South Shields. God bless you, Miss Fidge. This little last blossoming of earthly affection is touched somehow, I think, by 'caritas', the divine love; which should however be centred on no single individual but should hold out arms to the whole universe: in the manner of the heroes of God.

Last night after tea one of the Scabra girls came to the manse. Her mother and father had been fighting over at Anscarth – an old story, but Tilly seemed to be frightened. I took her hand to comfort her. My heart trembled for the trembling child, with pity, yes, but – I recognize it now – with something different and new and utterly unexpected.

She sat beside me in the car.

When we got to Anscarth all was sweetness and light again. But Arthur's smiling face had a long scratch down it.

The younger children were asleep all about the slatternly place: rosy tranquil tear-stained faces.

Angela made me a cup of coffee. 'That Tilly!' she said. 'Fancy disturbing you like that, Mr Gillespie! I'll talk to her, the little bissom.' . . .

For Tilly was no longer there. She was ashamed, obviously, of raising that false alarm; she had made herself scarce.

That white face kept me from sleep all last night.

A FRIDAY OF RAIN

I might have known. I might truly have known. What a fool. I might as well have sat on my arse. I might.

She must have crossed over last night or early this morning. That's it. She must have been in Quoylay all last week, taking her stink and her whine with her from door to door.

Friday is my day. Friday's the day I do my rounds. The whole wide world knows that, including Annie. Friday, Jake Sandside's day. She, and anybody else, can have the rest of the week.

Selskay, on a Friday, belongs to me.

It is not grudged, the bite I get here, the sup I get there. It is well recognized what I did in my youth, for my country, in His Majesty's navy, twenty-one years, man and boy, four war years and more, among burnings and drownings. They know, all right. People don't forget. (Well, some do.) There's always a copper for an old sailor, a pair of boots, a plate of broth. Friday, Sailor Jake's day. Now this old bag has come poaching.

I'll speak to the laird. I will.

I'll speak to Mr Gillespie up at the manse, though he has troubles of his own. Still, a word.

What's she ever done, except frighten children, and steal eggs, and pretend she had the evil eye when a fist or a face in a doorway was hard? An old bag. A boil on a decent community.

I served my country. There's the discharge papers and the fifteen bob a week pension (that wouldn't keep a libbed cat of course, but still).

In the shop, early on, I got the first hint of something wrong. 'Nothing today,' he says, his mouth like a trap. 'Sorry. No broken biscuits. The end of the ham has been taken.' So, there was an intruder.

'Good day to you,' I said with straight sailor shoulders and a salute. I keep my courtesy in every trying circumstance.

He turned away to his desk and cash-book.

It began to look then as if the wolf in the fold was Annie. But she had never been known to come on a Friday before . . .

I stood on the road outside. It had begun to rain. Where now? If

I could track the old bag down, I could – not for the first time – put the weight of my tongue on her. My English words, that I learned in the navy, always make her uncomfortable.

I did not see Orphan Annie anywhere in the village. She must be calling, I concluded, at farms in the hinterland. She would be leaving the village till evening. Good thinking – then the roadmen would be home with their wages. The baskets of fish would be on the pier.

A raindrop hit the back of my hand.

The morning village was mine, at least.

Jake, old friend, your wits are losing their edge. Mr Sandside, you are drinking too much of that wine and meth. The village had been broached before breakfast time. The great queen Annie had hardly waited for the women to get their knickers on. She was out of the village, loaded, and up among the hill farms.

It was 'Nothing today, sorry', all along the village street, like an echo. 'Nothing. Call next week.' I am always polite. Perhaps they are tired of me, after thirty years at the game. I touch my cap. 'Is there any firewood to break? Kittens to be drowned?' There was nothing.

Sure enough, there was the imprint of an ancient boot in the mud, beside the pump. Her Majesty had stopped for a drink.

Outside the doctor's that big black-and-white dog took me by the sleeve. I put a stone in his mouth.

Despised and rejected.

I had been confined to the house Monday and Tuesday with rheumatism in my leg. It wasn't better still.

Up among the crofts the evil old mouth would be whining for eggs, and a bit of butter – and saying, 'Oh, that's the sweetest ale, now, I swear to God I ever put in my mouth.' The locust is in my field. While I slept it came.

In that village, only at the hardest door did I get charity. Gurness the fisherman, he gave me a fill of my pipe and a clutch of matches.

It is very strange, Friday and fishermen. They are always kinder and gentler on a Friday. How is that? Do they still remember their patron, Peter, cursing and swearing and denying that Friday morning in the courtyard of the high priest, while inside the

Man of Sorrows began to enter upon his agony? All the generations
of fishermen have been sorry ever since. The Catholics have their
fish on a Friday. There might be something in it. I don't know.

'Don't stuff in any more shag,' said Gurness. 'That's half an
ounce you've taken. Your pipe'll break.'

'Much obliged,' I said, and touched my cap-brim. 'It's Friday.'

'What is there about me?' said Gurness. 'You're not the first this
morning. That old hag – what's her name, Annie – she was here
when I was having my breakfast. I gave her a piece of salt fish to get
rid of her.'

I saluted again, and left Gurness pulling his sea-boots on, with a
spatter of rain on his window.

It amounted to this: I might not starve at the weekend, but I
would be on iron rations: a turnip, limpets, tap water.

Which road had the old trash taken? She was quick as an otter,
but she couldn't cover the whole island in one morning. If I took
the opposite way, there might still be a picking or two. Also, there
was the chance I might meet her half way, near the crossroads.
Then I would have something to say to her ladyship.

I reckoned, in this rain, she would take the fertile end of the
island first, the region of the big farms. Towards nightfall she
might drop among the hill crofts, for a last over-brimming to her
bag. It was the poverty-road for me, then.

I was right. I got a sup of oatmeal and butter-milk here, and a
dried cuithe there, and an end of cheese in the other place. Near
Anscarth the kids threw clods at me. It was worth enduring that
black earth-storm to discover that the ale they had put on last
weekend was ready and was being broached by Arthur and Angela;
and in the middle of the day too, with a teething infant yelling from
a crib in the corner. They are kind and reckless, as far as their
means go, at the croft of Anscarth at ale-time. So, I got my cup
filled maybe half-a-dozen times . . . The climate suddenly changes,
for no reason, at an ale-session. Arthur and Angela turned from
singing and laughing to say, had I heard about their lass Tilly and
the minister, and what folk were saying, but they didn't care, Mr
Gillespie was a fine man. Arthur said that was right. His daughter
too, Tilly, she was a gem of a lass. Tilly and John (fancy, to call the

minister by his Christian name!) were very fond of each other. But Angela said that Tilly was a little tart . . . At that Arthur and Angela glared above their ale-mugs at each other: but only for five seething seconds. Then it was time to dip in the mugs again.

Rain drops shone and tinkled from the lintel. Outside the Anscarth children played in the downpour.

I told Arthur and Angela some of my war-time adventures in the Med and the North Atlantic and the Arctic. My only ambition, in those terrible times, had been to come home to my own folk, with my wound, and throw myself on their care, and so end my days in peace. But even that – I said – was not to be. A thief from another island, that very day, was taking the bite out of my mouth. 'O never never,' I said, and I cherished the gathering glitters in my eyes, 'give old Annie Ross, that bitch of hell, a bite.'

Angela, to comfort me, filled up my mug again.

The truth is this – I hardly remember leaving Anscarth. I didn't mind the rain on the road at all – it fell on me like wild sweet dew. They make their ale strong at Anscarth. (It's a good job old Mrs Scabra, who was president of the temperance guild in her day, isn't there to see their kirn and their mugs.) The sole of one of my boots was going flip-flap, splash-splurge, along the road and through puddles. For half-an-hour I didn't mind Annie Ross at all. Let her get what she could. We have a short time only.

I lost my joy in the doorway of Fiord. A face looked at me as if it had lain for a month in a deep-freeze. *Off with you.* And a dog growling inside. Rain bounced off the flagstones. The door quivered in its frame. A virtue went out of me.

I gave myself once more to the road and the weather. The rain had begun to search to the roots. My sinus throbbed, my left lung whistled. Drink should never be taken before the sun is under the yard-arm. Mr Sandside, when will you ever learn?

Now the weather began to concentrate on my rheumatism. It plucked at my thigh-bone till the whole left leg, from haunch to knee, made mad music. On I went, hirpling and hobbling. Bubbles gathered and burst at the lace-holes of my boots. I stood against a wall to add my dribble to the sky-tumults.

I edged, after a time, into the barn of Ingarth.

I took off my jacket and trousers and drawers and boots, and crept under the straw. I hung inside a yellow shaking wave. After a time I must have drowsed . . .

Words dragged me back out of a good sea-dream. *Where are you? Come on, Sailor Jake. I saw you going into the barn. No use hiding in the straw. I've got something here to warm you.*

When a man is old and wretched, and near death, shame leaves him. I raised naked shoulders through the straw. Rosie Houton stood there with a steaming bowl between her hands.

I put my face among the fumes. That broth was well worth the lecture I got. *Been at the meth again. No use denying it. Folk are getting tired of you. Very very tired. That's a fact. Do you realize what you're doing to yourself?*

Spoonful after spoonful after spoonful of the thick golden-gray stuff I put into my mouth. I burned my tongue. Bits of crust stuck in my beard. I rose and fell in the wave of straw.

Killing yourself, that's what you're doing. Your pension – spending it all on meth and cheap wine. And wandering about in all weathers.

The spoon rasped the bottom of the bowl.

'I have not drunk any meth,' I said. 'And it's Friday. I always go out on a Friday.'

Listen to that chest of yours! – You've got severe bronchitis. It might turn into pneumonia. Half-starved you are too. How much of your pension have you got left? For goodness sake buy some bread and cheese and margarine. Let me hear of you drinking meth again, I'll report you to the authorities. They'll sort you out. They'll put you in their home.

I thanked Mrs Houton for her wonderful soup.

The good woman; while I slept she had taken my clothes indoors and dried them at her fire. They steamed gently on her arm.

'You better go home soon,' said Rosie. 'The rain's stopped. Fred's in the village. Fred doesn't like tramps in his barn.'

'I am *not* a tramp. I am a pensioned sailor of the Royal Navy,' I said with as much dignity as a naked man in straw can summon.

You would never think Rosie Houton was the daughter of that misery down at the shop. She turned round while I put my clothes on. She knelt and tied the string on my boots in the barn door. *Now remember, straight home with you. No more drink.*

'Don't give anything to Annie Ross,' I said from the end of the farm road. The sun had come out. The pools on the road were burning mirrors. The rain had crossed the Sound to Torsay. The hills of Torsay were hung with sackcloth – the Selskay air was purest crystal.

I met Fred Houton near the smithy. He stopped for a word. I didn't tell him about the barn and broth. No sense in taking the edge off their charity. (He gave me a shilling.)

I called at the big house where Miss Fidge lives alone. Miss Fidge likes sailors. Her father was skipper of a coaster. Miss Fidge gave me two slices of ginger cake in a paper poke. I enjoy Miss Fidge's ginger cake with a cup of tea.

I was done in. I was completely buggered. The Anscarth ale slumbered still in the marrow of my bones. The weight of old rain was on me. Bad thoughts too wear out the spirit.

My feet dragged homewards. The rat began to gnaw again at my haunch-bone.

I wondered whether I should call at the manse. Tilly Scabra stood outside, on tiptoe, scouring the study window. Her little fist went round and round and then another pane glittered among the salted panes. Officially she's the manse housekeeper. Things are building up to a crisis there. There's to be a meeting of the kirk session on Tuesday evening next, I hear. I decided not to intrude upon Mr Gillespie and his troubles.

I turned the corner and there was my own cottage down beside the loch.

I took the silver whistle out of my trouser pocket and blew two blasts – a signal to the whole of Selskay isle that Sailor Jake was nearing port.

The dog of Skaill barked in the distance.

I *was* tired. I fell asleep in the rocking-chair beside the dead fire, a thing I hardly ever do so early in the evening.

When I woke up it was night. My paraffin lamp was lit. A few flames tumbled in the hearth.

There had been an intruder.

The room was different. Someone had shifted a chair. The water bucket was filled to brimming. There were strange shapes on the bed.

I hirpled over to investigate. A turnip – potatoes – eggs in a stone jar – butter in a saucer – a pot of rhubarb jam – bannocks and oatcakes – a poke of tea – a poke of sugar – brown serviceable boots – a jersey with darnings at elbow and neck.

What good ghost had come through the night to visit me?

I handled each item with lust and gratitude. All was well. The weekend was saved. My pipe with its tight knot of tobacco was on the mantelpiece. If only I had a sup of wine, I wouldn't have called the queen my cousin. (My tongue, after that Anscarth ale – need I say it – was like a flap of old leather.)

A presence was standing in the door with a bottle.

'I thought you were never going to waken,' said Annie Ross, and set the wine on the table. 'I had a job getting drink out of old Wasdale at this time of night.'

I couldn't say a thing.

'I heard,' said Annie Ross, 'that you were bad with rheumatics. A man told me that on the pier at Kirkwall yesterday. *Laid up*, he said – *the sailor's in his bed not able to stir. Looks as if this might be the end of him* . . . So I thought, *Tomorrow's his day. Friday. And what'll Jake do if he can't get round the houses?* I thought, *I better see what's what.* So I got a lift in Tomison's lobster boat this morning early.'

John Sandside, you are a fool.

'There's your takings,' said Annie, 'over there, on the bed. It's a fair haul. Them boots should see you through till the spring. I got enough money for a bottle of wine. There's your change.' . . . She put a couple of coins on the dresser.

You are a slanderer, John Sandside. You have taken away the character of an angel of light.

'It's started to rain again,' said Annie. 'Can I bide to my supper?'

'Yes,' I said. 'Thank you, Annie.'

'I did it for the sake of the old times,' said Annie. 'Though you haven't got a good word to say for me a many a time, and you blacked my eye the last Hamnavoe market. I did it because we were sweethearts once.'

'Forgive me, dear,' I said.

We had a good supper of bannocks and cheese and jam, and we finished the wine.

Annie stayed the night. She got a passage across the Sound in Gurness's boat on the Saturday morning.

My rheumatics, I'm sorry to say, are none better.

SEED, DUST, STAR

A community maintains itself, ensures a continuance and an identity, through such things as the shop, the kirk, the stories told in smithy and tailor-shop, the ploughing match, agricultural show, harvest home, the graveyard where all its dead are gathered. (It is the same with all communities – city or island – but the working-out of the ethos of a community is best seen in microcosm, as in the island of Selskay.) Most of all the community ensures its continuance by the coming together of man and woman. There will be a new generation to plough and fish, with the same names, the same legends, the same faces (though subtly shifted, and touched with the almost-forgotten, the hardly-realized), the same kirkyard.

The place where the community lives is important, of course, in perpetuating its identity. There is that cave under the crag with a constant drip of fresh water from its ceiling; a seaman called Charlie was thrown into the cave by a surge, miraculously, when his ship foundered one day in the year 1824, and Charlie lived for a week on the sweet cave-drops before he found courage to climb up to the crofts above. So any place is enriched with quirks of nature and of chance, that make it unique . . . That the same hill was there ten thousand years ago, and will still stand solid under the blue-and-white surge of sky in ten thousand years' time, moves even the coldest islanders to wonderment with mysteries of permanence and renewal (though the hills are shadows too). And at night, in the north-east, the same star shines here as everywhere else in the northern hemisphere; but here alone it smoulders on the shoulder of the hill Foldfea and sparkles in Susill burn, and puts a glim on the hall of the laird with its brief heraldry.

The people themselves are moulded by the earth contours and the shifting waters they live among. They are made of the same dust as the hills they cultivate. It would be sentimental to say the islanders love the island they live in. Nowadays many of them say they do, and genuinely in some cases; but their great-grandfathers had an altogether different relationship with the land and the sea. They saw no 'beauty' at all; at least, if they did, no record of it has come down to us. Men and the elements had a fierce dependence on each other, a savage thrust and grappling, that was altogether different from what we commonly think of as 'love' in these gentler times. Perhaps their attitude to their women was not so very different. They would grow old; there must be a new strong generation to bring in harvest and consider the drift of haddocks; so a wife was taken as a promising seed-vessel, not a creature of transient scents and gleamings and softnesses.

The croft children came weeping into time, one after another. So the ancestral acres remained 'real', and might not still – through barrenness or bad luck or improvidence – crumble into shadow. The love that croft parents two hundred years ago put on their children had a desperateness and depth in it that modern islanders hedged with security can hardly conceive of.

Yet who could bear to root a child in the womb, and have it cherished there and brought out into time, who stopped to consider for a moment what grief, pain, disgrace, violence, destitution, madness he was releasing into the world; if not for this immediate one, then inevitably, by natural shifts and permutations, for some or other of his descendants, even in the course of a century or two? No family tree from the beginning but has had put upon it, this generation or that, every variety of suffering. These outweigh the little compensatory joys – the boy with his lure and line, the linkings of lovers, the old man's pipe and ale.

There must be a starker more compelling summons into life than anything imagined by either the 'realists' of art and fiction or the 'romantics'.

For the Greeks, the actions of men were shadows projected by archetypes. The bread that we sow and reap is a tastelessness in comparison to that 'orient and immortal wheat'. The weave we put on our bodies, however comfortable and beautiful and well-cut – what are they to 'the heaven's embroidered cloths'? All the elements we handle fleetingly 'is diamond, is immortal diamond'. And all loves and affections become meaningful only in relation to Love itself. The love of a young man and girl in a small island is cluttered always with jealousy, lewdness, gossipings in the village store. But the mystics insist that Love itself 'moves the stars'. They say that, in spite of the terror and pain inseparable from it, 'all shall be well' – in the isolate soul, and in the island, and in the universe.

The meanest one in the community feels this occasionally; he could not suffer the awful weight of time and chance and mortality if he didn't; a sweetness and a longing are infused into him, a caring for something or someone outside his shuttered self.

Mr James Wasdale the merchant locked up his shop and rattled the door twice, to make quite sure.

On a Tuesday, twenty years previously, Paula had died. Every Tuesday therefore, when it was weather, Mr Wasdale visited the kirkyard and stood beside Paula's tombstone for a decent time. Then he touched the stone and came away.

The sun was almost down. The chiselled gilt letters filled with shadow. Mr Wasdale turned from the dust of his wife with one cold finger.

He walked for almost a mile into a magnificent sunset. He passed Sailor Jake's hovel. He passed the empty manse whose windows brimmed with cold fire. (The new minister and his family had not yet moved in.) Down below, at the shore, the croft of Anscarth was sunk in shadow: a hand put a lamp in the window.

Mr Wasdale walked on.

Before him one gable and chimney of a croft house detached itself from a cluster of smouldering green hillocks. Rosie was there, inside, hidden – his daughter who had left him for an ignorant poor crofter. There was a child in the cradle, and another – so he had heard – in her body. He held no communication whatsoever with the people of Ingarth. They got their provisions from the Tennants' travelling shop every Monday.

Mr Wasdale took a walk most evenings, before his supper;

always in the other direction though, towards the crags and the sea. Why had he come this way tonight? He hesitated. He would not go a step further. He imagined for a moment what it would be to knock at the door of Ingarth. He smiled. He would rather lose a hundred pounds than do that. But, standing between the dead and the unborn, he was moved a little; as if, after long drought, a crofter had come out of the rust of his stable and smelt rain in the wind.

Mr Wasdale turned. He walked back through the darkening island. Jake Sandside leaned, puffing a pipe, against the door-post of his hut. Mr Wasdale raised his hand. Sailor Jake looked the other way.

The kindness that he felt every Tuesday for his dead wife (in spite of repeated meannesses dealt out to her while she was alive, in the name of thrift), his possessiveness and ambition for his daughter Rosie – and they were the only people, apart from his mother, that he had ever cared for in any way – that 'love' still existed. He would not deny it. But it was different now. It had nothing whatever to do with money or prestige. Age and estrangement and death had removed the seed from his keeping; it was part now of the precarious continuing life of the island.

A star shone out at the shoulder of Foldfea. His feet stirred the dark dust.

The village was all lighted squares and darkness and sea-sounds when he came back once more among the houses.

Mr Wasdale fitted his key carefully into the lock.

WRITINGS

Anscarth, Selskay,
12 August

Dear Tony, You have read about it in all the papers, of course, so there's no point in repeating the stark fact that I am out of the kirk. A month ago I resigned – it might have been braver if I had hung on until they sacked me. But I have caused enough distress to everyone. Let's hope there'll be no more fireworks display from the newspapers. (I nearly throttled the last two reporters who called at the manse.) I'm living with Tilly's folk at a croft called Anscarth, just above the beach; but not permanently; I hope to get a place of our own soon, preferably before the baby comes. The Scabras – that's Tilly's folk – are a broody family: the house is in tumult from morning to night. It's small too – Tilly and I have to share a back room with two other infants. It's as different as can be from the silence of the manse: the situation calls for more sweetness of soul than I possess. 'Dear God', I pray a dozen times a day – seething inwardly – 'give me patience.' . . . Besides which Angela (the mother – she hails from Edinburgh) is forever brewing and sampling the fruits of her labour. And the old man is forever hanging around. To put it brutally, he is lazy. But there's a gentleness and a kindness about him that puts an ex-parson like me to shame.

What am I doing, then? How do I earn a living? The answer is that I am earning not a black penny; but I hope soon to be a breadwinner, for I have made a start at learning to be a fisherman. My tutor is Tilly's brother, a pleasant 19-year-old called Jerome. (The Scabras all have grand names, to compensate maybe for their tatters and crusts.) Jerome at present is fishing with Bert Gurness, a surly chap who owns a boat called *Thistle*. Jerome intends to break with Gurness and fish on his own account, with me as his partner. (We're already bargaining for a yawl – I think I have enough saved up to buy it – J. says she's a good boat.) Jerome's difficulty at this minute is to make the actual break with Gurness. I should think there's no problem. Gurness pays him only £7 a week. But J. is so shy. However, I've screwed up his courage for him as well as I can. Today is the day of the Agricultural Show in the island. Jerome means to give notice to Gurness among the cows and the roosters and the cheap-jacks.

I shudder to think what Professor Allardyce is saying about me. But there may be more charity in the world than I think now, in my present morbid state, after my dealings with elders and (especially) reporters.

I spent this morning down at the shore, selecting stones to weight our lobster creels: we have about fifty of these in the shed outside. I seemed to be alone in the island – every Selskay able-bodied person has gone to the show in a field at the heart of the island. While I was stooping and rising at the beach, selecting stones, I could hear the sounds of the fair surging and ebbing on the wind. All the Scabras have gone. Tilly wouldn't miss the annual junketings for anything. Angela has even whipped wee Marilyn out of the crib. So I sit in a blessed silence writing to you, my dear old friend of the days of our theological studies.

If you see my mother, give her my deep and genuine love. I wrote to her and all my folk a month ago, but have had no answer. I must have hurt them bitterly.

Do not you forget me, or the world would be a sterile promontory indeed.

So, picture me now, old friend, with a speckled black-and-white fisherman's jersey on me, and trousers stiff and gray with salt, working day after day on the shore, under the immense northern sky.

I try to keep off the road as much as possible, for I am an embarrassment to certain of the island folk. Some of my erstwhile choristers, for example, swerve away on to a sheep track when they sight me on the horizon. The shopkeeper – one of my elders in the old days – serves me with tobacco as though I was a spy or a criminal. There is one sweet balmy old lady, Miss Fidge, who makes no difference. 'Your sermon last Sabbath, my dear, it was so beautiful, a masterpiece . . .' I have not preached to Miss Fidge, or anybody else, for three months . . . In time, I hope, the island will forget, and accept me for what I have become.

Even in Anscarth, to begin with, I caused much uncertainty and some embarrassment. A minister, come down in the world, because of their Tilly, and now come to live with them, among all their uninhibited noise and squalor and on-goings! The awe didn't last long. But I do believe that Angela doesn't swear quite as much as she used to.

Rev. Anthony McLean, I a poor fisherman ask for your prayers and continuing concern. I know you will not plead with me to repent and come back to the fold: that would be impossible, because in a sense I have never left the fold. Not one jot or tittle of any belief has been shaken by what has happened. And if I were to 'repent', in that vulgar sense of the word, what would become of

Tilly and the child that's not yet born? I love her more now than that first evening when she stood on the manse doorstep, with tears in her eyes, mumbling something about a fight.

When I dropped in on Orkney last weekend, all my vague knowledge of these northern islands was confined to an 850-year-old cathedral, heroic lifeboatmen, some neolithic stones on a wine-dark moor. Then in my hotel in the main town, Kirkwall – it calls itself, proudly, a 'city' – I was told that I simply *must* visit one of the agricultural shows. There are, it seems, a whole cluster of shows about now. The Selskay show was to be on Tuesday. I booked on the little nine-seater plane and on Tuesday morning was set down in a field half-a-mile from where the show was.

It proved to be one of the most hectic days in my life. (I had come to Orkney expecting peace, silence, solitude.) I made a tour of the animal pens, and viewed superb bulls, handsome orange-tinted sheep, cockerels in cages giving the sun a ringing salute every minute, well-groomed ponies, new gleaming farm machinery . . . All the islanders were there in their Sunday best – and they know how to dress, believe me – and the girls' complexions and skins would break the hearts of the world's leading cosmeticians.

In an adjacent field, like old mushrooms, were the booths of itinerant showmen from the south.

I had a snack in the tea tent, presided over by a gracious lady, Mrs Dale from the farm of Fiord. A snack, did I say? In London a meal like it would have cost three pounds. There were Orkney cheese, Orkney oat-cakes, Orkney crab, Orkney ham, Orkney chicken. At the end of the gastronomic treat the bill came to about fifty pence!

Later I was glad of that lining on my stomach.

How delightful to move about in a crowd and know that not a soul is there with the intention of 'doing' you or conning you in any way. There was one exception, an old ex-navy man, but he was such a delightful yarn-loaded character that I didn't mind passing a few minutes with him and parting with five bob – it was worth it. (By the way, why don't some of our writers hard up for a theme get in touch with such folk as Jack Sandside, or 'Sailor Jack', as he is affectionately known in Selskay?)

Drawn by a crowd of merry youths in the entrance flap, drinking beer out of cans, I entered the whisky tent.

Because of the press of farmers in good thick tweeds, it was quite a feat to struggle through the marquee to the counter. I was greeted from far and near as if I had lived all my life in the island. Whiskies were set before me by men I had never seen before – not your English tot either, but a brimming noggin of Orkney malt whisky. It was as if I was tasting the essence of all I had seen and experienced that day. It takes a long time to learn how to handle the elixir.

Merriment, song, reminiscence all round me; and I was made to feel at home in the midst of it all.

Only one incident marred a perfect day. Two of the locals, a fisherman and a farmer, had a fight. In the midst of the revelry they suddenly fell on each other, and began to beat the daylights out. The crowd in the marquee seemed to expect this, and even to enjoy it. The tall strong fisherman seemed to be no favourite. Shouts went up for 'Fred' to finish the b— off. It was quite violent while it lasted; but eventually the police arrived; and the two pugilists were handcuffed, still struggling and swearing, and frogmarched away . . . I feel that one might have to live in a place like this for a decade at least before understanding of the folk begins to dawn – as the doors of the Black Maria opened to receive them, Fred and the fisherman were smiling at each other, and they seemed to be trying to do a difficult thing – embrace with shackled hands . . .

I was assured that the two were old enemies. They used to fish together in the same boat, but had quarrelled two years previously, and since then were at daggers drawn. The Selskay men, smiling, pushed more nips of the island whisky in front of me . . .

When I went out into the fresh air later, the whole bucolic festival began to waver about me like a merry-go-round. It's like I said – it might take ten years to understand these folk, but it takes a whole lifetime to learn how to hold their heroic whisky.

Two Selskay men, Frederick John Houton (27), crofter, Ingarth, Selskay, and Albert Sigurd Gurness (31), fisherman, Ness Cottage,

Selskay, appeared in court last Tuesday charged with committing a breach of the peace at the Selskay Agricultural Show on 12th August.

Both pleaded not guilty.

The Procurator Fiscal stated that the alleged offence took place in the beer tent in the course of the afternoon. The two accused assaulted each other with such violence that Gurness's nose was subsequently found to be broken and the lobe of Houton's ear was almost bitten through. There had, it seemed, been bad blood between Houton and Gurness since they had sundered their lobster-fishing partnership two years previously. They were apprehended with some difficulty by the police in the beer tent, and after being handcuffed were taken to the police station in the police van. On the way there they continued to struggle with one another. A blood test showed that both had consumed a considerable quantity of alcohol. They made no comment when charged. Their attitude continued to be so truculent that they were detained at the station overnight. Gurness asked that they be lodged in the same cell, so that 'they could have it out' – a request that had not been complied with.

Both the accused were unrepresented.

Jerome Scabra (19), fisherman, Anscarth, Selskay, stated that he had gone to the show-park about 1 o'clock on the afternoon of the 12th. He always went to the Show but on this occasion he had a particular errand: to tell the accused Gurness that he would no longer be able to help him in his lobster boat after Saturday, as he was intending to go to the fishing with his brother-in-law. He had seen Gurness at the bingo tent, and told him.

Fiscal – Was Gurness drunk at that time?

Scabra – No, sir. At least, he didn't appear to be.

Fiscal – How did Gurness take the news?

Scabra – I'm sorry, I don't follow . . .

Fiscal – I mean, that you would no longer be going lobster-fishing with him after the Saturday.

Scabra – He said there was no need to wait till Saturday. He was giving me the sack, he said, there and then. Then he told me to clear off, he couldn't hear the man shouting the bingo numbers. I asked him for my wages, seven pounds. He said as I had only worked four days that week he was only owing me four pounds. If I came to his hut that night, he said, he would pay me . . .

The witness went on to say that the next time he saw Gurness that day was in the whisky tent. Gurness was standing beside the tent pole drinking with another man. Witness approached Gurness with the intention of placating him – he did not wish them to part on bad terms, as he had a high regard for Gurness as a fisherman and as a person. But before he could reach Gurness through the crowd there was a disturbance at the counter – Fred Houton and a stranger he had never seen before were having a loud disagreement. The next he saw, Gurness had come between them and separated them. But immediately afterwards Houton and Gurness began fighting with each other. He had seen some fights in Selskay, but never any like that. They resisted all attempts on the part of the public to tear them apart. At last the police arrived, and took them both in charge.

Fiscal – Do you think now, that what you had told Gurness earlier, I mean, that you wouldn't be fishing with him any more, had perhaps upset him?

Scabra – It might have. We had both got on well together. He would have difficulty in getting somebody else to fish with him. He is not the most popular man in Selskay. It wouldn't be easy for him to fish in a boat like the *Thistle* alone – dangerous, I should say.

Houton had nothing to say in his own defence.

Gurness stated that it had been a most enoyable fight. He did not know when he had enjoyed a fight more. Everybody should have a fight like that occasionally. It would make for a better island.

The Sheriff said it was disgraceful, when people were gathered together on a festive occasion like an agricultural show, that their pleasure should be spoiled by two drunken brawlers. If they couldn't hold their drink they should leave the stuff alone. He fined them each five pounds.

'After I'm dead, everything of mine goes to Fred Houton of Ingarth, Selskay. The hut, the boat *Thistle* and all gear, the money in the post-office, the furniture such as it is, and all else whatsoever – A. S. Gurness.'

The above document was found in the table drawer of Ness Cottage, Selskay, after the death of Albert Sigurd Gurness in a storm off Borough Ness on the afternoon of 6th November that same year. The deceased was fishing alone at the time. His lobster boat *Thistle* was completely broken up. The body was taken from the sea a week later by two other Selskay fishermen, John Gillespie and Jerome Scabra.

The Burning Harp

A STORY FOR THE EIGHTIETH BIRTHDAY OF NEIL GUNN

Two nights before Yule in the year of 1135 a farmer called Olaf and his wife Asleif and all their household were sitting at supper in their house at Duncansby in Caithness, when a kitchen girl looked up and said that there was a fire in the thatch. They all looked up; the roof was burning. Then Anna a dairy girl pointed; the window was all flame and smoke. 'We should leave the house now,' said Olaf. 'We are not going to die of cold, that much is sure,' said his wife Asleif. The door was two red crackling posts and a crazy yellow curtain.

'I think we are having visitors for Yule,' said an old ploughman who was sitting with an ale-horn in the corner. 'I am too old for such boisterous guests. I think I will go to bed.' While the women ran from wall to wall yelling the old ploughman stretched himself out on a bench and seemed to go to sleep. Olaf and Asleif kissed each other in the centre of the room. 'I am glad of one thing,' said Olaf, 'our son Sweyn is out fishing in the Pentland Firth.'

The whole gable end of the house burst into flames.

Outside there was snow on the ground and beyond the burning house it was very dark. A dozen men one by one threw their torches into the rooted blaze. They took out their daggers and axes in case anyone should try to escape from the fire. A thousand sparks flew about like bees and died in the white midden and the long blue ditch.

A man called Ragnar said, 'There are innocent ones inside, servants and children. We have no quarrel with them. They should be let out.'

Oliver threw a bucket of water over the door. He shouted, 'Servants of Olaf, and any children, you are to come out now.'

A few girls ran out into the night with glaring eyes and rushed past the besiegers and were lost in the darkness beyond. A boy came out. He turned and looked back at the fire once, then he ran laughing after the servants, rising and falling in the snow, wild with excitement.

'I don't think we should have done that,' said Nord. 'These servants will tell the story of the burning all over Caithness. You know how women exaggerate. People here and there will think poorly of us for this night's work. That boy will grow up and remember the burning.'

Now that the girls were out of the house all was much quieter inside. Even the tumult of the flames was stilled a little. In the silence they heard the sound of a voice praying.

'Valt the priest is inside,' said Oliver. 'I had forgotten that he might be here at this time of year. We would not be very popular with the bishop or the monks if Valt were to die. Throw another bucket of water at the door.'

Father Valt came out with a scorched cross between his fingers. There was soot in his beard. He said to Oliver and the other besiegers, 'God pity you, my poor children.' Then he turned and absolved the dead and the dying inside, and walked away slowly towards the church at the shore.

'We didn't get much gratitude out of that priest,' said Nord. 'In my opinion it was a mistake to let a man like that go. With Father Valt it will be hell-fire for all us burners from now until the day he is able to preach no more. We will have no comfort at all, standing in his kirk.'

They heard a few faint harp-strokes through the snorings and belchings of flame.

'It is my opinion,' said Ragnar, 'that there is a poet inside.'

'Well,' said Nord, 'what is a poet more than a miller or a fisherman or a blacksmith?'

'From the sound of the harp,' said Oliver, 'from the way it is being played, it seems to me that the poet in there is none other than Niall from Dunbeath.'

'Well,' said Nord, 'and what about it? What is Niall more than other string-pluckers, Angus say, or Keld, or Harald?'

'Nord,' said Oliver, 'you are very thick in the head. I would keep my mouth shut. Niall is the poet who made the ballad of the silver shoals in the west. He also sang about the boy and the fishing boat – if I am not mistaken that was the first story he told. He was the one too who made us aware of the mysterious well of wisdom. He made that great song about the salmon.'

'It would be a pity indeed, I suppose,' said Nord, 'if the harp of a man like that was to be reduced to a cinder.'

'Nobody in Scotland sings with such purity and sweetness as Niall,' said Oliver. 'We would be shamed for ever if we stopped such a mouth with ashes. The world, we are told, will end in this way, some day soon, in ice and fire and darkness. But how can a harp stroke given to the wind ever perish, even though there are no men left on earth? The gods will hear that music with joy for ever.'

So another bucket of water was thrown over the threshold and the name of the poet Niall was called into the red-and-black dapple inside. Presently an old serene man carrying a harp walked from the burning house into the snow. He seemed not to see the lurid faces all about the door. Honoured, he sought the starlit darkness beyond the lessening circles of flame.

Sealskin

(i)

A sealskin, lying on the rocks – well, he could make use of that all right. Somebody must have dropped it. Simon didn't intend to ask too particularly: put a notice in the window of the general store, for example, or hire the beadle to ring his bell round the parish. Simon rubbed the pelt with his finger. It was a good skin. It might make a waistcoat for his father, he thought, walking back to the croft. His mother might want it for a rug for the best room. He rolled up the skin. He opened the door of the barn. He threw the skin among the low dark rafters.

His mother had the broth poured out. Three of them sat at the table – his father, his mother, himself. His father could work no more because of rheumatism; the trouble had grown much worse this past winter; it was as if his body was newly released from a rack. His mother's only concern was Simon, to see that he was kept warm and well-fed, so that he wouldn't think of taking another woman into the house – at least, not until she herself was dead in the kirkyard. If ever Simon looked at a woman – on the road to the kirk on Sabbath, for example, or when the tinker lasses came to the door with laces and mirrors – a great silent anger came on her. For the rest of that day the old woman spoke to no-one, not even to the dog or the cow. No other woman would share her spinning-wheel and her ale-kirn.

Thank the Lord, she thought, Simon is an ugly boy. That kept some of the parish Jezebels away. Even more important, Simon seemed not to be interested in the lasses at all. That was a great comfort to her.

There had been another son, Matthew, much older than Simon.

One spring he had gone to the whaling in the north-west and never returned. That was ten years ago.

Eventually, she supposed, Simon would have to marry. Well, let him, but only after she was dead.

The old man raised his twisted hand and blessed the meal. They lifted their horn spoons and silently dipped them in the soup bowls.

(ii)

In the afternoon Simon went down to the rocks for limpet bait. He did a little fishing now and then. He struck the limpets from the face of the rock into his wooden bucket with a long blue stone. The bucket was half full when he heard the first delicate mournful cry, a weeping from the waters. He looked across the bay. A girl was kneeling among the waves. She was naked.

Simon left the limpets. He stumbled up the rocks and loose clashing stones. He ran across the links to the croft. The old ones on either side of the fire gaped at him. He took his mother's coat from the nail in the lobby, and ran and slithered down the foreshore to where he had seen the girl. The sea was rising about her. She seemed to be quite exhausted. She didn't even cry out when Simon dragged her by the hair on to a rock. He threw the coat over her. Then he carried her in his arms up to the croft and the fire and the pot of broth.

'What's this?' cried the old woman. 'Where does she come from? Not a stitch on her! A strange naked woman. She doesn't bide here. Out she goes, once she's had a bite to eat.'

The old man nodded, half asleep over the embers.

Once the girl was fed a shiver and flush went over the cold marble of her flesh. She slept for a while in Simon's bed. The old woman, grumbling, looked for woollen garments in her clothes chest. 'That's my Sabbath coat you put about her,' she said. In the late evening the girl awoke and sat beside the fire. She was not a girl from any farm in the island. Simon had never clapped eyes on her at the Hamnavoe market. They spoke to her. They asked her questions. She looked at them and shook her head. She uttered one or two sounds. She pointed through the window at the sea.

She is a very bonny lass, thought the old woman bitterly. She doesn't look at Simon with any kindness at all, so far. But there would be days and nights to come.

'Well,' said the old man, 'I think she's a foreign lass. She doesn't make anything of the English I speak, anyway. I haven't heard of any wrecks from Hoy to Westray this past week, though.'

'She can't bide here,' said the old woman, swilling out the pots with cold water near the open door.

'We're supposed to be Christians,' said the old man, and began to fill his pipe beside the fire.

Simon said he thought they would have to keep the girl for a night or two at least. She could sleep in his bed. There was plenty of warm straw in the barn where he could lie down.

The girl looked timorously at the faces in the firelight – the hostile face of the old woman, the blank face of Simon, the kind suffering face of the old man.

'You'll stay, my dear,' said the old man.

The girl smiled.

The old woman set the iron pot down on the flagstone. It clanged like a passionate bell.

(iii)

The old woman was dead. Her life had dwindled away all summer and autumn like a candle-end. She lay now in her plain cloth-covered coffin with her hands folded over her breast. The old man sat in his chair at the fire. His withered eyes grew brilliant and brimming from time to time; then he would dab at them with a huge red handkerchief. Simon arranged plates of bread and cheese and fowl round the whisky flagon that stood in the centre of the table.

A face looked in at the window and presently James Scott their neighbour from Voe came in. There was a shy knock at the door – more a kind of powerful hand-flutter – and Walter Anderson the blacksmith came in. Presently there was the sound of many random feet on the cobble stones outside – one by one men from every croft in the parish entered the house.

Simon poured whisky into a small pewter goblet for each mourner as he entered.

Everybody spoke in praise of the dead woman: her thrift, her cleanliness, her decency, the golden butter and the black ale she had made.

A horse's hooves clattered outside. A tall man in blackcloth entered, carrying a black book. The room went silent as he entered.

Simon poured whisky for the minister.

'Later,' said the Reverend Jabez Grant. He opened his bible and cleared his throat.

The old man, after two attempts, heaved himself up from his chair to hear the holy words. He hung awkwardly over two sticks.

The minister began to read above the shut waxen face in the coffin.

Through the window Simon could see Mara down at the beach, turning over swathe after swathe of seaweed, probing behind every rock. What was she looking for? Some days she came up with a lobster in her fingers, and once a trout flashed in her hands like living bronze.

'Amen,' said the minister.

(iv)

'I delivered the bairn,' said Martha Gross, 'one night in March. It was a very hard birth. Simon came for me near midnight.'

'Just answer the questions,' said the session clerk, Mr Finlay Groat (who was the general merchant down in the village).

'So back I goes with Simon,' said Martha Gross. 'When we got to the gap in the hills, I could hear the screaming of her. It was such a cold high frightening sound. "Hurry up for God's sake," says Simon.'

'Thank you,' said Rev. Jabez Grant. 'That's all, Martha.'

'It was the hardest birth I was ever at,' said Martha Gross. 'A right bonny bairn when he did come, all the same. Lawful or lawless, that's not for me to say. I do declare he was as bonny a boy as ever I saw.'

The beadle plucked Martha Gross by the sleeve.

'Call Simon Olafson,' said Mr Finlay Groat.

Simon entered the vestry as nervous as a colt in a market ring. He agreed with every proposition they put to him, almost before the words were out, so eager he was to be out of this place of high authority.

Yes, his father Ezekiel Olafson of Corse employed the woman Mara Smith as a servant-lass. Yes, he had carnal knowledge of the said Mara in the barn of Corse, also in the seaward room of Corse, on sundry occasions; once in a cave under the crags. No, he was not married. The said Mara was not married either, to the best of his knowledge. Yes, he was aware that he had offended seriously against God and the kirk. Yes, he was willing to thole any public penance the kirk session might see fit to lay on him.

Simon left the table, dabbing his quicksilver face with the sleeve of his best Sabbath suit.

The girl entered, led by William Taylor the beadle. She put a cold shy look on one after the other of the session. She seemed to have no awareness of the purport of the proceedings at all. She answered the opening questions with a startled askance look, like a seabird on a cliff ledge when men with guns are on the rocks below.

'Look here, woman,' said Mr Finlay Groat at last, 'do you know why you're here?'

She frowned at him.

Their hard questions hung in the air unanswered. Incomprehension grew. The men turned in their chairs, they frowned at each other, they tapped their teeth. A great gulf was fixed between this girl and the kirk session of the parish of Norday in conclave gathered.

They turned away from the girl. They discussed the matter among themselves, in veiled voices. Her origins. Found on the shore. Possibly from a shipwreck. What shipwreck? No shipwreck that winter. Or forcibly got rid of out of some Baltic ship, put ashore in a small boat. Ignorant of the language. Ay, but the holy signs and symbols – the Bible, the christening stone, the black ministerial bands – all Christendom should recognize them. She didn't seem to. A heavy mystery indeed. What then? . . .

'She is said to be a seal woman,' said Walter Anderson (who was the blacksmith and rather fond of the bottle when he was not a member of this holy court).

'Mr Anderson,' said the minister coldly, 'I think we will not adulterate our proceedings with pagan lore.'

Walter Anderson, chidden, muttered into his beard.

'A thing should be said in favour of Simon Olafson,' said Saul Renton the joiner. 'It was a hard thing for Simon to stand here this day. Simon is a good lad. Simon of his charity took this woman, whatever she is, into Corse, and fed her and warmed her. It is more than likely that Simon saved her life. I think – apart from the fornication – it was a good and godly thing that Simon did.'

'Let her step down, I think,' said Mr Finlay Groat. 'We can make nothing of her.'

'Yes,' said the minister. 'I agree.'

There was a concurrence of heads round the table.

The beadle tapped Mara on the shoulder.

Mr Finlay Groat stated that he had a letter from Ezekiel Olafson of Corse. *Reverend elders*, the session clerk read, *I am sore afflicted with rheumatics in haunch and knee, and so unable to obey your summons this day. Simon must thole his punishment. He is in general a dutiful son. He labours hard on the land. There are worse fishermen. His lechery has been towards this one woman alone who has no speech or name. The bairn Magnus is a joy, he greets but seldom and that for a gripe or for a soreness in his gums, like all bairns. Simon has offended and so must be punished. They wish before harvest to be married in the manse if it so be the minister's good will.*

'A righteous letter,' said Walter Anderson.

'The usual thing, I think,' said Mr Finlay Groat. 'Three Sabbaths on the stool of penitence, before all the congregation, to suffer rebuke.'

Another sagacity of heads round the table.

The beadle was sent to bid Simon Olafson and Mara Smith return into the court, to hear judgement.

(v)

Simon and Mara were married in the manse of Norday at Michaelmas that year. The wedding feast was held in the barn of Corse. Guests came from all over the island to it.

The girl refused to sit at the supper board. She stayed in the house beside the child, though other women had offered to feed him and rock him to sleep. But when the fiddles struck up and the feet began to beat round in ordered violent circles Mara put on her shawl and crossed the barn yard. The dancers saw the white figure standing in the door, half in shadow. The fiddle sang like some wild bird from the world's farthest shore. Mara lingered in the door. Simon caught a glimpse of her through the whirling circles of the dance. He refused the whisky that was going round just then. He was vexed that he had had to sit alone at the bridal table. The hot whisky had made him arrogant and masterful. At least Mara must walk with him in the bridal march. No wedding was complete without the grand bridal march, led by the bridegroom and bride. He would compel her.

But when Simon reached the barn door, through all those stampings and yells, his wife was not there.

He crossed the yard to the house. The old man was in bed already. He did not hold with whisky and fiddles. For him the wedding was over with the giving of the ring and the minister's sacred pronouncement. He moaned softly in the darkness. He was having bad pain that winter in both his legs.

Simon opened the door of the seaward room. The lamp burned on top of the clothes chest, and flung a little wayward light on the darkness. Mara was bent over the cradle, singing in a low voice to the child.

> I am a man upon the land,
> I am a selkie in the sea,
> And when I'm far from any strand
> My home it is in Suleskerry.

The child lay asleep in his crib, quiet as an apple.

From another world came broken fragments of laughter, voices, clattering plates. The fiddle screamed suddenly, once. The barn fell silent again. A voice commanded. The fiddle moved into a sequence of urgent cadences, and the feet of the men moved over the barn floor to where the line of women sat at the wall with veiled expectant eyes.

'Mara,' said Simon, 'they want us in the barn. It'll soon be time for the bridal march. You must come.'

She knelt over the crib, her head enfolded in the soft sweet breathings of her child.

The old man sighed in the darkness next door.

A slow anger kindled in Simon's belly. It would be a disgrace to Corse for generations if the things that must be done at every wedding were not done.

'I am your man,' Simon said. 'You will come now.'

In the barn the dance whirled in ever-quicker circles to the last frenzied circle when the fiddler's elbow twitches like ague and the girls are almost thrown off their feet.

Mara took off her bride-gown and hung it at the hook in the wall. From her nakedness, gently laved by the flame of the lamp, came an intense white bitter coldness: the moon in the heart of an iceberg. Simon in his thick Sabbath suit trembled. His wife climbed into the bed and covered herself with the patchwork quilt.

The taking of the maidenhead had been accomplished twenty months previously. There would be no need for that ceremony again. She breathed softly and regularly on her pillow.

The light and the darkness wavered and interfolded and gestured on the walls of the bedroom like two ancient creatures in a silent dialogue.

Simon took his uncertain shadow away. He went on tiptoe through his father's room. The old man was muttering what seemed to be a fragment of scripture.

Sick at heart, Simon returned to the barn. The reel was over. The barn was full of smoke and sweat and red faces. It was time for more refreshment. A brimming whisky-vessel was thrust into Simon's hands.

'Where's your wife, man?' said Frank the boatman, mockingly.

(vi)

It was strange how the soul of old Ezekiel clung to his ruined body. He had always been a truly religious man. He loved his nightly readings of the bible. Even in the days of his strength the words of Ecclesiastes had comforted him:

> I returned, and saw under the sun, that the race is not to the swift, nor the battle to the strong, neither yet bread to the wise, nor yet riches to men of understanding, nor yet favour to men of skill; but time and chance happeneth to them all. For man also knoweth not his time: as the fishes that are taken in an evil net, and as the birds that are caught in the snare; so are the sons of men snared in an evil time, when it falleth suddenly upon them.

It was good that a young man should know how in the end all was bitterness and emptiness. He had never had any fear of death – indeed for the last six or seven winters he would have welcomed death heartily, like a friend. But death was still reluctant to knock on his door.

He waited upon the Lord, he said.

An unexpected sweetness had fallen upon his latter days: his grandson. Surely the goodness of the Lord was never-ending. The delight was perhaps all the greater because the marriage of Simon and Mara had quickly gone sour. They moved about the croft and did their appointed tasks in the due season, but they no longer took any comfort from one another. They broke the family bread with cold hands. They listened to the scripture reading with cold faces.

His own marriage had gone cold like this in the end; but first he had had a dozen joyous lusty years with old Annie who was lying now in the kirkyard at the shore. A year, and Simon and Mara spoke only when it was needful.

It was a great sadness to him. He thought about it one summer morning. The sun shone. He was sitting in front of the cottage in the deep straw chair.

Mara was baking bread inside.

Simon was bringing a cow out of the quarry field. He had to take that one, and Bluebell, to the pier in the village before the boat sailed. They were to be sold at the mart in Kirkwall.

Old Ezekiel heard distant shouts from the hill. It was Mansie and the neighbouring boy from Voe. The shouts dwindled. When they came again they had a new thinness and clarity. The boys were playing along the shore, where sea and sky are the twin valves of one cosmic echoing shell.

The sun went behind a cloud.

And yet he should not complain. Simon was a respectful son to him. And the girl, the stranger, did everything for him that was necessary. It was not the loving ways of a daughter, of course. Still, he should not complain. He knew he must be a great nuisance to them both.

If only the dark courteous guest would knock soon on his door.

The shouts came from the end of the house. A solitary small boy danced round the corner. The lap of his gray jersey was full of shells and buttercups and stones from the beach. Mansie showered this treasure over his grandfather. Then he leapt into the old man's lap and flung his arms about his neck.

'Ah!' cried the old man in agony, for now the rheumatism was in his shoulders too.

'Get down!' cried Simon, leading the black cow in. 'Go back to the shore!' Young flesh disentangled from writhen flesh. The boy ran behind the peat-stack. They heard soon the flutter of his bare feet on the grass of the links.

The old man's face was still twisted with agony.

'You should be inside,' said Simon. 'The wind's freshening. You should be sitting inby at the ingle.'

'Mara is baking,' said the old man. 'I would only be in her way.'

'You should have on your coat then,' said Simon. 'It'll get colder.'

'My coat's on the scarecrow,' said the old man, and smiled a little to think that his next coat would be a coat of heavenly yarn.

Simon fingered his chin, considering.

A freshet of wind blew in from the sea and brought with it a little shrill fragment of song. The boy was communing with the seals on the rock. Another sleek head broke the water, and another. The seals were coming close in to listen.

Mansie, thought the old man, always liked best to play by himself. He never played for long at a time with the other boys of the district. He was lonely as a gull.

'Wait a minute,' said Simon. He went into the barn.

The blue hot reek of baking drifted from the open door.

Verily I should be very thankful, thought the old man drowsily. The wind on my face. Mansie down at the shore. Seals, sunbursts, singing. The hillside tossing with green oats. The good smell of bread from the hearth inside . . . His head nodded on his chest.

Simon came out of the barn carrying the sealskin that he had found on the beach seven years before and had almost forgotten. He shook husks and stour out of it; the wind was gray for a moment. His father was asleep in the chair now. Simon draped the skin gently over the old man's shoulders.

Mansie, having lured the seals with his singing, began to throw stones at them. Stones splashed in the sea. There was the gentler splash of departing seals.

Simon lifted the rope from the dyke and led the black cow across the field to the road. 'Bluebell,' he called, 'Bluebell!' A red-and-white heifer that had been munching grass in the ditch ambled towards him. The two cows were seeing their last of Corse.

The old man slept peacefully in his chair.

The boy was running on the hill now, and creating panic among the sheep. He barked like a dog among them.

The wind blew colder from the sea. The sun was lost behind a huge cloud mass.

After a time Mara came and stood in the doorway. She was white to the elbows with meal.

'Leave them alone, the sheep!' she called in her strange bell-like voice. 'Come back. Come here.'

The boy stopped. The sheep were huddled in a gray agitated mass in one corner of the field. He turned. He ran across the shoulder of the hill towards the peat-cuttings.

He would only come home now when he was hungry.

The old man slept in his chair. Mara looked at him. Salt still

encrusted the veins that had been nourished too long with corn
and milk. She touched the sealskin that covered the shoulders of
the old man.

(vii)

'So,' said the stone-mason, 'what you want is one gravestone of
Aberdeen granite to be erected in the churchyard of Norday.'

'That's right,' said Simon.

They were standing in the stone-mason's yard in Kirkwall,
among hewn polished half-inscribed stones. Simon and Mansie
his son had come in that morning from the island on the weekly
boat. It was no idle excursion. Simon had business to do, at the
auction mart, in the lawyer's office, with the seed merchant and the
ironmonger, and now last with the maker of gravestones.

Mansie was not there. He had gone off to buy something with
the few pounds his grandfather had left him – he refused to say
what, until the thing was actually in his possession.

'The stone is for my father and mother,' said Simon.

The stone-mason wrote the names down in his notebook:
EZEKIEL OLAFSON and ANNIE OLAFSON. The chiselling of the
names would cost sixpence a letter, he told Simon.

Simon had been meaning all winter, since the old man died,
to erect a memorial over his parents. It looked so mean, them
lying in a nameless piece of earth in the midst of the blazoned
dead of Norday. Forgetfulness had caused the delay – a willed
forgetfulness, in a way, for to tell the truth Simon found it
unwholesome, all this tearful lauding of the dead that had lately
become the fashion; and the stark bones hidden under a heap of
wax flowers. The laird's wife even had a stone angel weeping
over her.

'It is usual nowadays,' said the stone-mason, 'to have something
like this, *In Loving Memory.* And then, at the base of the stone,
some text from scripture, such as *Not Lost But Gone Before* or
Asleep in Jesus.'

'Nothing like that,' said Simon. 'Just the names and the dates of
birth and death.'

The stone-mason licked his blunt stub of pencil and wrote the dates in his notebook under the names, 1793–1869 and 1797–1860.

A thick-set fair boy entered the yard from the street, bearing a shape wrapped in sheets of newspaper.

The stone-mason looked up from his notebook. 'I think you are a widower, Mr Olafson?' he said.

'Yes,' said Simon, 'I am.'

'Then,' said the stone-mason, lowering his voice a little, 'should there not be another name on the stone?'

Mansie began to tear the paper from the parcel.

'No,' said Simon. He shook his head. 'She came out of silence and she went back into silence. I don't even know her right name. Whatever it was, it shouldn't be on a Christian stone.'

'I see,' said the stone-mason.

It was a fiddle that Mansie held up. The strange exotic shape shone among the blank and the half-inscribed tombstones that were strewn about the yard.

'I saw it advertised for sale in *The Orkney Herald*,' said Mansie to his father. 'It was made in 1695 in Gothenburg by Rolf Gruning. He was a very good fiddle maker.'

'A waste of money,' said Simon.

Mansie plucked a string. The fiddle shivered and cried.

(viii)

This story is really about a man and his music.

At the turn of the century there was a stirring in the two Orkney grammar schools of Kirkwall and Hamnavoe. Suddenly, within a few years – as if in complete vindication of the Education Act of 1872 – they produced a crop of boys of outstanding intellect. These young men went on to one or other of the universities of Scotland, afterwards perhaps to Oxford or Cambridge. Most of them made brilliant careers for themselves, mainly in the Dominions (for they still kept some drops of viking blood; their bodies too were restless). All these clever Orcadians were men of science – medicine, botany, theology – and this practicality too was a viking inheritance: even the old sagamen kept to the factual truth in their

marvellous stories, and were suspicious of the imagination and all
its works.

The sole exception in that feast of scientific intellect was a young
man from the island of Norday called Magnus John Olafson.

After tasting the disciplines and delights of two universities, and
being uncertain for a while about his ultimate career – for he
showed, in common with his peers, considerable aptitude in
mathematics and physics – he turned finally to music.

He achieved a certain measure of fame while he was still in his
twenties. Edinburgh, London, Prague heard his music, and approved.

His compositions are out of favour, with most things Victorian
and Edwardian, nowadays; one occasionally hears on the Third
Programme his Symphony, his tone poem *Eynhallow*, his elegy for
piano *The Blue Boat*, his settings of the twelfth-century lyrics of
Earl Rognvald Kolson, his ballet *The Seal Women*, and most of all
perhaps his Violin Concerto with its few spare lovely melodies
among all that austerity, like flowers in an Arctic field.

Magnus enjoyed his fame as composer and conductor for a
decade and more; then gradually it lost its savour. With fame had
come a modest amount of wealth. He did not know what to do
with it. One summer he went back to the islands; first to the little
town with the red cathedral at the heart of it; then, the following
day, on the weekly steamer to Norday.

He did not want acknowledgement of his gifts here, and he did
not get it. On the steamer he was the sole passenger, except for a
boxed-in horse and a few cows complaining in the hold. He signed
in at the hotel at the pier. The bar fell silent when he walked
casually in. (They had spoken familiarly enough with him there ten
years previously.) One by one the farmers slipped away. He was left
with his lonely dram in his hand.

This was their way. They were shy and independent.

All these years he had carried Norday with him wherever he
went, but his memory had made it a transfigured place, more like a
piece of tapestry than an album of photographs. The great farm-
houses and the small crofts had appeared, in retrospect, 'sunk in
time'. The people, viewed from Paris, moved like figures in an

ancient fable, simple and secure and predestined, and death rounded all. He knew of course that there was poverty, and such sins as lust and avarice and pride. He had smiled often, for example, to think of the devious lecheries of Walter the black-smith; and how Willie Taylor, up in the hill in the springtime to cut peats, took his bowel-fruit home in the cart to enrich no land but his own; and how the mouth of Finlay Groat the merchant shone with unction even when it totted up the prices of sugar and tea and tobacco in his shop at the pier.

It was in a fable that these people seemed to move; and Magnus thought that if each man's seventy years could be compressed into a short time, his laborious feet, however plastered with dung and clay, would move in a joyous reel of fruition.

He was to be bitterly hurt and disillusioned as his holiday went on; for the people were changed indeed, but in an altogether different way.

They avoided him as if he was the factor or the exciseman. When the farm women saw him coming on the road they moved shyly out of the fields into barn or byre.

Even the boys who had sat beside him at the school desk, Willie Scott of Voe and Tom Anderson who had followed his father at the forge, spoke only when he spoke to them, and then in a painfully shy embarrassed way; and they were obviously glad when there was nothing more to say and the stranger had passed on.

A coldness gathered about his heart.

A revealing incident happened during his two-week stay in the island. A boy was drowned off the East Head – his fishing boat had been swamped in a sudden squall. Magnus was there with the other islanders at the village pier when the body was taken ashore. It was what the local newspapers called 'a tragedy', and the reporters went on to describe the 'affecting scenes' and 'the stricken island' . . . Magnus saw the women standing along the pier with their dabbling hand-kerchiefs, and the men gulping and turning their faces away as the shrouded stretcher was borne slowly up the road to the church hall.

He himself felt nothing – only a little irritation at the sloppiness of their mourning.

He stood utterly outside this festival of grief. He shook hands with the boy's father (with whom he had been at school) and murmured words of sympathy; but he was quite cold and unmoved.

Standing on that pier, the scales fell from his eyes – the change was not in the islanders but in himself. An artist must pay dearly, in terms of human tenderness, for the fragments of beauty that lie about his workshop. (Later that year, in London, he wrote *The Blue Boat*, an impressionistic piece for piano. It was a time of much give-and-take in the arts – poets had their preludes, composers their ballades and landscapes, painters their nocturnes and symphonies . . . Olafson's *The Blue Boat* is what music perhaps should never aim at – it is a description of a passing storm at sea. When at last the wind has swept away the thunder and the rain-clouds there is a brief silence, the dove broods upon the water; and then the piece is brought to a close with a last brief phrase. This is indeed a mystery of art, that a few musical notes, in a certain pattern and tempo, should suggest the fall of a wave on an Atlantic shore; since even in impressionistic music there is no similarity in the sound the piano makes to the actual sound made by salt water spending itself on pebbles, sand, rocks, seaweed. The music nevertheless subtly suggests the phenomenon. And why, more mysteriously still, should the same pattern of notes impress the listener with sorrow, with a grief that belongs to the sea alone, with youth gathered untimely into the salt and the silence? The end of *The Blue Boat* is all heartbreak; as if the tears shed at Norday pier that summer day had been gathered and given over to the limbecks of art for an irreducible quintessence.)

The day before he left Norday that summer he visited the kirkyard at the shore. Fifty years before a new ugly kirk had been built near the centre of the island, but the islanders still laid their dead in the earth about an ancient roofless (probably Catholic) chapel. Magnus remembered well where the family grave was. A new name had been cut in the stone.

SIMON OLAFSON
(1837–1884)

He remembered his father and grandfather with sudden deep affection. He wandered from tombstone to tombstone, pausing to read familiar names: Walter Anderson, Martha Gross, Rev. Jabez Grant.

Surrounded by these dead, he felt human and accepted for the first time since he had returned to Norday. He murmured the names on the stones with gratitude.

A dark comforting power rose from the vanished generations.

His wanderings had brought him back to the place where he had started. There was room at the foot of the Olafson stone for another name to be carved. It struck Magnus with a sudden chill that the islanders he loved might not want his dust to be mingled with theirs.

Next day he left Norday. Nobody said farewell to him at the pier. The old ferryman – a friend of his father's – accepted his generous tip and covered up his embarrassment with dense drifts of smoke from his clay pipe. Magnus wandered for an hour in a stone web, the piers and closes of Hamnavoe. A steamer received him; he was borne across the disordered surges of the Pentland Firth. The islands dwindled. At Thurso the train bore him south to new orchestras, to brilliant friends, to the new compositions that were already shaping themselves in his imagination.

These were not paltry delights that Magnus Olafson went back to.

He had many good friends in the cities of Europe: musicians, dancers, students, writers, art lovers. They received him back into their circles with pleasure. He went with them on their summer picnics in the forests and mountains. They experienced together the new poetry of Rilke and Blok, and discussed it late into the night; and experienced the new music of Mahler, and analysed it till the rising sun quenched their lamps. Magnus Olafson was well enough liked by his cultured friends; his clumsiness with their languages endeared him; and how he whose early life had been shaped by the starkness of sea and earth was at a loss with railway timetables, cheque books, wine lists.

He often felt, in moods of depression, that he was caught up in some meaningless charade in which everyone, himself included, was compelled to wear a mask. He would take part in their passionate midnight arguments about socialism, the ballet, anthropology, psychology, and he would put forward – as well as his clumsiness with German or French allowed him – a well-ordered logical argument. But deep down he was untouched. It didn't seem to matter in the slightest. It was all a game, to keep sharp the wits of people who had not to contend with the primitive terrors of sea and land. So he thought, while the eyes flashed and the tongues sought for felicitousness and clarity all around him. He was glad when the maskers had departed and he was alone again, among the cigarette ends and the apple cores. Occasionally, out of the staleness, would emerge a thread of melody; he would note it down on the back of an envelope and, too tired to work that night, begin to loose his boot straps. (In the morning, after breakfast, he would fall on the music paper with controlled lust.)

And his guests would say, going home in a late-night tramcar, 'Is he not charming, this Magnus? And how shy! And underneath, such talent!' What they were describing was the mask; few of them had seen the cold dangerous Orphean face underneath.

And they would say, lingering on pavements in the lamplight, 'He is so gentle and sensitive, this man from the north.' . . . But Magnus Olafson had long given up the idea that artists are the sensitive antennae of society – art is, rather, the ruthless cutting edge that records and celebrates and prophesies on the stone tablets of time. A too-refined sensibility could not do that stern work.

He had a friend, a painter, who used to argue that art was no separate sovereign mystery, with its own laws and modes and manners, answerable only to itself; 'art for art's sake'. 'No,' said this friend, 'in this way art will wither from the earth.' . . . Art, he argued, must become once more the handmaid of religion, as it had been in Greece and in the Europe of the Middle Ages. Magnus remembered the harshness of the Presbyterian services in Norday, when he was a boy, and shook his head. He went with his friend one Christmas eve to a midnight Mass in Notre Dame. The endless liturgy bored him, but he was moved a little by the homeliest thing in the huge church – the crib with the Infant in the straw, the Man and the Woman, the Beasts and the Star and the Angels. It reminded him of the byre at Corse, and how there had seemed to be always a kind of sacred bond between the animals and the farm-folk who were born and died under the same thatched roof . . . He left the church before the Elevation.

So Magnus Olafson had many pleasant friends, but found himself lonely among the rugs and poems and wine-cups. There is a deeper intensity, love – surely he found release there . . . He had the thick peasant body that rises in a slow fruitful surge of earth to the sun, and falls away again. It cannot be denied that this woman and that came to Magnus Olafson's bed – modern memoirs are frank and explicit – but none of these intelligent and attractive girls remained his mistress for long. The spring was choked, and in what loins did the stone of impotence lie, when most of these women afterwards became adequate wives and mothers? His seed, it seemed, had the coldness and barrenness of salt.

So he wandered among the cities of Europe, increasingly celebrated and lonely, and found no place (the gates of his Eden being shut against him) to establish his house.

Lately a new problem had begun to nag at him a good deal – the use of art. In this too he had a peasant's practical outlook. Everything about a croft is there for some specific purpose: the plough, the oar, the quernstones, the horse-shoe, the flail. Each implement symbolized a whole segment of labour in the strict cycle of the year, so that the end might be fruition, and bread and fish lie at last on a poor table. But this fiddle, the symbol of his art – he had squandered all his skill on it, and in return it had drained him of much human warmth and kindliness – what was the use of it after all but to titillate a few rows and boxes of cultured people on a winter evening?

If he allowed himself to brood too much on this, a desolation would come over his mind.

One autumn, after a year in which he had done little work, he thought of writing music – a tone poem, perhaps, or even an opera – with Celtic themes. In the library of Trinity College, Dublin, he was shown an ancient Gaelic manuscript. In the margin, in faded exquisite script, some student had scratched out a translation.

Thou hast heard how Jupiter changed himself into the
likenesse of a Swan or a Bull. Many a country spell hath
turned a Princesse into a Paddock. Girls have put on leaves
and branches and become very Trees. Such Metamorphoses
happen now never, or seldom, for it was the curse of the
Angel in the Garden, that each creature should seek out its
own isolation and build a wall about itself. Then Man (the
prime sinner) took after a season a foolish pride in his
separateness, for, said Adam with the Apple seed yet between
his teeth, We have graces not given unto Plants and Stones
and Beasts. Cannot I measure Stars and atoms of Dust with
the span of my fingers, and utter subtleties with my Tongue,
and lord it over the Ox and the fish? This was a false and a
foolish thought, that came nigh to tear asunder that most
intricate Web of Nature that God Himself spun on the Six
Dayes of Creation. If Chaos be not come in againe, the
reason is, that the delicate thin spunne Web I have spoken of
still holds, though grievously riven in sundry partes. There
be rocky places yet in the West and North where young men,
finding shy cold creatures of no tongue or lineage, have led
the same home to their mothers' Doors, and begotten
Children on them; they have laboured and grown bent
and grey together, and at last lain twined in the one Grave.
This is to say, Man hath taken a deep primitive draught, and
gotten drunk, and so pledged himself anew to the Elements.
Likewise this is said, that many a country Maid, taking the
shore road home from Mass or Market, hath vanished out of
mortal ken, but she hath been fleetingly glimpsed thereafter
lying upon a Rock in a great company of seales, or (it may
be) lingering alone in a little bay and looking with large
sorrowful eyes upon the Bell and Arch at the shore where she
hath learned in her childhood to say her *Credo* and her *Ave
Marias.*

Magnus Olafson was entranced, in a complex way, by the crude
paragraph. He who had never shed a tear for the vanishing of his
mother or the death of his father felt a swelling in his throat as he

read. At the same time his eyes and lips smiled at the quaintness and innocence of it all. The homily – it was from an old Irish sermon – seemed to treat of the question that had troubled him all that winter.

He thought of the men who had thrown off all restraint and were beginning now to raven in the most secret and delicate and precious places of nature. They were the new priesthood; the world went down on its knees before every tawdry miracle – the phonograph, the motor car, the machine-gun, the wireless – that they held up in triumph. And the spoliation had hardly begun.

Was this then the task of the artist: to keep in repair the sacred web of creation – that cosmic harmony of god and beast and man and star and plant – in the name of humanity, against those who in the name of humanity are mindlessly and systematically destroying it?

If so, what had been taken from him was a necessary sacrifice.

The Girl

In the high narrow rocky sea-inlet on the north coast of the island the men were making ready for the fishing. Ploughing and sowing were finished. The cattle, let out of the dark byres, drifted among the new sweet grass like tranced creatures. Down here, hidden from the women and the animals, the crofters turned their faces to the dazzle of the sea. It was a beautiful morning in April.

'Well,' said an old silky-bearded man, 'that was some day, I'm telling you. That was a day that will not be forgotten in this parish for a long time. I spat salt for a year after.'

Carefully he applied a brushful of tar in long fluent strokes to the flank of an upturned boat. When the tar thinned out he thrust his brush once more into the metal tar drum.

A thin dark twist of a man lifted his head from the rock and the pool where he was gathering limpets.

'Tell us, James of Dale,' he said. He turned and winked at the other men as much as to say, *Wait till you hear this lie.*

A girl appeared at the high sea-bank above the beach. She was shawled and she wore a long gray worsted skirt. She looked at the group of crofter-fishermen working below. She lingered uncertainly, as if she heard from far off the voices of women calling to her from the wells and peat-stacks. Then she crouched down on the grass, half turned away from the men, her hand on her bare instep.

'I was fishing that day,' said James of Dale, 'with my father and my grandfather under Scabra Head in Rousay. We were fishing for haddocks. That was all of fifty years ago. I wasn't long finished with the school. The razor had maybe touched my cheek once. Well, it was a fine day and we fished and we fished and we caught nothing. "Now," said my grandfather – he's been in the kirkyard thirty-two years come Michaelmas – "that's a funny thing," said he. "I could tell from the look of the sea beyond Scabra there were haddocks here, any God's amount of them." We drew in our lines and still there was not a fish on the hooks. After a time my father said, "There's a queer motion on the sea today." Then a shadow fell on us and I looked round and there beside the boat rose an island as big as the Brough of Birsay. And this whale, he hosed the sky through his blowhole. And he sent sheet after sheet of spray flying over us. I'm telling you. And his wash nearly turned us right over. I sat at the tiller and I never saw men rowing like my father and my grandfather. One moment they would be closed up on the thwart like jack-knives and the next they would be straight as boards, leaning far back. The blades sang like fiddlestrings. And the boat – *Dayspring*, that was her name – she skimmed the sea like a skarfie till we got back to this beach where we are now.'

The limpet-gatherer sat down on the flat dry rock and his shoulders jerked with merriment. The laughter came out of him in a thin wheeze that ended in a bout of coughing. Then he wiped his distracted eyes on the back of his hand.

'Thu may laugh, Sander Groat,' said James of Dale gravely, 'but what I'm telling thee is the God's honest truth.' He sank his brush deep into the jet-black lake, and began to stroke the *Mary Jane* tenderly and sensuously.

The girl on the sea-bank laid off her shawl. She plucked a long stalk of grass and put it in her mouth. From far inland came the fragile bleat of a sheep; nearer at hand a croft woman cried sharply to a child to keep out of the cornfield. The girl's hair was drawn back in a tight coil of bronze.

The youngest fisherman left his line and hooks on the rock where he was sitting and looked out to sea. It was still ebbing fast; he could hear the slow suck and drench of the sea as it was withdrawn from tangle and sand and rock crannies. He put his elbows on his knees and his face in his hands and looked out over the slowly shrinking ocean.

'Thu won't fill thee belly that way, Tom,' said Sander Groat. 'Thu has a hundred hooks to bait yet if thu has one.'

Tom rose to his feet and walked down to the ebb. Sometimes his bare feet slipped in the seaweed and then he described a wild pirouette and his hand would seize a spur of rock to keep himself from falling. Gracefully he swayed across the glittering red swathes, down to the shrinking edge of the water. Sometimes he would linger beside a rockpool and angle his face in that mirror, pushing out his lips, touching his curled blond hair with his fingers. On he swayed and slithered and hesitated to the sea fringe.

'Far too good for the likes of us, that one,' said Sander Groat. 'They're poor folk up at Estquoy, but this one, you'd think from the way he carries on his mother had given some duke or prince a night's lodging. He's going to Canada, fancy that! He's written to the emigration agent in Liverpool. His fingers are far too long and white to rip the guts out of a herring. He wants to sit at some office desk in Toronto. Then some summer he'll come home to Estquoy for a holiday and he'll be wearing tweed knickerbockers, and by God, he'll look at us like the far end of a fiddle.'

Sander Groat turned and spat among the shells. Then he raised his blunt stone and began rhythmically to knock limpets off the rock.

Up above, on the sea-bank, the girl had strewn her lap with a scatter of daisies, and she began to link them together, slow and silent and totally absorbed, a long thin pink-and-white halter.

Occasionally the silence of the boat noust was split by the rasp of a saw. Two men were working beside an upturned boat with a rectangular hole in it. A long white board lay on the stones. One man, stout and breathless with the exertion of sawing, hovered between the board and the gap in the boat, making anxious measurements and calculations. He marked the board with a crumble of red sandstone. Then he and the other man lifted the board and leaned it against a flat rock. He began to saw furiously. The song of the saw rose to a thin high shriek. A white stub fell off and the stout man once more fitted the board against the hole in the *Sea Harvest*. 'She'll need a thumb-length off yet,' he said.

'Have a rest now, Howie,' said his mate. 'Smoke thee pipe.'

'And by God I need a rest, Peter,' said the fat man. 'I'm all silver under my sark with sweat.'

'There is never any need to take the name of the Lord in vain,' said Peter.

Howie filled a clay pipe with tobacco from his pouch. 'It was done deliberately,' he said. 'Who would have done a thing like that now? If I get hold of him I'll twist his bloody neck.'

'Swearing never did any good at all,' said Peter. 'Nor unchari-table thinking either. The strake was rotten. Look at the pieces. You can crumble them in your hand like a bit of old bannock.'

Howie held the still flame of the lucifer over his pipe and sucked it down into the bowl. He blew out three clouds of smoke. 'I'll murder the bastard,' he said. 'Somebody smashed it in with a stone in the winter time.'

Up above, the girl brushed the daisies out of her lap, petulantly. She leaned forward from her haunches, looking out to sea, her face tilted high, lips apart, looking far out over the heads of the fishermen as if she saw a splendid ship on the horizon. Her eyes moved slowly over the delicate thin line of the horizon. Her brow fell, a shutter, and made shadows of her eyes. She was utterly absorbed in the furthest reaches of the ocean.

'For God's sake,' said Sander Groat, his stone hammer poised over a cluster of limpets, 'a seal.'

A sleek head flashed in the water, sank, rose again, shook a scatter of salt from its tight burnished pelt. A hand rose and arched and clutched at the water and disappeared. Then another hand. Arms beat the water like slow millwheels. The feet made a long rhythmic agitation. A shoulder flashed and sank, flashed and sank. Tom of Estquoy swam leisurely between the two skerries.

'I suppose he wants to wash the clay and the dung off him,' said Sander Groat. 'He can't go to Canada smelling like us poor folk. O no, that would never do.'

Old James of Dale dipped his brush, very finicky, around and between the faded blue letters MARY JANE at the bow of his boat. 'I mind the time,' he said, 'I swam from this same noust here to the island of Rousay for a bet. It was a winter day. Benjie Berstane wagered me a half-crown I couldn't do it. I had to swim against sea and snow.'

Nobody encouraged him this time. It was getting towards noon and the sun fell hot into the deep cove. They were beginning to feel hungry.

The old man mumbled away over the shining black curves of his boat.

There was one shed on the beach where two young men were working. They were so very like each other that they must be brothers; they might well be twins, for they seemed to be equal in possessiveness and authority. They kept themselves somewhat apart from the other fishermen. They spoke to each other privately, in harsh whispers; occasionally one or the other would look round to see if they were being overheard.

One brother was carrying out of the shed, three by three, a stack of lobster creels, and piling them against the outside wall. The other examined every creel carefully. Every now and again he would take a defective creel and lay it aside; it would have to be repaired with twine, perhaps, or the eye was twisted so that a lobster couldn't get in, or the wooden frame was smashed. And all the time they kept up their low harsh secret dialogue. Sometimes they would break off and face each other. Then it was like a man possessed glaring deep into a mirror.

'The shed is mine,' shouted one of them at last. 'He always said that. The shed and the creels and the tackle are mine.'

'Is that so?' said the other. 'I never heard him saying that. All right, then. You can have them, so long as the boat comes to me.'

They both realized at once that they had spoken too loud. They looked round guiltily at the other fishermen. They moved closer to each other, whispering, gesturing wildly with their hands, pointing inside the shed, pointing over the rim of the noust to their croft hidden in a fold of the hills. But even though they kept their voices down, the other men could hear an occasional word, 'ox' and 'plough' and 'spinning-wheel'. At last one of them gripped the other by the shoulder and their faces were close together, transfixed and yawing like cats.

Peter Simison rose to his feet and went over to the shed. 'Come now, Abel and Harald,' he said. 'What kind of way is this to behave? Your father's still not cold in his grave. Think shame of yourselves.'

'The two cows are mine,' shouted Abel to Peter. He still had a creel in his hand. 'Daddo took me into the byre one day just after New Year and he said, *Be good to them, Abel, after I'm gone.*' . . .

'Right,' cried Harald. 'I get the barn then. That's only fair.'

Peter stood between them. 'It's a great pity,' he said, 'that thee father died without making a proper will. What was he thinking of? He might have known it would come to this.'

'The fiddle on the wall is mine,' shouted Abel.

'The sensible thing to do,' said Peter, 'is for one of you to take the croft of Lombist and for the other to take the fishing boat *Trust* and all her gear.'

'A croft is ten times more valuable than a fishing boat,' said Howie the carpenter, his face like two immense apples behind a drift of tobacco smoke. 'That's the trouble.'

'And they're twins,' said Sander Groat from the rockpool. 'That makes it worse than ever.'

'Twins, maybe,' said Howie. 'But they didn't burst on the world at exactly the same time. One must have been dropped before the other. Who was the midwife? She would know.'

'My wife Mary Jane was the midwife,' said James of Dale. 'She's been in the kirkyard twelve years come the fourth of March. So we won't get much enlightenment from her.'

'Settle the business peaceably between yourselves,' said Peter to Abel and Harald of Lombist, 'or I'll tell you what way it'll end – you'll be two old tramps on the road eating a crust here and a fish-head there. Take charitable council one with the other.' He admonished them gravely, shaking his finger between them like a referee at a fight.

Chidden, the twins returned silently to their work. Harald brought out, four by four, the creels from the shed. Abel examined every creel carefully; every now and then he would lay one aside to be repaired. They did not look at each other. But the air seethed between them in the hot noon.

The girl stretched herself out in the new grass. She lay down and writhed about slowly like a cat. Then she was still, her eyes closed against the sun. Her eyelids pulsed slowly. She stretched her legs apart. Her closed fists lay on each side of her head like a child asleep. There was a faint puzzled smile on her face. All that could be noted of her existence now from the noust was a trembling in the tallest grasses.

'We won't get the new plank in her today,' said Howie the carpenter. 'I doubt it.' He scraped the dottle out of his clay pipe carefully and set the pipe on a rock ledge.

'It's just past noon,' said Peter Simison. 'There's a whole day before us.'

'I know,' said Howie. 'But I have to take this board home, and I have to plane the ends of it. Two miles there and two miles back. Then the riveting and the putty and the tar.'

'Well,' said Peter. 'There's no hurry.'

'And even then,' said Howie, 'she won't be tight till she's been in the water a day or two.'

Tom of Estquoy came up from the sea, shuddering with cold and fastening the band of his trousers. His worsted shirt was flung about his shoulders.

'Were thu trying to slip away quiet-like to Canada?' said Sander Groat. 'Losh, man, that'll never do at all. There must be a lot of ceremonial for an important chap like thee. I'm telling thee, the pier'll be black with folk the day thu leaves Orkney. The road to Hamnavoe will be one long lamentation of women.' Sander Groat gave a little snort of mockery.

Tom of Estquoy let on never to hear. He spread his gray shirt on the rock and lay back on it. His long arms gleamed like marble in the sun. The new red-blond hairs across his chest flickered like fire. His ribs were pearled with water. He closed his eyes against the light. He still shivered occasionally from the wetting of the ocean.

'Canada or no Canada,' said Sander Groat, 'thee father's a poor man like the rest of us. He'll have to go on fishing from this coast to keep thee mother and sister out of the poorhouse. He'll be wanting his lines baited for tomorrow morning.'

Presently, taking his time, as if the other fishermen in the noust didn't exist, Tom sat up and looked about him. He reached for his shirt and pulled it on. He yawned. He lifted a hook from the coiled line. He drew the tin of bait towards him. He stuck a piece of mussel on the barb. His nose wrinkled.

The last of the creels was out of the shed now. Abel and Harald sat against the black wall with one ball of twine between them. They worked expertly at the holes in the creels, knitting and knotting, passing the knife from one to the other. Whenever one had finished a repair job he held up the creel for the other's approval. Then they would nod, one after the other; and the mended creel would be added to the stack of sound ones.

They whispered together like two grudging ghosts.

'I don't want her at all,' whispered Harald. 'You can have her.'

'Are you sure?' whispered Abel.

'Him that's dead would have wanted it,' whispered Harald. 'His heart was set on that. I heard him speaking about it at the last Dounby Show to Tor her father, in the whisky tent.'

'But I thought you liked her,' whispered Abel. 'You danced with her all night in the barn at Estquoy last harvest home.'

'No, I don't like her that much,' whispered Harald. 'You can have her.'

'Well then,' whispered Abel, 'in that case the croft's yours. That's fair enough.'

'No,' whispered Harald, 'what way would you both live? You're not tinkers, you couldn't live in a ditch. I'll take the boat and the shed and the creels.'

'You heard what Howie said just now,' whispered Abel, 'Lombist is ten times more valuable than the *Trust*.'

'I don't care,' whispered Harald. 'Fishermen should be bachelors. The sea's no place for a new-married man. Look what happened last November to the *Jewel*. One wave made a new widow and three new orphans up at Clodberry.'

'Well then,' whispered Abel, 'you can bide with us up at Lombist. You'll eat and sleep there.'

'I will not,' whispered Abel. 'We can't bide the sight of one another. You know that fine. And with *her* at my mother's hearth it would be worse than ever.'

'Where will you bide then?' whispered Abel.

Harald nodded at the shed. 'In there,' he whispered. 'I'll get a stove put in.'

'It's falling to pieces,' whispered Abel.

'A few nails,' whispered Harald. 'A board or two. That's all it needs. I'd like fine to live here, next the sea.'

'You wouldn't last a winter,' whispered Abel. 'The cold and the damp.'

'Mind your own bloody business,' whispered Harald. 'Don't try to dictate to me.'

They worked together in silence for a while.

'Pass the knife,' said Abel.

James of Dale laid his tar brush carefully across the tar bucket. The *Mary Jane* was all tarred now except for the stern, and the name had to be painted in in blue. James sat down in the shade of the boat. He took a length of twist from his tobacco pouch and began to cut thin dark slivers with a knife into his half-closed palm.

'Did I ever tell you men,' he said, 'about the time I put down the travelling wrestler at the Hamnavoe Market? I put him down three times.'

'An old man like you will soon have his Maker to meet,' said Peter Simison gravely. 'You should be thinking thoughts of peace and of truth.'

Peter set the board along a flat rock with a bit of the end protruding.

'Ten bob this fair-man offered,' said James of Dale, 'to any man in the crowd who could beat his champion. You never saw such a girth on a man, like a hogshead he was, twice as big as Howie over there. Nobody stirred in the crowd for a while. Then, thinks I, the whole of Orkney will be disgraced –'

Howie put his knee to the board. He squinted along the pencil mark and applied the saw. The wood shrieked its torture between the high walls of the noust. For two minutes nothing else could be heard. Old James of Dale's mouth opened and shut silently, telling the story of how he beat the fair-ground wrestler.

At last the board was shorter by another thumb-length.

'– and so,' said James of Dale, 'there he lay in the centre of the ring, that great ox, panting and groaning, and me on top of him pressing his shoulders flat down on the canvas. You should have heard the cheers of the crowd! This man with the check suit and the cigar steps up and puts a half-sovereign in my hand. Next day the wrestling tent was away from the fair-ground. It was never seen in Orkney again.'

A sweet tremulous cry possessed the air. A cluster of kittiwakes dipped and circled above them. They had risen from the loch a mile inland; and now they hovered and dropped, a flashing disordered throng, and furled themselves on the still sea beyond the weeded rocks. The girl's startled face watched their flight through a screen of grasses.

'The tide's turned,' said Sander Groat. He wiped his slimy hands on his trousers and walked over to the crag. He took from a sandstone fissure a large stone jar. He prised the cork out of the neck and sniffed the contents. 'This is strong stuff,' he said. 'It's been in the jar since before Christmas.' He set the jar down on a flat rock in the centre of the noust.

The fishermen gathered round it, unwrapping their pieces. James of Dale sank his gums into a wedge of new cheese; the pale juice ran down into his beard. Abel Bews of Lombist had two cold smoked cuithes. Harald Bews cracked the delicate gray-blue shell of a duck egg on a stone. Peter Simison took from under his jacket a large round bannock, thickly buttered. Howie the carpenter had two boiled crabs. Peter and Howie shared their food. Tom of Estquoy sat slightly apart from the other men. He had a slice of bread from the baker's in Hamnavoe, doubled over, with honey in the middle. 'I never eat when I'm drinking,' said Sander Groat, and winked, and raised the ale-jar.

Peter laid his bonnet on his knee. He bowed his head and murmured a grace. When he looked up again Sander Groat's throat was convulsing with the ale. Old James of Dale took the ale-jar from him. He tilted it till it eclipsed the sun. He sighed. He was very content. His tongue licked one amber drop from his moustache. He offered the jar to Abel Bews of Lombist. Abel drank, scowling, as if it was bitter herbs. He would not pass on the jar to his brother. Instead he reached it back to the provider, Sander Groat. Sander Groat lurched to his feet and stooped with his precious burden over Harald Bews. Harald wiped the mouth of the jar with his shirt sleeve; he tilted first his head and then the jar at their different angles, and his adam's-apple jerked thrice in his well-sculpted throat. He sighed bitterly and gave the ale-jar to Peter Simison. Peter passed it on at once to Howie the carpenter; he did not drink himself. Howie drank for both of them. He held the fat jar with great tenderness to his mouth, as if he was dandling his first-born, his heart's-desire, the marvellous fruit of his loins, with a prolonged passionate kiss. 'I think thu're drunk enough,' said Sander Groat anxiously. Howie yielded up the jar reluctantly. Sander Groat stood in front of Tom of Estquoy whose mouth shone with honey and white crumbs. 'Nothing for you,' he said. 'No work, no drink.' He stood in the centre of the rock and drank the last of the ale himself, tilting the stone jar till it was completely upside down and empty. He sighed and scattered the last few drops on the rock.

'I'll tell you what I could do with now,' he said. 'A woman.'

'Sander Groat,' said Peter Simison sternly, 'thu has a wife and fourteen bairns up at Otterquoy. I'm surprised to hear a man like thee saying such things.'

Sander Groat began to laugh. His thin dark face twisted, his shoulders jerked, and the laughter came out of him in thin jets and wheezes. Then they were all laughing in the noust. Even the twins laughed, narrowing their eyes and showing their fine teeth and gums in exactly the same way; the sound of their laughter passed between them wonderingly, like an echo. Tom of Estquoy ate the last of his bread-and-honey and smiled superiorly. Only Peter Simison did not laugh. He waited till Sander Groat's mirth expired in a few coughs and gasps. Then he said, 'We'll get back to work now, I think, if it's the will of the Lord.'

Howie picked up his saw.

There was a new sound on the sea, as if a wondering hand had strayed over a harp. The lowest rocks were awash with the flowing tide. What had been pools a half-hour before no longer existed. Slowly the flood encroached. Forlorn brown swathes of weed were gathered once more into the great translucent Atlantic garden. The kittiwakes rejoiced in the new cold fecund waters.

There was a new sound on the land too. It began as a faint flutter. The rapid rhythm grew louder. Sometimes it was lost in a fold of the hills, then it came stuttering on, louder than ever. The girl's face flashed with excitement. The new sound came closer. It hammered the afternoon apart.

The girl rose up from her grass couch. She stood for a moment and looked down contemptuously at the fishermen who were turning their refreshed hands to the monotonies of the coming summer. She turned towards the hill and ran up the broken road to the crofts above; and a collie tore across the field to meet her, barking blithely; and a drift of ducks waddled in panic from her bare feet, filling the ditches with their gabble.

A motor cyclist came careering down the broken road towards her.

The Drowned Rose

There was a sudden fragrance, freshness, coldness in the room. I looked up from my book. A young woman in a red dress had come in, breathless, eager, ready for laughter. The summer twilight of the far north was just beginning; it was late in the evening, after ten o'clock. The girl peered at me where I sat in the shadowy window-seat. 'You're not Johnny,' she said, more than a bit disappointed.

'No', I said, 'that isn't my name.'

She was certainly a very beautiful girl, with her abundant black hair and hazel eyes and small sweet sensuous mouth. Who was she – the merchant's daughter from across the road, perhaps? A girl from one of the farms? She was a bit too old to be one of my future pupils.

'Has he been here?' she cried. 'Has he been and gone again? The villain. He promised to wait for me. We're going up the hill to watch the sunset.' Again the flash of laughter in her eyes.

'I'm sorry,' I said, 'I'm a stranger. I only arrived this afternoon. But I assure you nobody has called here this evening.'

'Well now, and just who are you?' she said. 'And what are you doing here?'

'My name is William Reynolds,' I said. 'I'm the new schoolmaster.'

She gave me a look of the most utter sweet astonishment. 'The new – !' She shook her head. 'I'm most terribly confused,' she said. 'I really am. The queerest things are happening.'

'Sit down and tell me about it,' I said. For I liked the girl immensely. Blast that Johnny whoever-he-is, I thought; some fellows have all the luck. Here, I knew at once, was one of the few young women it was a joy to be with. I wished she would stay for supper. My mouth began to frame the invitation.

'He'll have gone to the hill without me,' she said. 'I'll wring his neck. The sun'll be down in ten minutes. I'd better hurry.'

She was gone as suddenly as she had come. The fragrance went with her. I discovered, a bit to my surprise, that I was shivering, even though it was a mild night and there was a decent fire burning in the grate.

'Goodnight,' I called after her.

No answer came back.

Blast that Johnny. I wouldn't mind stumbling to the top of a hill, breathless, with a rare creature like her, on such a beautiful night, I thought. I returned regretfully to my book. It was still light enough to read when I got to the end of the chapter. I looked out of the window at the russet-and-primrose sky. Two figures were silhouetted against the sunset on a rising crest of the hill. They stood there hand in hand. I was filled with happiness and envy.

I went to bed before midnight, in order to be fresh for my first morning in the new school.

I had grown utterly sick and tired of teaching mathematics in the junior secondary school in the city; trying to insert logarithms and trigonometry into the heads of louts whose only wish, like mine, was to be rid of the institution for ever. I read an advertisement in the educational journal for a male teacher – 'required urgently' – for a one-teacher island school in the north. There was only a month of the summer term to go. I sent in my application at once, and was appointed without even having to endure an interview. Two days later I was on an aeroplane flying over the snow-scarred highlands of Scotland. The mountains gave way to moors and firths. Then I looked down at the sea stretching away to a huge horizon; a dark swirling tide-race; an island neatly ruled into tilth and pasture. Other islands tilted towards us. The plane settled lightly on a runway set in a dark moor. An hour later I boarded another smaller plane, and after ten merry minutes flying level with kittiwakes and cormorants I was shaking hands with the island representative of the education committee. This was the local minister. I liked the Reverend Donald Barr at once. He was, like myself, a young bachelor, but he gave me a passable tea of ham-

and-eggs at the manse before driving me to the school. We talked easily and well together all the time. 'They're like every other community in the world,' he said, 'the islanders of Quoylay. They're good and bad and middling – mostly middling. There's not one really evil person in the whole island. If there's a saint I haven't met him yet. One and all, they're enormously hospitable in their farms – they'll share with you everything they have. The kids – they're a delight, shy and gentle and biddable. You've made a good move, mister, coming here, if the loneliness doesn't kill you. Sometimes it gets me down, especially on a Sunday morning when I find myself preaching to half-a-dozen unmoved faces. They were very religious once, now they're reverting to paganism as fast as they can. The minister is more or less a nonentity, a useless appendage. Changed days, my boy. We used to wield great power, we ministers. We were second only to the laird, and the school-master got ten pounds a year. Your remote predecessor ate the scraps from my predecessor's table. Changed days, right enough. Enjoy yourself, Bill. I know you will, for a year or two anyway.'

By this time the manse car had brought me home with my luggage, and we were seated at either side of a newly-lighted fire in the school-house parlour. Donald Barr went away to prepare his sermon. I picked a novel at random from the bookcase, and had read maybe a half-dozen pages when I had my first visitor, the girl with the abundant black hair and laughter-lighted face; the loved one; the slightly bewildered one; the looker into sunsets.

The pupils descended on the playground, and swirled round like a swarm of birds, just before nine o'clock next morning. There were twenty children in the island school, ranging in age from five to twelve. So, they had to be arranged in different sections in the single large classroom. The four youngest were learning to read from the new phonetic script. Half-a-dozen or so of the eldest pupils would be going after the summer holidays to the senior secondary school in Kirkwall; they were making a start on French and geometry. In between, and simultaneously, the others worked away at history, geography, reading, drawing, sums. I found the variety a bit bewildering, that first day.

Still, I enjoyed it. Everything that the minister had said about the island children was true. The impudence and indifference that the city children offered you in exchange for your labours, the common currency of my previous class-rooms, these were absent here. Instead, they looked at me and everything I did with a round-eyed wonderment. I expected that this would not last beyond the first weekend. Only once, in the middle of the afternoon, was there any kind of ruffling of the bright surface. With the six oldest ones I was going through a geometry theorem on the blackboard. A tall boy stood up. 'Please, sir,' he said, 'that's not the way Miss McKillop taught us to do it.'

The class-room had been murmurous as a beehive. Now there was silence, as if a spell had been laid on the school.

'Please, sir, on Thursday afternoons Miss McKillop gave us nature study.' This from a ten-year-old girl with hair like a bronze bell. She stood up and blurted it out, bravely and a little resentfully.

'And what exactly did this nature study consist of?' I said.

'Please, sir,' said a boy whose head was like a hayrick and whose face was a galaxy of freckles, 'we would go to the beach for shells, and sometimes, please, sir, to the marsh for wild flowers.'

'Miss McKillop took us all,' said another boy. 'Please sir.'

Miss McKillop . . . Miss McKillop . . . Miss McKillop . . . The name scattered softly through the school as if a rose had shed its petals. Indeed last night's fragrance seemed to be everywhere in the class-room. A dozen mouths uttered the name. They looked at me, but they looked at me as if somebody else was sitting at the high desk beside the blackboard.

'I see,' I said. 'Nature study on Thursday afternoons. I don't see anything against it, except that I'm a great duffer when it comes to flowers and birds and such-like. Still, I'm sure none of us will be any the worse of a stroll through the fields on a Thursday afternoon. But this Thursday, you see, I'm new here, I'm feeling my way, and I'm pretty ignorant of what should be, so I think for today we'd just better carry on the way we're doing.'

The spell was broken. The fragrance was withdrawn.

They returned to their phonetics and history and geometry. Their heads bent obediently once more over books and jotters. I lifted the pointer, and noticed that my fist was blue with cold. And the mouth of the boy who had first mentioned the name of Miss McKillop trembled, in the heart of that warm summer afternoon, as he gave me the proof of the theorem.

'Thank God for that,' said Donald Barr. He brought a chess-board and a box of chessmen from the cupboard. He blew a spurt of dust from them. 'We'd have grown to hate each other after a fortnight, trying to warm each other up with politics and island gossip.' He arranged the pieces on the board. 'I'm very glad also that you're only a middling player, same as me. We can spend our evenings in an amiable silence.'

We were very indifferent players indeed. None of our games took longer than an hour to play. No victory came about through strategy, skill, or foresight. All without exception that first evening were lost by some incredible blunder (followed by muted cursings and the despairing fall of a fist on the table).

'You're right,' I said after the fourth game, 'silence is the true test of friendship.'

We had won two games each. We decided to drink a jar of ale and smoke our pipes before playing the decider. Donald Barr made his own beer, a nutty potent brew that crept through your veins and overcame you after ten minutes or so with a drowsy contentment. We smoked and sipped mostly in silence; yet fine companionable thoughts moved through our minds and were occasionally uttered.

'I am very pleased so far,' I said after a time, 'with this island and the people in it. The children are truly a delight. Mrs Sinclair who makes the school dinner has a nice touch with stew. There is also the young woman who visited me briefly last night. She was looking for somebody else, unfortunately. I hope *she* comes often.'

'What young woman?' said the minister drowsily.

'She didn't say her name,' I said. 'She's uncommonly good-looking, what the teenagers in my last school would call a rare chick.'

'Describe this paragon,' said Donald Barr.

I am no great shakes at describing things, especially beautiful young women. But I did my best, between puffs at my pipe. The mass of black hair. The wide hazel eyes. The red restless laughing mouth. 'It was,' I said, 'as if she had come straight into the house out of a rose garden. She asked for Johnny.'

Something had happened to the Rev. Donald Barr. My words seemed to wash the drowsiness from his face; he was like a sleeper on summer hills overcome with rain. He sat up in his chair and looked at me. He was really agitated. He knocked the ember of tobacco out of his pipe. He took a deep gulp of ale from his mug. Then he walked to the window and looked out at the thickening light. The clock on the mantelshelf ticked on beyond eleven o'clock.

'And so,' I said, 'may she come back often to the school-house, if it's only to look for this Johnny.'

From Donald Barr, no answer. Silence is a test of friendship but I wanted very much to learn the name of my visitor; or rather I was seeking for a confirmation.

Donald Barr said, 'A ghost is the soul of a dead person who is earth-bound. That is, it is so much attached to the things of this world that it is unwilling to let go of them. It cannot believe it is dead. It cannot accept for one moment that its body has been gathered back into the four elements. It refuses to set out on the only road it can take now, into the kingdom of the dead. No, it is in love too much with what it has been and known. It will not leave its money and possessions. It will not forgive the wrongs that were done to it while it was alive. It clings on desperately to love.'

'I was not speaking about any ghost,' I said. 'I was trying to tell you about this very delightful lovely girl.'

'If I was a priest,' said Donald Barr, 'instead of a minister, I might tell you that a ghost is a spirit lost between this world and purgatory. It refuses to shed its earthly appetites. It will not enter the dark gate of suffering.'

The northern twilight thickened in the room while we spoke. Our conversation was another kind of chess. Yet each knew what the other was about.

'I hope she's there tonight,' I said. 'I might even prevail on her to make me some toast and hot chocolate. For it seems I'm going to get no supper in the manse.'

'You're not scared?' said Donald Barr from the window.

'No,' I said. 'I'm not frightened of that kind of ghost. It seemed to me, when we were speaking together in the school-house last night, this girl and I, that I was the wan lost one, the squeaker and gibberer, and she was a part of the ever-springing fountain.'

'Go home then to your ghost,' said Donald Barr. 'We won't play any more chess tonight. She won't harm you, you're quite right there.'

We stood together at the end of his garden path.

'Miss McKillop,' I murmured to the dark shape that was fumbling for the latch of the gate.

'Sandra McKillop,' said Donald, 'died the twenty-third of May this year. I buried her on the third of June, herself and John Germiston, in separate graves.'

'Tell me,' I said.

'No,' said Donald, 'for I do not know the facts. Never ask me for a partial account. It seemed to me they were happy. I refuse to wrong the dead. Go in peace.'

There was no apparition in the school-house that night. I went to bed and slept soundly, drugged with fresh air, ale, fellowship; and a growing wonderment.

The days passed, and I did not see the ghost again. Occasionally I caught the fragrance, a drift of sudden sweetness in the long corridor between kitchen and parlour, or in the garden or on the pebbled path between the house and the school. Occasionally a stir of cold went through the parlour late at night as I sat reading, and no heaping of peats would warm the air again for a half-hour or so. I would look up, eagerly I must confess, but nothing trembled into form and breathing out of the expectant air. It was as if the ghost had grown shy and uncertain, indicated her presence only by hints and suggestions. And in the class-room too things quietened down, and the island pupils and I worked out our regime together as the summer days passed. Only occasionally a five-year-old would whisper something about Miss McKillop, and smile, and then look sad; and it was like a small scattering of rose-petals. Apart from that everything proceeded smoothly to the final closing of books at the end of the school year.

One man in the island I did not like, and that was Henrikson who kept the island store and garage, my neighbour. A low wall separated the school garden from Henrikson's land, which was usually untidy with empty lemonade cases, oil drums, sodden cardboard boxes. Apart from the man's simple presence, which he insisted on inflicting on me, I was put out by things in his character. For example, he showed an admiration for learning and university degrees that amounted to sycophancy; and this I could not abide, having sprung myself from a race of labourers and miners and railwaymen, good people all, more solid and sound and kindly than most university people, in my experience. But the drift of Henrikson's talk was that farmers and such like, including himself, were poor creatures indeed compared to their peers who had educated themselves and got into the professions and so risen in the world. This was bad enough; but soon he began to direct arrows of slander at this person and that in the island. 'Arrows' is too open and forthright a word for it; it was more the work of 'the smiler with the knife'. Such-and-such a farmer, he told me, was in financial difficulties, we wouldn't be seeing him in Quoylay much longer. This other young fellow had run his motor-cycle for two years now without a licence; maybe somebody should do something about it; he himself had no objection to sending anonymous letters to the authorities in such a case. Did I see that half-ruined croft down at the shore? Two so-called respectable people in this island – he would mention no names – had spent a whole weekend together there at show time last summer, a married man and a farmer's daughter. The straw they had lain on hadn't even been cleaned out . . . This was the kind of talk that went on over the low wall between school and store on the late summer evenings. It was difficult to avoid the man; as soon as he saw me weeding the potato patch, or watering the pinks, out he came with his smirkings and cap-touchings, and leaned confidentially over the wall. It is easy to say I could simply have turned my back on him; but in many ways I am a coward; and even the basest of the living can coerce me to some extent. One evening his theme was the kirk and the minister. 'I'm not wanting to criticize any friend of yours,' he said. 'I've seen him more than once in the school-house and I've heard that you visit him in the manse, and it's no business of mine, but that man is not a *real* minister, if you ask me. We're used with a different kind of preaching in this island, and a different kind of pastoral behaviour too, I assure you of that. I know for a fact that he brews — he bought two tins of malt, and hops, from the store last month. The old ministers were one and all very much against drink. What's a minister for if he doesn't keep people's feet on the true path, yes, if he doesn't warn them and counsel them in season and out of season, you know, in regard to their conduct? The old ministers that were here formerly had a proper understanding of their office. But this Mr Barr, he closes his eyes to things that are a crying scandal to the whole island. For example —'

'Mr Barr is a very good friend of mine,' I said.

'O, to be sure,' he cried. 'I know. He's an educated man and so are you too, Mr Reynolds. I spoke out of place, I'm sorry. I'm just a simple countryman, brought up on the shorter catechism and the good book. Times are changing fast. I'm sure people who have been to the university have a different way of looking at things from an old country chap. No offence, Mr Reynolds, I hope.'

A few moths were out, clinging to the stones, fluttering and birring softly on the kitchen window. I turned and went in without saying goodnight to Mr Henrikson.

And as I went along the corridor, with a bad taste in my mouth from that holy old creep across the road, I heard it, a low reluctant weeping from above, from the bedroom. I ran upstairs and threw open the door. The room was empty, but it was as cold as the heart of an iceberg, and the unmistakable fragrance clung about the window curtains and the counterpane. There was the impression of a head on the pillow, as if someone had knelt beside the bed for a half-hour to sort out her troubles in silence.

My ghost was being pierced by a slow wondering sadness.

Henrikson my neighbour was not a man to be put off by slights and reprovings. The very next evening I was fixing lures to my sillock rod in the garden, and there he was humped over the wall, obsequious and smiling.

It had been a fine day, hadn't it? And now that the school was closed for the summer, would I not be going off to Edinburgh or Brighton or Majorca for a bit of a holiday? Well, that was fine, that I liked the island so much. To tell the truth, most of the folk in Quoylay were very glad to have a quiet respectable man like me in the school, after the wild goings-on that had been just before I arrived . . .

I was sick and tired of this man, and yet I knew that now I was to hear, in a very poisoned and biased version, the story of Sandra McKillop the school-mistress and Johnny. Donald Barr, out of compassion for the dead, would never have told me. So I threw my arms companionably over the wall and I offered Henrikson my tobacco pouch and I said, 'What kind of goings-on would that be now, Mr Henrikson?'

Miss Sandra McKillop had come to the island school straight from the teachers' training college in Scotland two years before. (I am paraphrasing Henrikson's account, removing most of the barbs, trying to imagine a rose here and there.) She was a great change from the previous teacher, a finicky perjink old maid, and that for a start warmed the hearts of the islanders to her. But it was in the school itself that she scored her great success; the children of all ages took to her at once. She was a born teacher. Every day she held them in thrall from the first bell to the last. And even after school there was a dancing cluster of them round her all the way to her front door. The stupid ones and the ugly ones adored her especially, because she made them feel accepted. She enriched their days.

She was a good-looking girl. ('I won't deny that,' said Henrikson, 'as bonny a young woman as ever I saw.') More than one of the island bachelors hung about the school gate from time to time, hoping for a word with her. Nothing doing; she was pleasant and open with them and with everybody, but love did not enter her scheme of things; at least, not yet. She was a sociable girl, and was invited here and there among the farms for supper. She gave one or two talks to the Rural Institute, about her holidays abroad and life in her training collge. She went to church every Sunday morning and sang in the choir, and afterwards taught in the Sunday School. But mostly she stayed at home. New bright curtains appeared in all the windows. She was especially fond of flowers; the little glass porch at the front of the house was full all the year round with flowering plants; the school garden, that first summer after she came, was a delight. All the bees in the island seemed to forage in those flowers.

How she first met John Germiston, nobody knows. It was almost certainly during one of those long walks she took in the summer evenings of her second year. John Germiston kept a croft on the side of the Ward Hill, a poor enough place with a couple of cows and a scatter of hens. Three years before he had courted a girl from the neighbouring island of Hellya. He had sailed across and got married in the kirk there and brought his bride home, a shy creature whose looks changed as swiftly as the summer loch. And there in his croft he installed her. And she would be seen from time to time feeding the hens at the end of the house, or hanging out washing, or standing at the road-end with her basket waiting for the grocery van. But she never became part of the community. With the coming of winter she was seen less and less – a wide-eyed face in the window, a figure against the skyline looking over the sound towards Hellya. The doctor began to call regularly once a week at the croft. John Germiston let it be known in the smithy that his wife was not keeping well.

There is a trouble in the islands that is called *morbus orcadensis.* It is a darkening of the mind, a progressive flawing and thickening of the clear lens of the spirit. It is said to be induced in sensitive people by the long black overhang of winter; the howl and sob of the wind over the moors that goes on sometimes for days on end; the perpetual rain that makes of tilth and pasture one indiscriminate bog; the unending gnaw of the sea at the crags.

Soon after the new year they took the stricken girl to a hospital in the south.

Of course everyone in Quoylay was sorry for John Germiston. It is a hard thing for a young handsome man to work a croft by himself. And yet these things happen from time to time. There are a few cheerful old men in the folds of the hills, or down by the shore, who have been widowers since their twenties.

Somewhere on the hill, one evening in spring, John Germiston met Sandra McKillop. They spoke together. He brought her to his house. She stood in the door and saw the desolation inside; the rusted pot, the torn curtains, the filthy hearth. The worm had bored deep into that rose.

From that first meeting everything proceeded swiftly and inevitably. No sooner was school over for the day than Miss McKillop shook the adoring children off and was away to the croft of Stanebreck on the hill with a basket of bannocks or a bundle of clean washing. She stayed late into the evening. Sometimes they would be seen wandering together along the edge of the crags, while far below the Atlantic fell unquietly among shelving rocks and hollow caves; on and on they walked into the sunset, while near and far the crofts watched and speculated.

Night after night, late, as April brightened into May, she would come home alone. A light would go on in the school-house kitchen. She would stand in the garden for a while among her hosts of blossoms. Then she would go in and lock the door. Her bedroom window was briefly illuminated. Then the whole house was dark.

'I suppose,' said Henrikson, 'nobody could have said a thing if it had stopped there. There was suspicion – well, what do you expect, a young woman visiting a married man night after night, and her a school-teacher with a position to keep up – but I don't suppose anybody could have done a thing about it.

'But in the end the two of them got bold. They got careless. It wasn't enough for this hussy to visit her fancyman in his croft – O no, the bold boy takes to sallying down two or three times a week to the school-house for his supper, if you please.

'Still nobody could make a move. A person is entitled to invite another person to the house for supper, even though on one occasion at least they don't draw the curtain and I can see from my kitchen their hands folded together in the middle of the table and all that laughter going on between them.

'Mr Reynolds, I considered it my duty to watch, yes, and to report to the proper quarters if necessary.

'One Friday evening Germiston arrives at the school-house at nine o'clock. A fine evening at the beginning of May it was. The light went on in the parlour. The curtain was drawn. After an hour or so the light goes on in her bedroom. "Ah ha," says I to myself, "I've missed their farewells tonight, I've missed all the kissing in the door." . . . But I was wrong, Mr Reynolds. Something far worse was happening. At half past five in the morning I got up to stock the van, and I saw him going home over the hill, black against the rising sun. At *half past five* in the morning.

'That same day, being an elder, I went to the manse. Mr Barr refused to do anything about it. "Miss McKillop is a member of my church. If she's in trouble of any sort she'll come to me," he said. "I will not act on slanderous rumours. There's more than one crofter on the hill at half past five in the morning." . . . There's your modern ministers for you. And I don't care if he is your friend, Mr Reynolds, I must speak my mind about this business.

'By now the whole island was a hive of rumour.

'Neither John Germiston nor Miss McKillop could stir without some eye being on them and some tongue speculating. And yet they went on meeting one another, quite open and shameless, as if they were the only living people in an island of ghosts. They would wander along the loch shore together, hand in hand, sometimes stopping to watch the swans or the eiders, not caring at all that a dozen croft windows were watching their lingerings and kissings. Then, arms about one another, they would turn across the fields in the direction of the school-house.

'Ay, but the dog of Stanebreck was a lonely dog till the sun got up, all that month of May.

'One Tuesday morning she arrived late for school, at a quarter past nine. She arrived with the mud of the hill plastered over her stockings, and half-dead with sleep. "Hurrah," cried the bairns congregated round the locked door of the school. They knew no better, the poor innocent things. They shouted half with delight and half with disappointment when she gave them the morning off, told them to come back in the afternoon. They were not to know what manner of thing had made their teacher so exhausted.

'Of course it was no longer possible to have a woman like her for the island teacher.

'I had written to this person and that. Inquiries were under way, discreetly, you know, so as not to cause undue sensation. I think in the end pressure would have been put on her to resign. But as things turned out it wasn't necessary.

'One night they both disappeared. They vanished as if they had been swept clean off the face of the island. The school door remained locked all the next week. John Germiston's unmilked cow bellowed in its steep field. "Ah ha," said the men in the smithy, "so it's come to this, they've run away together . . ."

'Ten days later a fishing boat drew up the two bodies a mile west of Hellya. Their arms were round each other. The fishermen had trouble separating the yellow hair from the black hair.'

Henrikson was having difficulty with his breathing; his voice dropped and quavered and choked so that I could hardly hear his last three words. 'They were naked,' he mouthed venomously.

Moths flickered between us. The sea boomed and hushed from the far side of the hill. In a nearby croft a light came on.

'And so,' said Henrikson, 'we decided that we didn't want a woman teacher after that. That's why you're here, Mr Reynolds.'

We drifted apart, Henrikson and I, to our separate doors. Eagerly that night I wished for the vanished passion to fill my rooms: the ghost, the chill, the scent of roses. But in the schoolhouse was only a most terrible desolation.

On fine evenings that summer, when tide and light were suitable, Donald Barr and I would fish for sillocks and cuithes from the long sloping skerry under the crag. Or we would ask the loan of a crofter's boat, if the fish were scanty there, and row out with our lines into the bay.

The evening before the agricultural show was bright and calm. We waited in the bay with dripping oars for the sun to set behind the hill. We put our rods deep into the dazzle but not one cuithe responded. Presently the sun furled itself in a cloud, and it was as if a rose had burst open over the sea's unflawed mirror. Cuithe fishing is a sport that requires little skill. Time after time we hauled our rods in burgeoning with strenuous sea fruit, until the bottom of the dinghy was a floor of unquiet gulping silver. Then the dense undersea hordes moved away, and for twenty minutes, while the rose of sunset faded and the long bay gloomed, we caught nothing.

'It must have been about here,' I said to Donald Barr, 'that they were drowned.'

He said nothing. He had never discussed the affair with me, beyond that one mention of the girl's name at the manse gate.

A chill moved in from the west; breaths of night air flawed the dark sea mirror.

'The earth-bound soul refuses to acknowledge its death,' said Donald. 'It is desperately in love with the things of this world – possessions, fame, lust. How, once it has tasted them, can it ever exist without them? Death is a negation of all that wonder and delight. It will not enter the dark door of the grave. It lurks, a ghost, round the places where it fed on earthly joys. It spreads a coldness about the abodes of the living. The five senses pulse through it, but fadingly, because there is nothing for the appetite to feed on, only memories and shadows. Sooner or later the soul must enter the dark door. But no – it will not – for a year or for a decade or for a century it lingers about the place of its passion, a rose garden or a turret or a cross-roads. It will not acknowledge that all this loveliness of sea and sky and islands, and all the rare things that happen among them, are merely shadows of a greater reality. At last the starved soul is forced to accept it, for it finds itself utterly alone, surrounded as time goes by with strange new unloved objects and withered faces and skulls. Reluctantly it stoops under the dark lintel. All loves are forgotten then. It sets out on the quest for Love itself. For this it was created in the beginning.'

We hauled the dinghy high up the beach and secured her to a rock. A few mild summer stars glimmered. The sea was dark in the bay, under the shadow of the cliff, but the Atlantic horizon was still flushed a little with reluctant sunset, and all between was a vast slow heave of gray.

'I have a bottle of very good malt whisky in the school-house,' I said. 'I think a man could taste worse things after a long evening on the sea.'

It was then that I heard the harp-like shivering cries far out in the bay. The sea thins out the human voice, purges it of its earthiness, lends it a purity and poignancy.

'Wait for me,' cried the girl's voice. 'Where are you? You're swimming too fast.'

Donald Barr had heard the voices also. Night folded us increasingly in gloom and cold as we stood motionless under the sea-bank. He passed me his tobacco pouch. I struck a match. The flame trembled between us.

'This way,' shouted a firm strong happy voice (but attenuated on the harpstrings of the sea). 'I'm over here.'

The still bay shivered from end to end with a single glad cry. Then there was silence.

The minister and I turned. We climbed over loose stones and sandy hillocks to the road. We lashed our heavy basket of cuithes into the boot of Donald Barr's old Ford. Then we got in, one on each side, and he pressed the starter.

'Earth-bound souls enact their little dramas over and over again, but each time a little more weakly,' he said. 'The reality of death covers them increasingly with its good oblivion. You will be haunted for a month or two yet. But at last the roses will lose their scent.'

The car stopped in front of the dark school-house.

The Tarn and the Rosary

(i)

He was cast out of unremembered dark into salt, light, shifting immensities. A woman closed him in with hills, sweet waters, biddings, bodings, thunders and dewfalls of love. He sat among three sisters and one brother at a scrubbed table. Colm: that was his name. There were small noises from a new cradle in the corner. His mother was a little removed from him then. His father was in the west since morning. The cow Flos that belonged to the croft next door bent and nuzzled buttercups. Hens screeched round a shower of oats from old Merran's fist. A gentleness of beard and eyes came in at the door at thickening light with fish and an oar: his father. Then his mother and brother and three sisters and the old one went silently to their different places. The infant, Ellen, was lifted from cradle to breast. The lamp was lit. His father wiped plate with crust. His father filled his pipe. His father spoke from the chair beside the smoke and flame. His father opened a book. There was a silence. The boy closed his eyes. Then very ancient wisdom was uttered upon the house, a gentle deliberate voice prayed from the armchair: his grandfather.

(ii)

In the wide grassy playground the children whirled and chirruped and slouched. A whistle shrieked: the children were enchanted to silence. They stepped quietly past the teacher into a huge gloom, desks and globe and blackboard. Miss Silver said, more grave than any elder, 'A terrible thing has happened, a sum of money has been removed from my purse this morning. This is what must happen now. You will all empty your pockets on to your desks, every single thing, and then we will see who took the half-crown and the two sixpences . . .' Guilt whitened Colm's face like chalk (though he had done nothing). Soon the desks were strewn with bits of string, shells, fluff, cocoa tin lids, broken blades. Miss Silver strode among all this bruck, jerking her head back and fore like a bird. 'Very well,' she said. 'The thief has hidden his ill-gotten gains. It is now a matter for the police. The policeman will be taking the boat from Hamnavoe tomorrow, with a warrant, and also handcuffs, I have no doubt.' Colm felt like a person diseased, scabbed all over with coins, so that everyone could see he was the culprit (though he had only once seen a half-crown, between his father's fingers, the day his father opened his tin box to pay the rent; a white heavy rich round thing). 'We are doing the exports and imports of Mexico, I think,' said Miss Silver in a hurt voice, turning to the senior class. The school was a place of chastity and awe all that afternoon – the brand of crime was burned on it . . . 'I wonder if Jackie Hay will be long in jail?' said Andrick Overton on the way home from school. Torquil, Colm's brother, asked why. A surge of joy went through the boy because it was not being said among the pupils that he and only he was the thief. 'Did you see Jackie's mouth when the teacher was searching the desks?' said Andrick. 'He had slack silver teeth.' The older boys all laughed on the road, and Colm laughed too. The Hamnavoe policeman did not come and Jackie Hay was not sent to prison. Instead he bought the big boys who were with him lucky-bags and liquorice sticks next day, Saturday, from the grocery van. He smoked a packet of woodbines himself and was sick in a ditch. Nobody was sorry for Jackie Hay. Torquil's mouth was black and sweet all that afternoon.

(iii)

Colm came through the village carrying a basket of eggs and a pail of buttermilk from the farm of Wardings. 'What a kind body the wife of Wardings is,' his mother always said, her voice going gentle and wondering. It was true; he liked going to the farm for the eggs and kirned-milk on a Saturday morning. Mrs Sanderson always took him in and gave him a thick slice of the gingerbread she had baked herself. She asked him questions about the school and his family in a hearty voice. She didn't seem to mind if some golden breadcrumbs fell from his mouth on to her stone floor which was always so clean. The door into the whitewashed kitchen would open for sure, sometime when he was eating the gingerbread, and the dog come in. He didn't like dogs. He was nervous of dogs. But Rastus, the black-and-white collie, seemed to have some share in the kindliness and benevolence of Wardings. Boy and dog, after the first unsure moment, eyed each other trustfully. He patted the neck of the dog (but still with some reserve). Rastus licked the sweet crumbs from the fingers of his other hand. 'Mrs Sanderson,' he said, 'I'll have to be going now.' . . . Smiling, she stood in the door and waved goodbye to him.

It was steep, the road down through the village. One terrible morning, when he was five, he had fallen; every single egg was smashed and the buttermilk was spilt; red and gray tatters across the frosty road. He ran home yelling, empty-handed. He would not even go back to get the pail and the basket. Mary-Anne had to go and fetch them.

Today he stepped easily down the brae, holding the pail in one hand and the basket in the other. So delicate his going that the buttermilk only, at most, shivered into circles. It was pleasant, the dark rich tang of the gingerbread in his mouth. Mrs Sanderson was nice. He wouldn't mind biding at a farm like Wardings.

Huge strength and power broke the skyline. Tom Sanderson the farmer was ploughing the high field with his team. He shouted to Colm and waved his arm. Colm waved back.

It was dinner-time, surely. There was not a soul in the village street. The smell of mince and boiled cabbage came from the Eunsons' house; that made him feel hungry. The only living thing on the road was the merchant's dog, Solomon – a lion-coloured mongrel – and it lay asleep in the sun under a window with loaves and cream cookies and one iced cake in it. A bare curved knuckle-ended bone lay at the dog's unconscious head. Whose birthday was it? Colm looked through the shop window at the cake. It must be a boy or girl from one of the better-off families – from the Bu farm, maybe, or the manse, or the doctor's. From the house above the shop came the rattle of plates, a shred of vapour, a most delicious smell of frying onions. His dinner would be ready too, he must hurry. There was no candle – it was more likely to be a christening cake. With his left foot he eased the bone towards the wet black nose. The bone whispered in the dust. A name was written in pink icing on the white-iced cake: *Christopher Albert Marcusson.* That must be the minister's new baby. There would be marzipan inside, spices, sherry, raisins, threepenny bits. The tawny flank heaved once, gently. Sweetness, sweetness. Colm loved all sweet things – languors and dissolvings and raptures in the hot cave of the mouth. The road swirled. His left leg was draped in rage. Teeth and eyes flashed under him, and fell away. Two livid punctured curves converged along his left thigh; they began to leak; his knee was tattered with blood. He set the eggs down carefully on the road; the buttermilk quivered once and was still. The dog skulked across the road to the tailor shop; and it looked back at him once or twice balefully. He looked down at the lacerated leg. It was very strange, his leg wasn't sore at all. On the contrary, it felt warm and pleasant and refreshed (like when you draw it out of a cold pool and let it dry in the sun). Yet he had been bitten. The merchant's dog had bitten him. Nobody had seen it happen. His lip quivered. He picked up the basket and the pail and went slowly, limping, through the dinner-time village to the house at the shore. There was really no need to limp at all, but he limped. It was terrible – he had tried to be good to the dog, to put his bone near his mouth seeing that it was dinner-time, and this was the way the beast had repaid him. His throat worked, and he felt tears in his eyes. There was a numbness now in his thigh. He hurried on. His father was sitting on the wall smoking his after-dinner pipe. Some buttermilk slopped over, the eggs clacked gently. He sobbed. His father looked at him and said, 'You're late for your dinner,' and then saw with astonishment that something was wrong. Colm set down pail and basket on the flat quernstone at the door and with one loud wail flung himself into the fragrant gloom of the kitchen, and the startled faces, and the warm enfolding arms of his mother. He hid the mask of tears in her bosom. He held up his wounded leg. His mother said, 'There there' and 'Poor angel', and set him down on a chair. His mother issued calm orders: kettle on fire, a bandage, lysol. His three sisters dispersed about these tasks. 'That dog of Wardings,' said his mother. 'What do they call him, Rastus, I've never trusted him. The sly way he comes up to you. It's a wonder to me Mrs Sanderson lets the thing wander about freely like that. I'll speak to her.'

It was a secret. Nobody knew but himself. He wouldn't tell her till he was safely in bed that it wasn't Rastus, it was the merchant's dog, Solomon, that had bitten him. Maybe they would have to cut off his leg. He sat erect in the chair and gave out long quivering sobs.

Mary-Anne took a small round purple bottle from the cupboard and gave it to the mother.

Grand-dad muttered from his chair beside the fire, 'That's nothing, a clean bite. There's worse things than that'll happen to him. Fuss, fuss.'

His father had come in and was leaning against the kitchen doorpost, watching him, and his pipe glowed and faded in the interior gloom.

Great jags of flame went into his thigh. He screamed and held on desperately to his mother. 'It's all right, darling,' she said. 'I'm putting a drop of lysol on. That'll make you better.'

The disinfectant flamed and flickered and guttered in his white flesh. The faces came about him again. Freda was smiling – she seemed to be pleased at his sufferings. His father's pipe glowed and faded and glowed. He was the important person in the house that day. He sobbed and sniffed in a long last luxury of self-pity. His mother cut a piece of lint with the scissors.

(iv)

Colm crouched among the tall grasses of the dune. 'Colm, where are you? You must come home . . .' It was Ellen's voice that went wandering along the sea-banks, here and there, seeking him out. He wished Ellen would go away. 'Colm, something has happened . . .' His grandfather was dead, that's what had happened. He knew without Ellen having to come and tell him. The old man had lain ill for ten days in the parlour bed. A deepening silence had gathered about him. The mother and children passed from room to room in whispers. He lay there, a lonely stricken figure. 'Colm, mam wants you home now . . .' He pretended not to hear Ellen's quavering command. He scooped up a handful of sand and let it stream through his fingers. He left the dune and slipped like a shadow down to the shore. If Ellen came that way he would hide in the cave. 'Colm, it's grand-dad. Hurry up . . .' He wished Ellen would go away and leave him alone. He did not like people spying on his feelings. He did not feel anything, anyway, in the face of this suffering and death, except a kind of blank wonderment. He dipped one foot in a rockpool. A salt vice gripped his ankle. The coldness reverberated in his belly, tingled in his ear-lobes and fingers. He turned. His sister was going back across the field. Colm was the only person on that mile-long sweep of beach. The sea pulsed slowly over seaweed and sand. A wave smashed the bright calm rockpool.

The boy moved across a narrowing strip of sand. It must be nearly high tide. He sat down on a rock. What was grand-dad now, an angel? He stood up and sent a flat stone leaping and skidding over the highest gleam of the sea. It was full flood. 'There'll be more fun in the house now. We'll be able to sing and shout again.' He neither liked nor disliked his grandfather. Grand-dad was just a part of the house, like the cupboard and the straw chair he sat in. Grand-dad could be very grumpy and ill-natured. Grand-dad sat at the fire all winter putting ships into bottles. People on holiday, tourists, English trout fishers, came and bought them from him. Then grand-dad would be pleased, flattening out the pound notes, folding them, stowing them carefully into his purse. The ships-in-bottles were always the same: a three-masted clipper, a rock with a lighthouse, a blue and white curling plaster sea. Grand-dad had been a sailor when he was young. Then he had come home and gone to the fishing. He was very old now. It was grand-dad's house they were living in – would they be put out of it now that he was dead? Grand-dad had almost drowned one day off Braga Rock when he was coming home from the lobsters and a sudden gale

had torn the sea apart. He told the story so often that Colm knew it
by heart. This past winter grand-dad had added a few new words:
'Life was sweet then. A pleasant thing it was for the eyes to behold
the sun. Anyway, I got ashore. But now I would be glad to be taken
. . .' He had become very remote from them all lately. He smoked
his pipe still and spat into a spittoon on the floor. His mother had
to clean out the spittoon, a horrible job, long slimy clinging slugs of
spittle into the burn – the gushing freshness of the burn bore the
old man's juices out to sea. Colm and Ellen had to look about the
beach for gulls' feathers to clean the bore of his pipe; if they found
good ones grand-dad would open his purse carefully and give them
a ha'penny each. He stopped making ships-in-bottles soon after
New Year. More and more often he would pause in the arm-chair,
his pipe half-way to his mouth, as if he was listening for something.
For two whole days his pipe had lain cold on the mantelpiece. 'I
won't be a trouble to you much longer,' grand-dad had said to
mother. He frowned at Ellen and Colm, as if they were strangers
trespassing on his peace. The fishing-boat belonged to him too.
Would they have to sell it now? What way could his dad go to the
fishing if they had no boat? Maybe they would starve. Colm walked
up the cart-track from the beach. He sat down on the grass and put
on his sandals. The sea pulsed, a slow diastole of ebb; it surged in
still, but left shining fringes; the forsaken sand gleamed dully. They
would all have to wear black clothes, or at least black cloth
diamonds on the sleeves of their coats and jackets. That was
horrible. There would have to be the funeral, of course. His
grand-dad would be put deep in the churchyard: frail old bones,
silky beard, sunk jaws. The wood of the coffin would begin to rot in
the wet winter earth. Then spring would come, but grand-dad
would know nothing about it. There were cornfields all about the
kirkyard. In summer the land would be athrob with ripeness, the
roots in the kirkyard too. Grand-dad would have 'given his flesh to
increase the earth's ripeness': that was Jock Skaill the tailor's way of
looking at it. That, he assured Colm, was the meaning of death. But
most of the Norday women said nobody, least of all a child, should
pay attention to an atheist like Jock Skaill. Still, there was more in
what Jock Skaill said, in Colm's opinion, than in all that talk about

angels and harps and streets of gold. His grand-dad would be lost
in a heaven like that. 'My grand-father, Andrew Sinclair the
fisherman, is dead.' He could not really believe it. Merran Wylie
was flinging oats to her hens at the end of her croft. The boy and
the woman looked at each other in passing. Merran shook her head
sorrowfully, then emptied her aluminium bowl and went hurriedly
back in through her door. When he turned the corner there it was,
down at the shore, their house with the blinds drawn against the
sweetness of day. The whole house looked blind and bereft. The
door opened and a woman who had no right to be there shook his
mother's rug and went in again, leaving the door open: Jessie Gray
from Garth. All the village women had united to help his mother.
That's what happened whenever anybody died. Bella Simison from
the Smithy came to the open door and stood looking out over the
fields, shading her eyes with her hand. They were all wondering
about him, Colm, for of course he should be in the house with the
rest of the family at such an important time. He stood behind the
fuchsia bush in the manse garden till Mrs Simison had gone in
again. It was Saturday. He heard shouts from the end of the village:
the boys were playing football in the quarry field. Their shouts
sounded profane. They did not understand the gravity of what had
happened. Colm felt as if he was about to enter a solemn temple.
He heard voices over the high wall of Sunnybrae. 'Yes, so I hear,
Andrew Sinclair the fisherman . . . About ten this morning. He's
well relieved, the poor man. Two strokes in a week . . .' The
minister's wife and Mrs Spence of Sunnybrae, Captain Spence's
widow, were talking about the death of his grand-dad.

He ran swiftly and silently across the grass to the house of death.

He stood with fluttering breath in the open door. The kitchen
was full of gray whispers and moving shadows. He exchanged,
furtively, the light for the gloom of the lobby.

His mother's face was purified, as if a fire had passed through it.
She sat in the straw-back chair beside the dresser. The village
women fussed around her. One was making tea at the stove. One
was washing the best china in preparation for (probably) the
funeral meal. Jessie Gray was telling stories about Andrew Sinclair
– all the memorable things he had done and said in his life: from

time to time the other women shook their heads slowly and smiled. Mrs Sanderson from Wardings farm was baking bannocks on the girdle. The only grieving creatures in the house were the two younger girls. Freda and Ellen hung about with blubbered faces and large eyes in the darkest corner of the room. His father sat in the window-seat; he looked uncomfortable in the company of all these priestesses of death. Freda and Ellen glanced reproachfully at Colm as he entered, silently, the kitchen.

The village women turned grave complacent faces on the new-comer.

'Colm,' said his mother in a queer artificial voice, 'your grandfather's passed away.'

'I know,' he muttered ill-naturedly.

It was not death. It was a kind of solemn game with words and gestures, a feast of flowers and false memories.

He followed Jessie Gray into the parlour.

Even when he looked down on the strange familiar cold face on the pillow it was still all a mime to give importance and dignity to a poor house. Two of the village women looked smilingly down at the corpse from the other side of the bed. Grand-dad's face was a still pool.

'Touch the brow with your hand.' It was the tranquil voice of Jessie Gray, who knew all about the trappings and ceremonies of death; she had prepared a hundred corpses for the kirkyard in her time.

Colm put two fingers, lightly, to his grandfather's forehead; they winced from an intense and bitter coldness. He could have cried out with terror. Now he knew that his grandfather was dead indeed.

He saw the cold pipe on the bedside table. He remembered the gulls' feathers and the ha'pennies. His grand-dad had been a very sweet kind old man.

The women watched him slyly. He knew these women. They were waiting for him to burst into tears. That was the pious thing for a boy to do. Then they would come about the bereaved one with their false hearty comfortings. He hated to have his feelings spied on. He would not cry to please them.

'How peaceful he looks,' said Jessie Gray.

He looked earnestly into the cold pool that was growing rigid, even while he looked and wondered, with the frost of death.

(v)

'Alice, tell them what I mean by the phrase "colours of the spectrum",' said Miss Silver.

Alice Rendall was the cleverest pupil in the Norday school. When the ten-year-olds were arranged in order of merit at the start of each week, Alice sat always at the top seat with the class medal pinned to her jersey: a heavy lead disc with *For Merit* stamped on it. The little ring on top of the medal blossomed with a ribbon.

Colm sometimes had the feeling that Alice was made of china rather than flesh, there was such fragility and coldness and cleanness about her. She did not get into trouble of any kind – did not whisper to her neighbours or pass notes – did not suck pan-drops through her handkerchief – did not leave her coat in school when the sun broke the rain-clouds – had never been known to raise her hand, untimely, with an urgent 'Please, miss, may I leave the room?' Some of the girls were not above showing the fringes of their knickers to the boys under the desk; never Alice. Her face shone each morning from much soap-and-water and a soft towel.

Alice was good at nearly everything: sums, reading, writing, spelling, history, geography. She did not have much of a singing voice, it was true. Her drawings were not as good as Willie Hume's. And she could not run and somersault as well as most of the other girls. 'Alice Rendall, you have the highest marks this week again,' said Miss Silver regularly every Friday afternoon. 'You will sit at the top of the class on Monday morning. Well done, Alice. Second, John Hay. Third, James Marcusson . . .'

Colm was not particularly good at any subject. He liked history. He was bad at drawing and geography. He did a strange perverse thing every Friday: he deliberately falsified his marks, downgraded himself, so that he could share the bottom place in class with a boy called Phil Kerston. As surely as Alice Rendall was dux each week,

Philip Kerston was dunce. Phil was utterly ignorant of every subject on the school curriculum. But he could snare rabbits. He could light fires in a gale. He had taken eggs from the face of Hundhead, the highest cliff in the island.

Miss Silver gave Phil jobs to do, such as look after the school fire in winter, wipe the blackboard clean with a duster, and fill the ink-wells. In school he was good-natured and quiet.

Colm sat beside Phil Kerston whenever he could. The smell of rabbits and grass-fires attracted him. Another part of the attraction was that he was a little afraid of the strange wild ignorant boy.

One Friday afternoon Phil Kerston and Colm whispered to-gether on the front seat while Miss Silver wrote multiplication tables on the blackboard. Tomorrow, Saturday, they were to burn heather among the hills. Colm promised to bring a box of matches. He would buy it with the penny he got every Saturday from his father.

Colm ran through the gap in the hills, breathless, after Phil Kerston and Andrik Overton. The sun was hot on the gray rocks. A bee blundered from heather-bell to heather-bell. Colm stumbled up the cart track.

He stood between the two hills, Brunafea and Torfea, and looked back. Phil and Andrik had gone on ahead, into the heart of the island. Colm had never been as far as this before. He did not like to be too far away from his mother's door. He saw the village down below, and the beach with a few boats hauled up, and small moving toy cows in the field of Wardings.

So, up here was where the farmers and crofters dug their winter fires. The long deep black lines of the peat-banks stretched across a flank of Brunafea that could not be seen from the village.

But he would have to hurry. Phil Kerston and Andrik Overton were two lost voices, thin and sweet, answering each other from the interior of the island. They would not wait for Colm, who couldn't move as fast as them on account of the asthma that bothered him sometimes in the summer. They had taken his box of matches from him and gone on up.

Colm did not like to be alone in strange places. He had got his breath back now. He ran on, between the summer hills, in the direction of the voices.

He rounded a shoulder of Torfea, a little stony outcrop, and a world he had never seen before opened out before him; the barren interior of Norday. He caught his breath, it was so lonely and beautiful. There was not a croft in sight. There was nothing but sweeps of moor and bog, and, like a jewel among the starkness, a little loch. A hidden burn sang under Colm's feet. A lark, very high up, drenched the desolation with song.

Colm ran down towards the loch that was still half-a-mile away. It was Tumilshun Loch. He had heard his father and the other men speaking about it in the smithy. He had seen the English trout-fishers in summer setting out with rod and reel for the place. These men with the loud voices and thick tweeds would bide among the hills till sunset. A small shiver went over Colm's skin. He would not care to spend even an hour in such a desolate place.

Where were Phil and Andrik? He couldn't hear them any more. They might be gathering blackberries. Andrik had brought a tin can for that purpose. Colm went down a few paces more in the direction of the loch. A sprig of heather scratched his bare ankle. He put his hand to his mouth. 'Phil,' he called out, 'where are you?'

The shadow of a cloud moved across Brunafea.

It was unnerving, the sound of his voice. It was like blasphemy. It bounced off the craggy face of Brunafea. It seemed to shiver across the face of the loch. It came back to him, all eeriness and mockery, and died among the far hills. Colm listened, appalled. His heart pounded in his chest.

Why didn't Phil and Andrick answer him? He would not shout like that again.

It was then that the hinterland was drained suddenly of all its colour. The lark stopped singing. The sun had gone behind a cloud.

Tumilshun lay there below, a sheet of dead pewter. Colm remembered how his father had told him that it was a very deep loch: in his time two people had committed suicide in it. Fifty years ago a girl from the croft of Swenquoy was found floating among the reeds.

Colm faced quickly back towards the gap in the hills. He climbed like a goat, from rock to heather-clump, out of the awful landscape. He could not have uttered another cry – terror had numbed his throat. He fell and rose and fell among the clumps of heather. A flood of light came over the flank of Torfea and enveloped him. He ran on. Only when he could see a segment of ocean between the hills did he turn back: there Tumilshun lay, a dark blue gleam, far below him. And there, between the loch and the lower slope of Brunafea, was a red-gray smudge. Phil and Andrick had lit their fires, and gone on.

The lark, empty of song, eased itself down. It guttered out among the coarse grass.

With a surge of joy (but ashamed at the same time of his cowardice) Colm emerged from the sinister region and saw below him the squares of tilth and pasture, and the village: and Tom of Wardings cutting hay in his field with a flashing scythe. Further away, between the ness and the holm, the *Godspeed* entered the bay.

'Poetry,' said Miss Silver. 'William Wordsworth. "Fidelity". Page 35 in your books.'

Colm bent his head over the page. He read, silently.

> A barking sound the shepherd hears,
> A cry as of a dog or fox.
> He halts – and searches with his eyes
> Among the scattered rocks;
> And now at distance can discern
> A stirring in a brake of fern;
> And instantly a dog is seen
> Glancing through that covert green.

'You will learn this verse for recitation tomorrow morning,' said Miss Silver to the ten-year-olds.

Poetry was hated by the whole school. The children's natural style of recitation, a chant heavily accented, was condemned by Miss Silver (who had been taught Elocution at her teachers'

training college). 'No,' she said, 'You mustn't drone on monotonously like that. You must recite the poem with *expression*. Like
this. Listen.

> A *barking* sound the SHEPHERD hears,
> A CRY as of a *dog* or *fox* . . .'

The only poetry the island children knew were the surrealist word-
games – corn-spells, fish-spells, ancestral memories of murder and
grief and illicit love made innocent and lyrical – that they played in
the school playground.

> Water water wallflower
> Growing up so high
> We are all maidens
> And we must all die . . .

None of the island children could recite 'with expression'; Alice
Rendall could, a little. So they disliked poetry, especially when they
were given verses to learn by rote for Tuesday afternoon, which
was the time devoted to poetry and recitation. Every Monday
evening, therefore, in a dozen scattered crofts, the same ritual took
place: at the kitchen table, under the paraffin lamp, innocent
mouths moved silently and resentfully above the school poetry
book, again and again; until their own sweet natural rhythms were
crushed under the relentless stone.

> There sometimes doth a leaping fish
> Send through the tarn a lonely cheer;
> The crags repeat the raven's croak
> In symphony austere.
> Thither the rainbow comes – the cloud –
> And mists that spread the flying shroud;
> And sunbeams; and the sounding blast,
> That, if it could, would hurry past:
> But that enormous barrier holds it fast.

Colm read the verse idly, once, before bed-time. The book lay open
on the scrubbed table. *A lonely cheer.* His breath trembled on his
lip. He subjected the page to a silent absorbed scrutiny. It was a
lonely experience, like death or nakedness. His mouth moulded
the words: *mists that spread the flying shroud.* He hoarded the lines,
phrase by phrase.

It was the interior of Norday that was being bodied forth in a few
words.

The lamp splashed the page with yellow light.

This poet must have seen Tumilshun too, or else some loch very
like it. He had felt the same things as Colm. This was strange, that
somebody else (and him a famous dead poet) felt the dread, for
none of the other boys seemed to; at least, if they did, they never
spoke about it. But this was even stranger: there was a joy at the
heart of the desolation. Colm could not explain it. It was as if the
loch had a secret existence of its own. The hills stood about the
loch, silent presences; they were frightening too, when you were
among them, but the boy had an obscure feeling that his flesh was
made of the same dust as the hills. They bore with ageless patience
the scars of the peat-cutters on their shoulders. Colm felt a kinship
with that high austere landscape, a first fugitive love.

The poem had worked the change.

His lips moulded, again, the incantation.

> There sometimes doth a leaping fish
> Send through the tarn a lonely cheer . . .

'Colm, it's long past your bed-time,' said his mother. 'Your face is
white as chalk. Close that book now . . .'

Colm stood at his desk next afternoon, when his turn to recite
came. He uttered the magical words in a high nervous treble. He
looked down sideways at Phil Kerston. Phil Kerston had taken
trout out of Tumilshun with his hands; his father's croft was
thatched with heather from the flank of Brunafea; Phil was bound
to like the poem, far more even than he did himself. But Phil sat
knotting a piece of wire under his desk, idly, making a rabbit snare.
Poetry to him was just another cell in the dark prison of school.

'De-dum-de-dum-de-dum,' said Miss Silver. 'No, Colm. You have learned the words, good, but you destroy the life of the poem the way you recite it. Listen now. This is the way it should be spoken: "There sometimes doth a *leaping* FISH . . ." '

One day that same term Miss Silver said to the ten-year-olds, 'We have all learned at last to read, fairly fluently, out of our school text books, have we not? All except Philip Kerston, but Philip may learn to read in time. Don't worry Philip. There is something equally important – writing. You must learn how to express yourselves on paper. For, when you leave school, there will be letters to write. Now, won't there, Willie? You don't know? Of course there will . . . Perhaps one or two of you will be sailors far away from home, so you will want your parents to know how you are getting on, in Sydney, or Port Said, or Bombay perhaps. Even those who stay in the island will also need to know how to express themselves. For, perhaps Maisie Smith will be made secretary of the W.R.I. – no laughter, please – or Stephen Will of the Agricultural Society, and then Maisie or Stephen will be expected to make up minutes of the proceedings and also send a report to *The Orcadian* . . . Learning to write correctly is called what, Alice?'

'Composition,' said Alice Rendall.

'It is called composition,' said Miss Silver. 'We are going to write our very first composition this morning. Philip, fill the ink-pots that are empty or nearly empty. John Hay, pass round those new composition exercise books. The compositions are to be written in ink. I want your very best writing, remember. Does everyone have a blotter? Very well, then. Listen. The subject of the composition is this: "The World I see from my Door". '

A dozen pens scratched and hesitated across white pages for an hour.

Colm wrote idly to begin with, about the lupins in his mother's garden. They grew in summer between the rhubarb and the potato patch. If he stood on the low wall he could see the beach, his father's boat, the sea. Some days, after a westerly gale, Corporal Hourston would come to the shore looking for jetsam. The corporal was a beachcomber. One winter night he stood in the door and there were stars in the sky, hundreds of them, and a full moon. Snow had fallen all day. The furrows in a field at Wardings were long purple shadows. Some days he stood in the door watching for his father's boat to come back from the fishing. He was uneasy whenever *Godspeed* was late. Then everything he saw looked gray, the sea and the sky. The thoughts that went through his mind seemed to be gray too. One day he was alone in the house and he heard a knock at the door. He opened it. He saw a tinker wife standing there with a stumpy pipe in her mouth and a pack on her back . . .

Colm did not suppose he would be better at composition than he was at arithmetic or geography. He discovered that he could remember things much better writing them down than speaking them. When he had time to assemble his material the past ceased to be a confused flux; it became a sequence of images, one image growing out of another and contrasting with it, and anticipating too the inevitable exciting image that must follow. He liked making sentences. He put commas in, and full stops; in that way he could make the word sequences (which were, of course, inseparable from the image sequences) flow fast or slow; whichever seemed more suitable. He even put a semi-colon in the part about the moon and the snow, and then the sentence seemed to hang balanced like a wind-slewed gull. Writing gave Colm a small comfortable sense of power.

'Time up,' called Miss Silver. 'Blot the page carefully. Philip Kerston, gather the composition books and bring them to my desk.'

Next morning Miss Silver handed the corrected compositions back.

Alice Rendall sat, demure and erect, at the top of the class.

'You have a great deal to learn, all of you,' said Miss Silver, 'about how to write English properly. Spelling and punctuation were, on the whole, dreadful. On the other hand, some efforts were quite promising. Alice wrote a nice composition about the hill of Torfea, with its wild birds, it muirburn, its peat-cutters, etcetera. You can see all that from the door of your father's farm, can't you, Alice? However, the best composition of all was written by Colm

Sinclair. Well done, Colm. Colm, I want you to come out to the floor and read your composition to the school. Listen, everybody. It is really quite original and good.'

He stood beside Miss Silver's desk, his composition book in his hand, trying to control his nervous breaths. He read: 'The door of our house is made out of an oak beam that my great-grandfather found a hundred years ago at the beach under Hundhead . . .'

Then the school heard another new sound. A score of faces looked round, startled. It was Alice. Her head was down on the desk; her little fists trembled; spasm after spasm went through her body. The girl was sobbing as if her heart would break.

(vi)

After tea one Saturday night, it rained. Colm put on his coat and cap and went to the tailor shop at the end of the village. Jock Skaill the tailor was his best friend in Norday, though he was forty years older than Colm. The islanders could never make up their minds about Jock Skaill: the women were always gossiping about him in the store. – *Jock Skaill says there's no God . . . He's a communist . . . They say he has bairns somewhere in the south . . . Him and his drink . . . They say he was in prison for a while . . . He was the death of that wife of his, if you ask me . . .* The bitter mouths. The head-shakings. The shuttered brows.

Colm's mother wouldn't have it. She maintained always that Jock Skaill was a fine man. She knew him; they had attended school together; they had been neighbours in the village when they were children.

'Jock Skaill,' she would say, 'he's had an unfortunate life, if you think about it. He was the cleverest boy by far in Norday School, he could have gone on to the university and everything. But old Tom his father would have no grandiose nonsense of that kind. When Jock left school he had to go and sit at that tailor's bench. He hated it – you could see that he was like a young dog tied up in a shed. So when old Tom died he just put up the shutters and left the island without a word to anybody. I suppose he went to sea. What if he did have a wild year or two of it? It's a queer chap that doesn't sow

his wild oats in his twenties. There's many a good man been in jail
– John Bunyan for example, and James Maxton, and Gandhi. Well,
he came home and opened the shop again and he married that girl
from Hamnavoe, Susan Fea, and I'm sure no couple were ever
happier than them for a year of two. And then the poor lass, she
went into some kind of a decline, you know, consumption, and she
died in the sanatorium in Kirkwall. Between one thing and another
Jock Skaill's had a stony path to tread. It hasn't soured him at all,
that's the wonder. He's the kindest cheerfulest man in this
island . . .'

Thus his mother on Jock Skaill the island tailor, whenever the
subject was raised with malicious intent in her presence.

But Jessie Gray and Bella Simison would turn down their
mouths and keep on muttering about communists and atheists
and jailbirds . . .

Colm hung his damp coat on a nail in the door. Jock Skaill
cleared bits of cloth, shears, a tiny triangle of chalk, a few books,
the cat's milk saucer, from the end of the bench. He set out the
draught-board. He put a few peats into the stove.

They played silently that night, two dreaming faces over the
bench in the lamplight. It was a leisurely dance and counter-dance
of pieces across the board. Outside the rain drummed on the dingy
window-panes.

Jock Skaill only spoke when a game was over and he was filling
his pipe, and Colm was arranging the counters on the board once
more.

'Four years next Wednesday since Susan died. Susan was my
wife. "There is a happy land far far away . . ." Don't you believe it,
boy. She came out of the earth and we were happy for two years
and three months, and then she went back to the earth. That's the
way I think of her. She's a part of the rich beautiful earth . . .
There's the cat scratching on the door. Let him in out of the rain.'

Colm won the first game.

'It's a grand feeling, to know you have children. Get married,
boy, have children, but not too many – the world's full enough as it
is. I have a child that I've never seen. Withered folk, grandparents,
they came between the boy's mother and me. I had a great liking

for that girl. I'm glad that somewhere in England there's a piece of me, a living body that came out of my own body. He walks in the wind and the sun. He will make a new human being when the time comes. That's the only kind of immortality there is . . . That fire needs a few peats.'

Jock Skaill won the second game.

'The gossiping old women, I don't mind them at all. They've been at it since the world was young. The Greek choruses began with the likes of Jessie Gray and Bella Simison. What grieves me is the change that's come over the men in this island. They used to tell stories, not the old women's tittle-tattle, but the legends of the island, what their great-grandfathers said and did. That's the source of all poetry and drama. Not now – they discuss what they read in the newspapers and hear on their wireless sets, they have opinions about Free Trade and the Irish Question. I swear to God it makes me laugh to hear them going on about Ramsay Macdonald and Life on Mars, down there in the smithy. All so knowledgeable and important, and not one original idea among them. The marvellous old legends, that's beneath them now . . . I'm boring you, I expect. If you open that drawer you'll find a poke of butternuts.'

Jock won the third game also.

'Progress, that's the modern curse. This island is enchanted with the idea of Progress. Look at what we have now – reapers, wireless sets, free education, motor bikes, white bread. Times are much easier for us than for our grandfathers. So, they argue, we have better fuller richer lives. It is a God-damned lie. This worship of Progress, it will drain the life out of every island and lonely place. In three generations Norday will be empty. For, says Progress, life in a city *must* be superior to life in an island. Also, Progress says, "Here is a combine harvester, it will do the work of a score of peasants . . ." Down we go on our knees again in wonderment and gratitude . . . Will there be a few folk left in the world, when Progress is choked at last in its own too much? Yes, there will be. A few folk will return by stealth to the wind and the mist and the silences. I know it . . . Would you reach up for the tea caddy – the kettle's boiling.'

Jock won the fourth game also and so there was no need to play a decider.

They drank tea out of rather filthy mugs, after the draught-board was folded and put away. Then Jock Skaill told him about some of the old men in Norday that he remembered, and some of the shipmates he had sailed with.

Then he said, 'You better be getting home now, boy. Tomorrow's Sunday. Tell your mother I'm asking for her. Go home. They'll be saying in the store on Monday morning that I'm a corruption to you, if they aren't saying it already.'

(vii)

His mother said, 'Colm, go and see if you can find your father. He's in the shed, most likely.' Torquil and Ellen were spreading butter on their oatcakes. Suppper had begun without a blessing from the head of the house.

The shed on the pier was a black unlighted cube.

Colm wandered up the shore road to the village. His father was most likely in the smithy. A few of the village men gathered in Steve Simison's smithy in the dark evenings. What would they be talking about tonight? The last time Colm had been in the smithy they had been discussing The Yellow Peril.

He entered the smithy shyly. A paraffin lamp hung from the rafters. There were a few men sitting round the anvil. Steve Simison had taken off his leather apron and washed his face and hands; he had a white pure look about him. There indeed was his father, sitting on the bench.

The black maw of the forge gave out a warmth still.

None of the men let on to notice the boy.

Colm tried to catch his father's eye but the company was deep in some discussion: grave tilted faces under the lamp, furrowed brows.

Colm listened. They were talking about the date of Easter.

'I can't understand it,' said Mr William Smith the general merchant. (He was probably the most important man in the island, now that the laird had declined into genteel poverty. He kept the shop in the village and his merchandise comprised everything: groceries, wine, bread and cakes, footwear, butcher-meat, confectionery, fruit, flowers and wreaths, draperies. In addition he was the county councillor for the island, and vice-president of the local Liberal Party, and session clerk, and registrar, and Justice of the Peace. Everyone heard him always with the greatest respect.)

'I can't for the life of me understand it,' he was saying. 'It shifts about from year to year. *I'll be wanting the usual lilies and daffodils for Easter – would you order them please?* says Miss Siegfried in the shop a fortnight ago. So, thinks I to myself, there's plenty of time. In she comes again this morning. *I'll take the flowers now,* says she, *if they've come.* I had been meaning to write all week to the florist in Kirkwall. *I think we should wait till nearer the time,* says I. *Then they'll be fresh* . . . She looks at me like the far end of a fiddle. *Tomorrow's Good Friday,* she says. *This is Maundy Thursday. I require the flowers for the chapel on Easter morning. I'm afraid it might be too late now.'*

'Easter was a lot later indeed last year,' said Dod Sabiston, 'if I'm not mistaken.'

'*This is Maundy Thursday,*' said William Smith, imitating quite well the loud posh English accent of Miss Siegfried the laird's sister. 'Of course they're Episcopalians up at The Hall. So there I was in a fine fix, I can tell you.'

'But why should it be?' said Colm's father, Timothy Sinclair the fisherman. 'Why should Easter be one date this year and another date next year? I could never fathom that.'

Colm stood there silently, his eyes going from face to face.

'God knows,' said the blacksmith. 'Christmas now, that's the same date every year.'

There was silence for half a minute. Then Corporal Hourston cleared his throat and combed with his fingers his handsome moustache: a sign that he had something to say. Corporal Hourston was a retired soldier, and lived on a small pension at the end of the village, in a poor hovel of a place. He had gathered hundreds of bits of useless wisdom from Egypt, Hindustan, the Transvaal. The village men deferred to him, half mocking, half respectful.

'It's the Pope that decides,' said Corporal Hourston senten-
tiously. 'The Pope decides the date of Easter every year for the
whole world.'

They pondered this, gravely.

'The Pope,' said Mr Smith, offended. 'The Pope. The Pope has
no authority over *us.*'

'No, we're Presbyterians,' said Timothy Sinclair. 'We threw off
that yoke a long time ago.'

'The Pope indeed!' said Mr Smith. He turned to Colm's father.
'You're right, Tim,' he said. 'That was the Reformation. And it
didn't happen a moment too soon, if you ask me.'

'It was Martin Luther that saved us from the Pope,' said Dod
Sabiston of Dale.

'No,' said Andrew Custer the saddler, who was also a deacon in
the kirk, 'it wasn't Martin Luther. The English Protestants followed
Martin Luther. The Presbyterians followed John Calvin. Luther
was a German.'

They nodded, sagely.

'It's very hard to credit,' said Mr Smith, 'that people could be
taken in by such darkness.'

'We were all Roman Catholics once,' said Corporal Hourston.
'All our forefathers here in Orkney were Roman Catholics.'

'That was a long time ago,' said Timothy Sinclair. 'People were
very ignorant in those days. There was no education. They couldn't
read the Bible. They knew no better. They had to believe whatever
the priests told them to believe.'

'The Pope, though, he still rules a great part of the world,' said
Andrew Custer. 'France, Italy, Spain, South America.'

'And Ireland too,' said Corporal Hourston.

'The Irish people are very poor,' said Mr Smith. 'Very poor and
very oppressed. You'll find, if you study the matter, that all Roman
Catholic countries are very backward.'

The forge was sending out lessening circles of warmth. Colm
shivered a little. He moved nearer to the wise deliberate lit mouths.
He was glad that he did not live in Ireland or Spain. He was pleased
too that his father had a respected word in these smithy counsels.
His father had thought about things and formed his own opinions.

He was only a fisherman but the other men listened gravely whenever Timothy Sinclair opened his mouth. There was a stack of books in their house, in the window shelf. His father read for a long time every night in winter after the young ones were in bed. *The Rat Pit* by Patrick MacGill. *My Schools and Schoolmasters* by Hugh Miller. *People of the Abyss* by Jack London. *Now Barabbas* by Marie Corelli. *Selected Poems and Letters of Robert Burns.* These were only a few of the titles on the window shelf. His father was well respected in Norday for his earnestness and literacy. He was another one who could have 'gotten on' if poverty hadn't kept him tied to his fishing boat.

'You would hardly credit it,' said Andrew Custer, 'but they worship the Virgin Mary.'

A new face appeared from behind the forge. Mrs Bella Simison stood there. She had come no doubt on the same errand as Colm, to get the breadwinner in to his supper. But she saw the ring of contemptuous slightly shocked faces, and stood listening.

'When I have sinned,' said Mr Smith, 'I ask for God's forgiveness. We all sin, we are frail mortal clay, the best of us. But your Catholic, he goes to a priest to be forgiven, he tells his sins to a man who is a sinner like himself.'

'That's not all, William,' said Dod Sabiston. 'He has to give the priest money to forgive him.'

Timothy Sinclair and Steve Simison shook their heads incredulously. Only Corporal Hourston seemed unmoved: he had known worse things beside the Brahmaputra – sacred hens, crocodiles, cows, widows and infants laid alive on burning pyres.

'That there should be such darkness in the human mind,' said Mr Smith. 'When I want to talk to my Maker, I pray. I tell him how things are with me. I ask for guidance. Your Roman Catholic takes out his rosary beads. He counts them over and over. He mumbles the "vain repetitions" that we are warned against in scripture.'

The Virgin Mary. Priests in black, accepting money from sinners. Rosary beads. Colm shivered with supernatural dread. The dark pool of the human mind. He moved closer in to the fading warmth of the forge.

'Then they die,' said Mr Smith. 'But they do not go like you and me to glory or the bad place, according as we have lived our mortal lives. O no, they go to Purgatory, a place that as far as I know is nowhere mentioned in scripture.'

'No, William,' said Andrew Custer, 'but money comes into that too. You pay to get your friends out of Purgatory. The more you pay, the sooner they get out. That's what they believe.'

Purgatory: another word to add to his sinister hoard.

Corporal Hourston cleared his throat. 'I fought beside Irishmen at Ladysmith,' he said. 'They were all Roman Catholics. They were very good soldiers. Lord Lovat was the commander-in-chief. If I'm not mistaken Lord Lovat was a Roman Catholic too, but of course he was a Scotsman.'

'I once went into a Roman Catholic kirk in Glasgow,' said Dod Sabiston. 'It was full of statues that they prayed to. There was this old woman lighting candles in front of a plaster saint. Graven images everywhere. And the smell of incense, I'm telling you, it was enough to make a man's stomach heave.'

Colm noticed a face that he had not seen at first when he came into the smithy. Tom Sanderson of Wardings had been sitting silent all the time in a dark corner that was studded with old rusty horse-shoes. He was smiling quietly to himself. He took his pipe out of his mouth. He looked over at Colm and shook his head gently and smiled.

Bella Simison spoke up from beside the forge in her deep rapid stacatto. 'Don't tell me about Catholics, them and their carry-on, I have a book in the house, Tina Wasbister took it from Edinburgh, *Maria Monk*, that's the name on it, about nuns in a convent, O my God what a carry-on, them and the priests, supposed never to marry, and babies born every now and then, first done away with, then buried, the poor innocent things, in quick-lime. Well, this Maria Monk, she was a nun too, and she tried to get out and . . .'

'That's all right,' said Steve Simison coldly to his wife. 'I'm just closing up. Then I'll be in for my supper.'

'You can't tell me anything I don't know about Roman Catholics,' cried Bella. She turned her flushed face from one to the other. 'I'll give you the book to read, anybody that wants it, a loan of.' Then she withdrew, in the darkness, to the smell of kippers that came from the open door beyond the forge.

One by one the men got to their feet. Colm's father lowered himself from the bench. Steve Simison closed the forge and put on his jacket. It was beginning to be very cold in the smithy.

'No doubt but it is a great abomination,' said Andrew Custer solemnly. 'It is The Scarlet Women spoken of in the Bible. It is the Whore of Babylon. It is the abomination of desolation.'

Steve Simison raised the lamp glass and blew out the flame.

They moved one after the other towards the door, feeling their ways.

'I'll tell you a very strange thing,' said Mr Smith. 'When I was a boy the gravedigger was old Thomas Wylie. None of you will mind him. Well, Thomas, he was called on to dig a grave in the oldest part of the cemetery, you know, beside the ruined wall where there are no stones at all, only a shallow hump here and there. That's where the people were buried when Orkney was a Catholic place. Well, when old Thomas was digging the grave he came on a hoard of silver and gold coins. The story was told often when I was a boy. I marvelled at that and I still do – burying money with a corpse.'

They stood together on the dark road outside the smithy. Corporal Hourston clicked his heels and, grave and erect, marched off in the direction of his cottage. Steve Simison closed the smithy door and barred it from the inside. Colm put his cold hand into his father's great warm rough hand. There were squares of light here and there in the darkling village.

'What I can't understand,' said Mr Smith, 'is why they can't grow their own daffodils and lilies. They have a big enough garden. God knows, up there at The Hall, and it's all choked with weeds!' . . . He gave his imitation of Miss Siegfried's cut-glass accent, '*I assure you, Mr Smith, tomorrow is Good Friday, and I require the flowers for the chapel on Sunday, and you promised, you know, you promised.*'

Dark fragments of laughter, and 'goodnights'. Colm walked with his father to their house: to the fire, the table with its milk and oatcakes, the bed where he would soon kneel and say his one simple good Presbyterian prayer.

(viii)

The young man, because of asthma, had hardly slept all night. His breathing was always more laboured in the city in the middle of summer. There had been three or four warm July days – hot days even, for Edinburgh. The canyon of the street where he lodged kept still, after midnight, some of its gathered warmth. It brimmed through the high dark window of his bed-sitter. He sweated under his single blanket, and longed for morning.

He must have drowsed for an hour or so; when he looked again the window was a silver-gray square. There would be dawn over the North Sea now, trying to burn its way through the early mists.

The man had done no work on his novel since the start of the golden weather. The sun from morning to night, among the city streets, even across the handsome squares and gardens, distracted him. His imagination was dislocated. Writing became a burden not to be borne. For the past two days he had taken a bus out to the village of Cramond on the Firth of Forth, thinking that the sea might help him. He had sat on the rocks, smoking, and watched the picnics, the children bathing, the sailing boats. But even here there was no release: he felt his loneliness like a pain. He envied the happy young folk with their towels and bottles of coke. Yesterday he had gone to Cramond again, but he had spent most of the day in the Inn, drinking iced lager.

He wished, this cold northern man, that the sun would stop shining, so that he could put his loneliness to some use, and get his writing done. He wished, alternatively, that he could pack his bag and settle with Mrs Doyle his landlady and take a boat north. And the longing and the loneliness ground out between them this asthma that distressed his daytime and kept him awake half the night.

The window brightened, quite suddenly. The sun, hidden by the tall tenements of Marchmont, had ruptured the sea haar. It was going to be another breathless idle day for him. He looked at his watch; it was passing five o'clock. He decided to get up and, before the day made him inert, write a letter.

'Dear Jock – I am not coming north this year. There are it's true so many things I want to see – Tumilshun and the hills, the churchyard, the school, the piers where I fished and the ditches where I burned my fingers. But there are other places that give me a pain at the heart when I think of them – the doorless houses in the village, the *Godspeed* rotting on the beach, the black forge, the mill with its great stones dusty and silent.

'I can only finish this new novel in a cold neutral unhaunted place.

'Thank you for that last letter. That you liked *The Rock Pastures* gives me more genuine pleasure than if, for example, Dr Leavis or Professor Trilling had signified their approval. "It tastes of earth and salt. The folk in cities will be none the worse of that", you say. "That is the good thing about all you write. That is your best gift to the world. Even old Tom Sanderson liked it. He told me so, between laughter and head-shakings, when he was here the other day about his new Sabbath suit . . ."

'Then all those thunderings at the end of the page, against the "idolatry" and the "supersition" that spoil everything! "I will never never understand" you write, "why you have been enchanted by that mumbo-jumbo to such an extent. Giving up old Calvin and his works, that was well done, but you have opened your door to seven devils worse than the first. When you come to Norday in August, in time for the agricultural show – if there is to be one this year, that's to say, for not a month passes but another farmer leaves the island – you must tell me what made you do it . . ."

'I will try to tell you now, in writing, for I have as you know a heavy awkward peasant tongue. You always beat me in an argument. If I *have* to argue, all I can offer is an unfolding sequence of images: stations that lead to a stone, and silence, and perhaps after that (if I'm lucky) a meaning. Where can I make a start? It isn't too easy, trying to assemble your thoughts at half past five in the morning in a cold Edinburgh bedroom, with the prospect of another day of hurt breathing.

'Who better to begin with – since you mention him – than old Tom Sanderson of Wardings in Norday?

'Tom Sanderson is a simple self-effacing man. In this evil time, indeed, he is ashamed of his coarseness and earthiness when he compared himself with such folk as grocers and clerks and insurance-men. He is, after all, bound upon the same monotonous wheel year after year. There is nothing alluring about the work he does. He wrestles with mud and dung to win a few crusts and flagons from the earth.

'Yet see this peasant for what he is. He stands at the very heart of our civilization. We could conceivably do without soldiers, administrators, engineers, doctors, poets, but we cannot do without that humble earth-worker who breaks the clods each spring. He is the red son of Adam. He represents us all. He it was who left the caves and, lured on by a new vision, made a first clearing in the forest. There he began the ceremony of bread. He ploughed. He sowed seed. He brooded all the suntime upon the braird, the shoot, the ear, the full corn in the ear. He cut that ripeness. He gathered it into a barn. He put upon it flail and millstone and fire, until at last his goodwife set a loaf and an ale-cup on his table.

'He exists in a marvellous ordering of sun and dust and flesh. I can hear Mr Smith the merchant saying, "Nonsense – it's simply that man has learned how to harness the brute blind forces of nature . . ." I can hear, among the cloth clippings and shears of Norday, a wiser explanation, "Man and nature learned at last to live kindly and helpfully with one another . . ." But that for me is simply not good enough; it leaves too much out, it doesn't take account of the terror and the exaltation that came upon the first farmer who broke the earth. It was a terrible thing he had done, to put wounds on the great dark mother. But his recklessness and impiety paid off at the end of the summer when he stood among the sheaves. Soon there were loaves on his table; he kept every tenth loaf back – the set-apart secret bread. Why? Because he sensed that there was another actor in the cosmic drama, apart from himself and the wounded earth-mother: the Wisdom that in the first place had lured him on to shrug off his brutishness – the quickener, ordainer, ripener, orderer, utterer – the peasant with his liking for simplicity called it God. Man made God a gift in exchange for the gifts of life, imagination, and food. But still the primitive guilts and terrors remained, for the fruitful generous earth would have to be wounded with the plough each spring-time.

'In the end, to reconcile the divine and the brutish in men, that Wisdom took on itself to endure all that the earth-born endure, birth and hunger and death.

'You have read and digested all those Thinker's Library books on your mantelpiece – Robertson, Ingersoll, Reade – and so you know that no such person as Jesus Christ ever walked the earth; or if indeed some carpenter at the time of Tiberius Caesar left his workbench to do some preaching in the hills, that doesn't mean that he was an incarnation of God – that was the fruit of a later conspiracy of priests and potentates, to keep the poor in thrall.

'But I believe it. I have for my share of the earth-wisdom a patch of imagination that I must cultivate to the best of my skill. And my imagination tells me that it is probably so, for the reason that the incarnation is so beautiful. For all artists beauty must be truth: that for them is the sole criterion (and Keats said it 150 years ago). God indeed wept, a child, on the breast of a woman. He spoke to the doctors of law in the temple, to a few faithful bewildered fisher-men, to tax-men and soldiers and cripples and prostitutes, to Pilate, even to those who came to glut themselves on his death-pangs. With a *consummatum est* he died. I believe too that he came up out of the grave the way a cornstalk soars into wind and sun from a ruined cell. After a time he returned with his five wounds back into his kingdom. I believe that a desert and a seashore and a lake heard for a few years the sweet thrilling music of the Incarnate Word. What is intriguing is how often the god-man put agricul-tural images before those fishermen of his: "A sower went forth to sow . . ." "First the blade, then the ear, after that the full corn in the ear . . ." "The fields are white towards harvest . . ." "I am the bread of life . . ." No writer of genius, Dante or Shakespeare or Tolstoy, could have imagined the recorded utterances of Christ. What a lovely lyric that is about the lilies-of-the-field and Solo-mon's garments. I'm telling you this as a writer of stories: there's no story I know of so perfectly shaped and phrased as The Prodigal Son or The Good Samaritan. There is nothing in literature so terrible and moving as the Passion of Christ – the imagination of man doesn't reach so far – it *must* have been so. The most awesome and marvellous proof for me is the way he chose to go on nourishing his people after his ascension, in the form of bread. So the brutish life of man is continually possessed, broken, transfigured by the majesty of God.

'What is old Tom of Wardings that his labour should be seen at last to be so precious? Goldsmith and jeweller work with shadows in comparison.

'It is ceremony that makes bearable for us the terrors and ecstasies that lie deep in the earth and in our earth-nourished human nature. Only the saints can encounter those "realities". What saves us is ceremony. By means of ceremony we keep our foothold in the estate of man, and remain good citizens of the kingdom of the ear of corn. Ceremony makes everything bearable and beautiful for us. Transfigured by ceremony, the truths we could not otherwise endure come to us. We invite them to enter. We set them down at our tables. These angels bring gifts for the house of the soul . . .

'It is this saving ceremony that you call "idolatry" and "mumbo-jumbo".

'Here, in a storm of mysticism, I end my homily for today.

'I will come back to the island sometime, but this year I must bide in Edinburgh, alone and palely loitering. I promise I will come when this novel is finished. I long to walk by the shore and among the fields, under those cold surging skies. If it rains, I will come and sit on a cloth-strewn bench and listen to monologues about the essential virtue of man, wild flowers, the things that were said and done in Norday before my time. We will perhaps broach a bottle of Orkney whisky. I think I will be content with that.

'I belong to the island. It grieves me to think I should ever be an exile. My flesh is Brunafea. The water of Tumilshun flows in my veins.

'To return for one last time to "idolatry". When first the subject troubled me I read book after book, for and against, and heard great argument about it and about, and got myself into a worse fankle than ever. I might still be lost in those drifts if, in the end, a few random pieces of verse and song – those ceremonies of words – had not touched me to the heart's core:

La sua voluntate e nostra pace . . .

Withinne the cloistre blisful of thy sydis
Took mannes shap the eterneel love and pees . . .
I want a black boy to announce to the gold-mined whites
The arrival of the reign of the ear of corn . . .

Thou mastering me
God! giver of breath and bread;
World's strand, sway of the sea;
Lord of living and dead . . .

You must sit down, says Love, and taste my meat.
So I did sit and eat . . .

Moder and maiden
Was never non but she:
Well may swich a lady
Godes moder be . . .'

Seeing that it would still be another hour before Mrs Catrian Doyle
shouted the length of the corridor that the ham-and-eggs was
dished, Colm laid his letter to Jock Skaill in his table drawer. He
splashed his face in cold water in the bathroom. He put on his
jacket and descended the tenement stair.

The chimney tops on the opposite side of the street were smitten
with the morning sun. It lay across the Meadows. It emptied itself,
a silent golden flood, into the city that was already beginning to
clang and chink with dust-bins and milk bottles.

In a beautiful square a quarter of a mile from his lodgings Colm
entered a church that from the outside looked like an ordinary
Georgian house. Upstairs there were a few elderly women kneeling
here and there. The celebrant entered. Colm had not seen this
particular priest before – he looked like an Indo-Chinese. Once
again, for the thousandth time, Colm watched the ancient endless
beautiful ceremony, the exchange of gifts between earth and
heaven, dust and spirit, man and God. The transfigured Bread

shone momentarily in the saffron fingers of the celebrant. Colm did not take communion. He had a dread of receiving the Sacrament unworthily, and he considered that the envy and self-pity he had indulged in these last few sun-smitten days were blemishes he would have to be purged of.

During the Last Gospel it came to him that in fact it would be the easiest thing in the world for him to go home. There was nothing to keep him here. There were still meaningful patterns to be discerned in the decays of time. The hills of Norday were astir all summer, still, with love, birth, death, resurrection.

The shops were opening when Colm walked back through Marchmont. Awnings were going up on the bright side of the street. Mr Jack the tobacconist stood in his shop door and waved to him. Colm waved back.

'Been to Mass, is it?' said Mrs Doyle. 'Well now, if it isn't the good religious lodger I have staying with me. The bacon got burnt.'

Colm told Mrs Doyle that he would be taking the boat from Leith northwards that afternoon at five o'clock. He would be away from Edinburgh, he thought, for three weeks at least. He would try to be back for the opening of his new play at the Festival. If Mrs Doyle would be good enough to keep his room open for him . . .

Back in his room, he tore up the letter that he had written that morning. He packed a few shirts and books. His breathing was much easier, now that the decision had been made.

The Interrogator

I was ordered to make a preliminary inquiry into the case on the last day of August.

Accordingly I set out for the Orkneys from Leith, and stayed in the cathedral town in the main island for two days before I got a passage to Norday in a fishing boat.

I was met at the pier by an old man who told me that he had been instructed to see to all my needs. He brought me to an inn in the village. It was a plain place, with simple food and a clean bed (I asked no more).

I told the old man that the inquiry would commence the next morning. I gave him a list of persons that he should summon.

The kirk session, he told me, had agreed to let me have the vestry of the church for my business. I would be quite comfortable there, he said; also it was very handy for him, as he was the church officer and also the gravedigger.

The road through the village next morning seemed to be busy with men and animals going one way. The old man told me that it was the annual agricultural show in the island, always the busiest day of the year. Some of the farmers eyed me with open curiosity, others turned away shyly. The great horses plodded past. Sheep huddled in a dense tremulous mass.

The old man led me through a field of ripening oats to a church. It was a square barn-like building with gravestones all round it. The door stood open. Beside the dark oak pulpit an interior door led to another room with a table and a few chairs. A black gown hung on a hook. My guide said that this was the place.

'Light a fire,' I said.

The old man blew at the meagre flame he kindled among the peats. A gray strand of smoke rose up the chimney.

'The witnesses,' I asked, 'have they been summoned?'

'They are sitting here and there among the pews,' he said. 'Did you not see them as you came in?'

'Fetch the first one on the list,' I said. 'William Paulson, farmer in Arngarth.'

William Paulson was the father of the girl. He sat down on the chair opposite me: an austere stubborn quick-tempered peasant.

'I don't know what way I can help you,' he said. 'I have heard nothing from Vera since the morning she left. She's well, I'm sure of that. She's the kind of lass that can look after herself. I'm sorry, I can't help you in any way. All I know is, she's not at Arngarth. She did not tell me where she was going the day she left. She was always like that, a sudden self-willed lass. She has a right to go when and where she pleases. She is twenty-one years old.'

'You are not concerned about what may have happened to your daughter?' I asked.

'No,' he said. 'Vera can look after herself. I have no great fears for her. She's chosen her road and she'll have to follow it to the end. I have three other lasses at home. Vera had a good Christian upbringing. What more could I do? She's in God's hand, wherever she is.'

The old man was a bit upset by the farmer's behaviour. 'Now William' he muttered, 'now William, the authorities. This gentleman is just doing his job.'

'You do not wish to say anything more, then?' I said.

'No,' said the farmer. 'Nothing. What's past is over and done with. I have two horses and a bull at the show. There might be inquiries about them, offers. Macpherson the dealer was there. I will not be in time for the judging. That's where I should be, in the yard. I've told you I know nothing about Vera. I am missing money.'

'Very well,' I said. 'You may go.'

The old man opened the door for the farmer. 'Now William,' he said, 'I think you should have tried to tone it down a bit, eh?'

I wrote in my notebook, *In the midst of them they have set up a little calf of gold.*

It was a beautiful morning outside. From the show field came, occasionally, the great blort of a bull, and the mingled shouts of farmers, and from the wrestling booth and the puppet show and the Fat Lady's tent scatters of laughter.

'Neil Garth,' called the old man into the hollowness of the church. 'You are to come now, please.'

Neil Garth, I read in my notes, was a boatman.

A young man in a blue jersey entered the vestry and was ushered into the seat opposite me.

'Vera Paulson,' I said. 'Does that name mean anything to you?'

'No, sir,' he said. 'At least, it didn't the only time I ever had dealings with her.'

'Did you row a young woman across the Bay of Norday on the day before midsummer?' I said.

'She was wearing a green dress,' he said. 'I didn't know her name at the time. Yes, sir, I took her across.'

'Now,' I said, 'where did the young woman get into your boat?'

'At the Taing,' he said. 'She asked me to row her across the bay. You see, anybody who wants to get from the south side of the island to the north side is much better to come in my boat. It saves a lot of time. She didn't say one word all the way across. When we got to the beach at Skaill on the opposite side she told me she had no money to pay her fare. They're like that, the crofting folk from the south side, poor as kirk mice. I wasn't pleased about that. The ferry-boat is my livelihood. I set her down and let her wade ashore. I'm sorry now I wasn't a bit kinder to her.'

'Why?' I said.

'They say something bad happened to her,' he answered. 'Everybody seems to think that. Of course I know nothing about it.'

'After she left your boat,' I said, 'did you see which way she went?'

'No sir,' he said. 'I was in a bad temper then. I never once looked. I was glad to see the back of her.'

'Thank you,' I said. 'You can go now.'

'You did very well, Neil,' muttered the old man to the boatman as he opened the door for him. 'You spoke up just fine. The gentleman is pleased, I can tell that.' . . . He turned back to me. 'Will I call the next person now?'

'In a minute,' I said. I wrote down in the notebook, *He wore for one day the mask of Charon.*

Through the window I could hear a distant cheering. 'That's the folk at the show,' said the old man. 'The champion animal has just been chosen. There'll be a lot of drinking in the whisky tent now.' The cheering went on. I imagined a bull being led in, a thick lumbering garlanded fecund cube.

'I am ready now,' I said.

The old man opened the door. His voice sounded like doom in the empty church. 'Andrina Moar,' he called. A stout country-woman entered: pleasant-looking enough on an ordinary day, I could believe, but now flustered as a hen.

'Now, now, Andrina,' murmured the old man, 'take peace on yourself.'

'Just tell what you know,' I said. 'I am inquiring about a young woman called Vera Paulson.'

'She came to my door,' said Mrs Moar. 'It was in the afternoon. Nobody was in the house but myself. I had just been out feeding the hens, my hands were all oats and bread-crumbs. No, that's wrong – I had been baking bannocks. There came this tap-tap at the door. Out I goes, wiping my hands in my apron. This Vera Paulson was standing at the door. I had never spoken to her till that day, but I knew her, I had seen her at the Lammas Fair in Hamnavoe last year with two other lasses. She was from the south end of the island, where all the small poor crofts are. Later the same day I saw her in the boat coming home, in certain other company. These young folk nowadays!'

'Andrina knows everybody,' said the old man. 'Every living soul in Orkney, all their cousins and all their kin. She does that.'

'Well, this particular day I saw she was in trouble of some sort,' said Mrs Andrina Moar. 'She was so tired she could hardly stand. Her legs were plastered with sand and seaweed. It was a very hot day at the height of summer. *Please*, said she, *can I come in and sit down for a minute?* So I took her in and sat her down in the big chair. And I gave her tea and bread and cheese.'

'You would have done that indeed, Andrina,' said the old man. 'Nobody goes hungry from Andrina's door in Stoorwall.'

'After a time,' said Mrs Moar, 'she said she felt rested, and thanked me, and she would be getting on now, she said, for she had a mile or two still to go. I thought of asking her what place she was going to, but of course it was none of my business, and in any case I had heard this and that. People will speak. I have eyes in my head too. But I thought to myself, and I said to my man when he came in from the turnip field, *A Paulson girl from the south side was here, she's in trouble of some kind.* And he said he had spoken to her too. He's like that, he'll stop whatever he's doing to speak to every tinker and tramp. She went anyway. The last I saw of her she was on the crown of the road, black against the sky. Then she went down the other side of the hill, and from that day to this I never saw her again.'

'Thank you, Mrs Moar,' I said. 'You've been very helpful. You may go now.'

'Thank you, sir,' she said in a loud ringing sincere voice, so pleased was she to be finished with me and my sheets of paper and my air of authority.

'He's very pleased with you,' the old man muttered to Mrs Andrina Moar of Stoorwall farm, showing her out.

There was a good fire burning now. Outside the wind was rising. It set the tall oats rustling in the Glebe field like conspirators. The hill beyond the village was a tumultuous driven dapple of sun and cloud shadows.

I wrote in my book, *The price of a virtuous woman is above rubies.*

'Please,' I said to the old man, 'do not speak to witnesses as they enter or leave. There should be a certain purity in these proceedings.'

The old man stood in the open door between vestry and church. 'Yes, sir,' he said to me over his shoulder. And into the church he boomed, 'Fenton Smith.'

A ragged creature with young eyes and a young mouth entered, and stood in the door looking at me with a mixture of impudence and servility.

'Now, Fenton,' said the old man, 'off with your hat. Remember where you are.'

'Sit down, please,' I said (though I would not have cared to be the next person to sit on that fetid flea-smitten chair).

'I'll tell you what I know,' said the man. 'It's about the Paulson girl, isn't it? I'll tell you the exact truth as I see it. I'm a poor man, mister. I have no education at all. But for all that I'll tell you what I know, the way I've pieced it out for myself.'

'You might have washed yourself, Fenton,' whispered the old man. 'You might have splashed your face.'

'What do you know about Vera Paulson?' I said.

'Nothing,' he said. 'I never heard her name spoken, mister, before the disappearance. Of course I knew about the farm of Arngarth, that folk called Paulson lived there. It's at the other end of the island to where I live. Crofts among the peat-bogs. I'd seen Paulson once or twice, in fact it must have been several times. I think I even spoke to him once, at the crags, about the time the *Archangel* was wrecked, that's a dozen years ago. But as for his family, I knew nothing about them at all. It's a big island, this. You might live here a lifetime and not get to know everybody. My kingdom is the beach.'

'Fenton, Fenton,' whispered the old man urgently, 'a little bit more respect. Say "sir", not "mister".'

'Then what are you doing here?' I said. 'You have plenty of talk but no information, it seems.'

'Wait a bit,' said Fenton Smith. 'I saw something, mister. I saw a girl standing in the ebb on midsummer evening. I didn't know her. I was working in the seaweed a mile or more away.'

'Fenton is a beachcomber,' the old man said, half to himself and half to me.

'I paid no attention to her,' said Fenton Smith. 'A girl among the rockpools, you can see that any day. They go down there to wash their feet sometimes, mister. You have no idea how vain they are, women. They'll sit watching themselves in a pool for hours. This one was facing west. She seemed to be looking into the sunset. She was nothing to me. Well, mister, when my sack was full I put it over my shoulder and I set out for the quarry.'

'Fenton lives in the quarry, except in winter,' said the old man. 'He has a kind of a tent there.'

'I found a body a month later a mile further round the shore,' said Fenton Smith. 'I'm sorry, mister, not a body, a ruckle of bones with a few wet rags about it. A thin tall skeleton – it could only have been a woman, and a young woman at that.'

'You informed the authorities?' I asked.

'I did,' said Fenton Smith. 'What do you take me for? I told the laird a month later when I happened to meet him on the road. Sometimes you get a reward. The laird said right away, "Vera Paulson." But when I led him to the cave mouth the bones weren't there any more. I turned the tangles over, this way and that. Sometimes the sea takes them back. They go out on the big Lammas ebbs. And that's the best thing that can happen, mister!'

'Thank you,' I said. 'That will be all.'

I wrote on the paper, *This hand has seen a light of silver.*

'Fenton,' whispered the old man, 'was there any need for you to spit in the fireplace like that?' . . . He pushed the ragged back through the door and intoned into the church, 'Theodore Hellzie.'

The agricultural show was over. I could hear the distant clop of a horse's hooves going home. Country voices called to each other on the roads. The hollows in hill and field filled slowly with shadows. In the village someone began to tune a fiddle. The daylight hours had passed quickly, and still our work was only half over.

A tall powerful man, rigged out in good tweed and leather, had entered the vestry. He nodded courteously to me. I indicated the seat opposite.

'Who won the championship?' whispered the old man. 'Was it Tom Mack again this year? Did his stallion get the cup?'

I rapped on the table. Mr Theodore Hellzie sat down as if he had never heard these irrelevances.

He answered each question in a rich deep voice, pausing for just a second in order it seemed to arrange his statements as clearly and accurately as possible.

Yes, his name was Theodore Hellzie. He was a farmer. He owned and worked the farm of Northvoe. He had inherited it from his father. It was so called because it was the most northerly farm in the island, and it was situated above a little bay. Yes, he remembered midsummer day this year quite clearly. It had been a sad day for him; while she was preparing the dinner his mother had had a slight stroke; at any rate, the knife fell from her hand into the basin of half-peeled potatoes, and there was a dumb twist to her mouth when he had asked what ailed her.

'Do you remember that day for any other reason?' I asked.

No, it was a day of farm work like any other day. His mother, he should add, had had a more severe stroke a fortnight later and had died late in July.

'A purposeful woman she was,' said the old man. 'Maria Marwick from Upland. She married Ezra Hellzie. I was at their wedding.'

At this point Theodore Hellzie took a flask from his pocket; light trembled dully across the pewter. He looked at me, mutely seeking permission. I nodded. He uncorked the flask and sipped. He smiled; then brushed an amber drop from the russet fringe of his moustache.

(The interrogation, I knew now, was a failure. The time had not yet come for a mouth to shine upon that troubled vanished day – a living mouth preferably, but, if not, one from foldless unfathomable depths. The tongues we had heard thus far were, as yet, loaded with the dross of vanity.)

'Did you not have a visitor?' I persisted.

He looked at me blankly. A visitor? Let him think. Gangrel bodies came about the place from time to time, tinkers and tramps and men selling tracts and bibles. On this particular day he was worried about his mother's illness. Let him think. O yes indeed, a girl had called in the early evening of that day. A girl in a green dress. He was threshing a sheaf in the barn and he turned to find this shadow in the door. At first he thought it must be some tinker lass come to sell pins and laces, or to scrounge a can of milk, but when he went to the barn door he saw her in full sunlight. She had a green dress on. She was an island lass, but from the south end of the island, and though he had seen her before once or twice, at kirk and market, he couldn't put a name to her. She was wearing a green dress.

Theodore Hellzie uncorked his spirit flask once more.

'Fortify yourself, Theodore,' said the old man. 'Your poor mother. I dug a deep grave for her.'

The girl had asked, very civilly, for a cup of water. He had taken her into the kitchen of the farmhouse. He had given her a cup of milk and an oat bannock. If his mother had been in her usual health the girl of course would have got something proper to eat; some broth, a plate of fish. But his mother – as he had said already – was sick that day. It was the first time he ever remembered his mother being taken sick. The first he knew of it was when the knife slipped out of her hand among the potatoes. His mother was lying speechless in the box bed when the girl was in the kitchen.

'That's the way it happens,' said the old man, shaking his head. 'A knife clattering. A thick tongue.'

'What conversation passed between you and the girl?' I asked.

At this point the old man lit the lamp on the lectern; and a new oblique shadow fell across the farmer's face, and clung there, a shifting web.

There had been very little talk, he said. He was depressed that day about his mother and didn't feel inclined for small-talk. Besides, to tell the truth, he had always felt uncomfortable in the company of women. It was a very ordinary kind of talk that they had, with long pauses between. The girl had thanked him at last for the bread and milk. He had asked her then what her name was and where she came from. She had not answered. She had then said the only remarkable thing he could remember; which was to inquire of him if he had seen a Norwegian fishing boat lying off the Ness. Indeed he had seen one that very morning, when he was out at his cattle; and he told her so. She had seemed satisfied at that, and smiled, and even gave a brief laugh. She had thanked him once more, and touched him on the hand and so left the house. The last he saw of her she was walking rapidly towards the beach.

I saw that the hand the girl had touched was trembling; so much so that the tilted flask put a dark stain of whisky on his handsome beard. The hand was more withered. The russet had streaks of gray in it.

'And that was the last you saw of her?' I asked.

'That was the last I saw of her,' he whispered. He had heard in the course of the following week that a young woman was missing, a daughter of William Paulson of Arngarth. He had then put two and two together. He remembered to have seen that very face in the Paulson pew in the kirk, on the rare occasions – Harvest Thanksgiving or Lord's Supper – when he attended the kirk. He had gone at once and informed the laird and the minister; for to tell the truth he had not cared to tell Paulson himself that his lass was consorting – so it seemed to him – with foreign fishermen.

I asked him if, in his opinion, Vera Paulson had gone away on the Norwegian fishing boat. And might she not in all likelihood be living in some Norwegian town, Bergen or Hammerfest, at that very moment, with nets drying at the sea-wall before her door?

He answered that in all likelihood this was what indeed had happened.

'Women are queer creatures,' said the beadle, chuckling a little. 'They take fancy ideas in their heads from time to time.'

What was astonishing was how old the man had grown in a half-hour, since the lighting of the lamp; so that he who had been so handsome and ruddy at the start took from the vestry a withered sick face; and even his good tweeds were sere and shiny (as if they hung from one who would soon be a ghost). The lamplight had made him all angles and spasms.

I nodded his dismissal.

Mr Theodore Hellzie went from the vestry without one more look at either the old man or myself. He left behind him only the hot rich reek of whisky. We heard his footsteps shuffling through the hollow church.

I wrote in my notebook, *In the heart live a rat and a stone and a rose.*

I saw through the tall window that the west was now faintly tinctured with primrose. A star fluttered softly above the village. With the coming of night the island began to strum with festal noise – the rant of a fiddle, the beat and whirl and onset of dancing feet, laughter, occasionally a low lonely poignant cry.

'Dancing, dancing,' said the old man, and lit another paraffin lamp on the mantelshelf. 'They'll dance their way into the grave but they won't dance their way out of it.' His eyes crinkled with merriment. He consulted his paper. He went over and boomed into the church, 'Joseph Blackburn.'

Joseph Blackburn, coastguard, stated that a Norwegian fishing vessel had fished off the island for a day and a night round about midsummer. Her name was *Lofoten*. The boat had approached the shore in the early evening. Two men had come ashore and walked in the direction of the village. He assumed that they had gone to buy provisions in the village store. They re-embarked, carrying a loaded sack, an hour later. He had seen no person, man or woman, in their company. Mr Theodore Hellzie from the farm of Northvoe had called at his lookout hut on the headland three days later and said was it not strange, he had seen the girl Vera Paulson down at the shore making signals with her arms to the Norwegian fishing boat. He too (Joseph Blackburn) must have seen that. The witness answered Theodore Hellzie that he had not. Theodore Hellzie said that was a pity, as there were bound to be inquiries about the girl, and they might not believe him unless somebody else had seen it too . . . Joseph Blackburn had been surprised to see Theodore Hellzie at his hut, for he had never called there before, to his certain knowledge. On this occasion, moreover, Hellzie had given him a gift – a half pound of Navy tobacco and a large cheese. His last words had been, 'Try hard to remember a girl on the shore. Fenton Smith saw a girl on the shore that day.' . . .

The lamplight mellowed the face in front of me. It was as if the gray and blue and slate of the sea had passed into his eyes, and they had the steady outgoing look of a man who is accustomed to probe the wide circle of the horizon in all weathers. I thanked him and sent him away and wrote on my sheet of paper, *A rock among these dark tumults.*

It was now quite dark outside. I told the old man to extinguish the two lamps in the vestry. The interrogation was over. (Privately, once more, I acknowledged that it had been a failure.)

In the porch the old man lit a lantern. I expected that he would see me out at the gate, or perhaps walk with me past the festive hall to the inn. He said, 'I'd better see that they're all safely home, after their outing.' He left the path and began to probe and pry with his lantern among the tombstones. I followed him, as best I could. The lantern lit, flickeringly, the inscribed face of this stone and that; the kirkyard was otherwise blocks of darkness.

JOSEPH BLACKBURN (1821–1886) *Home is the Sailor, Home from Sea.*

The gravedigger tracked across kerbs and withered wreaths, I stumbling behind him.

Sacred to the Memory of ANDRINA MOAR *who departed this life the third day of October 1872. Also her spouse . . .* I read here and there in the wavering circle of light. We moved on to an old tombstone with a fresh name among withered names. NEIL GARTH *drowned on* Daffodil, *the 16th of June, 1864.* The old man turned to face the kirkyard wall. There were a few humps there, the graves of nameless people, parish paupers and others. He patted one of the humps kindly and said, 'Poor Fenton, he took a bad cold one winter. He was only twenty-six.' . . . We made another brief crepuscular trek among the stones, then the light trembled over a hunk of granite . . . *also* MARIA HELLZIE, *wife to the above, fallen on sleep the twenty-third of July, 1862.* The bottom part of the granite still awaited the chisel and the gold-leaf.

I turned to go.

'Wait a minute,' said the old man. He swung the lantern around till its light splashed over an urn-crowned Victorian column. This part of Orkney was crammed with the Paulsons, that much was evident. The old man's forefinger touched one name half-way down the roll. WILLIAM PAULSON *farmer in Arngarth in this parish, twenty-three years an elder, entered into his reward, full of years, the fourth day of January, 1901.*

'Well,' said the old man, 'they're all safe folded again. That's fine. It's best to make sure. It won't be that long till I'm lying among them myself.'

To me what I heard then was the cold plaint of a seabird. The old man however stood among the tombstones, his fleet splashed with light, his head tilted, dark, intent, silent, listening to silence. 'It's Vera,' he whispered at last. 'There she is, over there by the window.' One shadow detached itself from the huge black block of the church, drifted towards us, then eddied once more into the deeper darknesses.

I had not expected so much. This was a soul from a dark circle beyond my powers to probe.

The old man entered the church once more. He said among the shadows and the dew of the doorway. 'We're glad you've come, Vera. The gentleman wouldn't have been able to do much without you.' . . . I followed him back to the vestry, and was aware of the rejected unshriven soul behind me: a cold intense current of air: a quintessence of winter.

When the old man set down his lantern on the table, I could see that there was a third presence in the room, a young woman. She stood at the table. She looked at me without a word, but there was pain and pleading enough in her eyes.

She could not speak until she was bidden, in the fashion prescribed for an earth-bound unquiet spirit; and one moreover who had left the light without valediction or blessing.

In the lantern-light she seemed a plain country girl, with dark hair drawn back and gathered into a bun, and a freckled face. In a city milliners and cosmeticians might have put a passable attractiveness on her. Here she seemed to be what peasant women have always been: a sturdy vessel – a bearer, for a year or two, of the precious seed, so that the generations of ploughman and hunter might never fail in the islands.

We watched each other in silence. The coldness intensified, even though the old man fed the flames with peat, and raked ash out of the ribs, and plied the bellows.

I charged her, using the prescribed Latin words, that she, being dead, should not trouble the abodes of the living unless she had seemly and charitable business to transact, the completion of which had been prevented by death; but if on the contrary she lingered on earth to be a disturbance to any living soul whomsoever, I bade her begone into the region which had been assigned to her and to trouble the thresholds of breath no longer.

These sonorities echoed through the ice-cold chamber.

'I have come to tell the truth,' said Vera.

I re-opened my satchel and withdrew sheets of foolscap.

'That's a good girl,' said the old man. 'Just you tell what you know.'

I adjured her to say simply and honestly what had happened to her on the twenty-third day of June in the year 1862.

She answered that that day had been the day of her death. It had not been death she was thinking of when she got out of her bed, it was such a bonny summer morning with sun and wind among the young oats, and that always made her happy. But across the breakfast table her father glowered at her once or twice, and her three sisters looked frightened. And later that morning when she was churning butter in the kitchen next to the hill her father had come to her in a great rage – she had never seen him so moved – and he said he saw well enough now with his own eyes that it was the truth they were saying in the smithy and the tailor-shop – and he had denied it to this one and that, including the minister – and he said such a disgrace had never befallen Arngarth before – and he called her a whore, and he struck her on the face, and he told her to go to the man who had got her into trouble, whoever he was, and get bread and shelter there, for here in Arngarth there was no place for her any longer.

She had wandered about the fields most of that morning, hardly knowing where she was going, but she found her feet taking her the road to the north, and that when she thought about it it was only natural, for where now could she look for help and shelter but to the man she loved and the father of her unborn child, who was Theodore Hellzie in the farm of Northvoe.

The more she thought about it the more anxious she was to get to Northvoe, for surely Theodore, when he heard how her father had cursed her and ill-used her, would have a kindly welcome for her, and fire and board and bed. And yet there was a doubt in her mind.

To get quickly to the farm of Northvoe it was best to take the ferry-boat across the bay, for thus a long roundabout way was cut short. So she was glad when she came to the beach that the *Daffodil* was tied up at the stone pier. She could see the ferryman Neil Garth sitting against the rock smoking his pipe. She went up to him and explained as well as she could that she wanted to get to the further side, but that she had at present no money, but if he was willing to wait for a day or two he would be paid. The ferryman never seemed to hear her.

Neil Garth went on smoking his pipe. She had heard that he was a morose man, but she was put out that he would not even give her an answer, and she was walking away, resigned to the ten-mile roundabout walk, when Neil Garth knocked the last ash out of his pipe and got to his feet, and when she turned round again he was pointing mutely at the boat.

'Faith, that's just like Neil,' said the old man.

All the way across the ferryman had said not a word to her, and the only sound was the plash of oars in the water. She sat in the stern. She remembered how sweet and cold the air was on her face. It had been very hot walking on the road . . . Here the young woman paused for a few seconds, and turned her eyes away, as if she was reluctant to go on.

'Keep on, Vera,' said the old man. 'You're doing fine.'

She sighed, and said after another pause that on the far shore Neil Garth had tried to force her into a cave that was there, for a purpose that was only too obvious. 'And that was another hard thing to bear,' she said, 'that every man from then on would look on me as a bad woman.' . . . She showed me the rent in her dress that Neil Garth had made, trying with promises and threats (for soon after the keel ground on the stones words burst out of this silent young man) to get her into the cave with him.

'I ran across the beach and over two fields,' she said. 'I must have been a poor distracted sight when I beat on the first farm door I saw. Nobody answered. I realized how hungry I was when I got the smell of new scones from the girdle inside, for if I had eaten one mouthful in the morning, before the rage burst on me, that was all. I saw a fleeting face at the window. I thought to myself, *She must be deaf.* I tried the door. You must know, sir, how kind and welcoming most of the country folk are. The bar had been slid across. Then I knew that here again I stood recognized and condemned. The hand of everyone was against me. The face appeared at the window once more. A hand made a sign of denial, and the mouth made shapes that were more horrible than any heard words. I was frightened. I turned away.'

'That's the way it happens,' said the old man, and set more peats to the fire that only sent out wave after wave of coldness.

'But then a good thing happened,' said the girl. 'A man came out of the turnip field of this same farm and stood in the way I was going. I turned aside from another hurtful thing, but he put his hand in his waistcoat pocket and brought out a shilling and offered it to me. I will not forget the look of pity and kindness on this face. "Take your time," he said. "You're tired, lass. There's a shop at the crossroads a mile on." I had the grace to say, "Thank you." And then, leaving him, I heard a loud angry voice. His wife was standing in the open door, white to the elbows with meal, and she was raging at him for the biggest fool and simpleton and spendthrift in Christendom. Her rage dwindled behind me as I trudged on over the shoulder of the hill.

'That was Robert Moar of Stoorwall,' said the old man, nodding his head; and I agreed, silently, that it had been a good thing the farmer had done; he had touched the purgation of a ghost with sweetness.

'Theodore Hellzie lived in Northvoe with his mother,' said Vera, 'a woman that I had met only once, in the time of my innocence, the winter before. You likely know, sir, that no mother willingly lets her son go into the keeping of another woman. It is a curious thing. It was a cold hard hand she had put in mine that first meeting. The three of us sat at the table. The mother hardly looked at me. Mother and son spoke to each other in low strained private voices. I was shut out from their communion. I might have been in another room. When at last the time had come for me to say goodnight, and Theodore was getting the gig ready in the yard, the old woman smiled, but to herself only, for it must have seemed to her then that she had kept what she most wanted to have in the world: the greater part of his love.'

'Maria Hellzie was always mistress of her own hearth-stone,' said the old man.

'I thought on that,' said the ghost, 'as I walked slowly down the road to Northvoe. If the ferryman and the baker of scones had treated me like a bad woman, how would old Mrs Hellzie, who disliked me already, welcome me and the bairn that her son had lawlessly put on me?'

(Every unborn child indeed cries out of the womb to its grandparents that the grave is waiting for them. The kisses that the old give to the young must always be bitter, even when there is love and kinship. What gall and vinegar would indeed be waiting for Vera in the fireside chair at Northvoe?)

The cold voice came again: 'The thought of it slowed my steps, when I saw at last the steading of Northvoe lying below me. I lingered uncertainly on the hill. I turned aside to the beach, to consider what I should say when at last the door of Northvoe opened to me. I saw a boat with a foreign rig off the headland. A man was putting seaweed into a sack at the far side of the beach. I stood among the rocks there for a long time. At last in the early evening I gathered up some courage. I left the empty shore and walked between the sandy fields to the farm. By this time I was very tired, but my mind was made up, and I began to feel a little happier. Wasn't it my sweetheart I was going to? What was I afraid of? The old woman wouldn't live for ever. Here were security and comfort. I was going, with my child, into our inheritance.

'Theodore met me in the barn door. He was changed. At first I hardly recognized him, with that shaking cheek and distracted eye. He seemed not to hear what I was saying. I don't think he was aware that I was there, to begin with. The sight of him made me forget my own troubles. "Poor Theo", I said, "what's wrong with thee?" And I kissed him gently on the throat.

'He shook my hand from him. He began to cry. I had never seen a man crying before. "What ails thee?" I said. "I'm Vera. I want to help thee." He said, between distracted gasps, that his mother was taken ill that day preparing the dinner, and he didn't know what to do.

'I said we would look after her together, till she was better.

'He said that was impossible. He looked at me then in a hard hurt angry kind of way. He said that we had done wrong. He said that it was because we had done wrong that his mother was the way she was. It was a punishment on him. His mother had brooded about their affair all spring. He said that the sight of me now, in my shameful state, would be the death of his mother. She was lying stiff in her bed in the room next the sea, but her eyes were open and watchful. She would know all right. I must go away.

'I said that here I was and here I would bide, whatever his mother thought. The bairn I carried was his. It would be born and reared at Northvoe. There was nowhere else I could go. I had been put out of my own house that morning.

'"She will die," he said, leaning his brow against the cold stonework. "She will die. O God, my mother will die."

'"She will," I said. "That is natural. It is right that you should mourn for her. But afterwards there will be another life in Northvoe. There will be a new and a more wholesome kind of love in this place."

'He gave me a look I will never forget. And then he turned away from me.' . . .

There was a long silence in the vestry. The old man sighed and stirred his poker among the bright twisting coldnesses in the grate. The ghost looked into her open palms as if she was finished with speech for ever.

'Well, go on,' I said, without much hope.

She shook her head.

'I know it is a hard thing you have to tell,' I said. 'But when you have said the last word you will be free, and so too will all the tangled dead you had dealings with that day.'

'Yes, Vera,' said the old man, 'that's the best way. Just do what the gentleman says.'

Her lips moved, as if they trembled on the verge of some deep utterance; her throat worked on the bitter stuff that rose up from her heart; but in the end her head dropped and she said nothing.

'I have commanded you to tell the truth,' I said.

'The truth is that I loved him,' she said. 'What more do you want me to say?'

'Your faithfulness is a credit to you,' I said. 'But it makes this court impotent. It lingers out your time in the flame.'

'I have suffered very much,' she said.

'Poor Vera,' said the old man. 'Poor lass.'

'Tell me about Theodore,' she whispered. 'How is it with him now?'

'He is still in Northvoe,' I said. 'The place is going to ruin round him. He is very much in debt. He has drunk heavily for years past – the barn is full of bottles. He is an old lonely sick man. He was never popular in the island – now even the tinkers don't go near his door.'

There was another long silence in the vestry.

'I think now,' said Vera, 'that there has been enough suffering.' I nodded.

Her lips moved. I hastened to put a strict conjuration upon her, before (such is the vanity even of the suffering dead) her tongue moved into deceits and delusions and self-flatterings. 'Let any utterance thou makest now be a true and a wholesome confession,' I said in Latin, 'lest thou exchange thy present healing flame for the unending brimstone. Be no bitterness or lies or uncharity in thy mouth, whatever in time thou hast endured.'

She smiled.

The old man had come to her side and was bending over her with one hand cupped to his ear.

I braced myself for the flash of the spade into her face, the battering of the flail, the mindless hands at the throat – whatever had finally thrust this girl out from the doors of the living.

'I gave myself to the sea,' she said.

It was as if momentarily she was enclosed in a cold glistering sheath, like one newly drawn out of a deep salt fissure. Then she was a tall fading gleam. Then she was nothing, but the table where her hand had lain was beaded and bright and wet.

'Well now,' said the gravedigger, 'that old man up at Northvoe will have a winter of peace yet before I dig his grave.'

When I left the church to go back to the inn, having arranged my papers and signed my name at the foot of every sheet, the daylight was coming in. The old man stood sharpening a scythe in the long grass at one corner of the churchyard.

The interrogation I had conducted was only a beginning. All these souls must now pass on to a higher court, to stellar deliberations, to flames and charities which did not concern a lowly recorder like myself.

On the road to the village I passed a man bearing homeward an exhausted fiddle.